THE BELL MOUNTAIN S

MW00639737

The Glass Bridge

Lee Duigon

STOREHOUSE
PRESS

VALLECITO, CALIFORNIA

Published by Storehouse Press

P.O. Box 158, Vallecito, CA 95251

Storehouse Press is the registered trademark of Chalcedon, Inc.

Book design by Kirk DouPonce (www.DogEaredDesign.com)

Printed in the United States of America

First Edition

Library of Congress Control Number: 2014959599

ISBN-13: 978-1-891375-67-5

ISBN-10: 1891375679

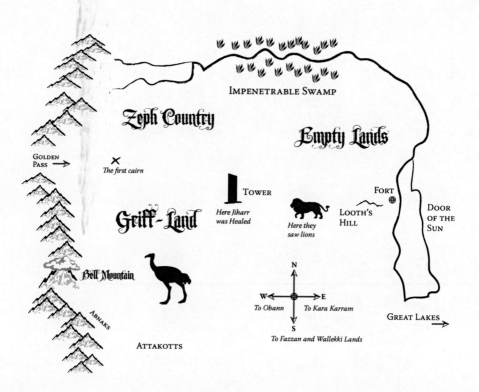

IMPENETRABLE SWAMP

Zeph Country

Empty Lands

GOLDEN
PASS →

× *The first cairn*

TOWER

FORT

Griff-Land

*Here Jiharr
was Healed*

*Here they
saw lions*

LOOTH'S
HILL

DOOR
OF THE
SUN

Bell Mountain

ABNAKS

N

W   E
To Obann   *To Kara Karram*

S

To Fazzan and Wallekki Lands

GREAT LAKES →

ATTAKOTTS

CHAPTER 1

How Ellayne Learned of Her Future

"And so when the princess went a-maying, the arch-magician set on his ogres to attack her knights; and when all the knights were slain, he spirited her away to his castle to be a prisoner there until her father should consent to her marriage to this wicked man, making him the heir to the kingdom.

"Now this was a castle made and upheld by magic. It was of the purest crystal, all sharp edges and points like spears. A keen-eyed man from a distance might see into the very heart of it and see the princess in her prison chamber, praying on her knees for deliverance. And there were a hundred doors and gates all around the castle, to go in and out.

"But this crystal castle was built upon a high rock, and all the way around that rock was a wide chasm; and this chasm had no bottom, so that any who fell into it would fall until the end of time.

"And when Abombalbap came and looked upon the castle, behold, a single bridge spanned the chasm. This was a bridge of glass, sparkling and intricately wrought, and so delicate that it would shatter at the lightest touch."

This was the story that Ellayne was reading to Jack and Enith on the back porch on a rainy day, when her father came out through the kitchen door and interrupted it.

"Ellayne," said Baron Roshay Bault, "your mother and I want to have a talk with you. Put the book down and come with me."

He didn't say "please," so of course Ellayne wondered, "Now what have I done?" She couldn't think of anything. Even so, it sounded like a serious matter. You could tell that from the expressions on Jack's and Enith's faces.

"Just Ellayne," the baron said. He looked at Jack. "It'll be your turn later," he said; and Jack thought that maybe he saw the hint of a twinkle in the baron's eye, but wasn't sure. The baron and baroness had formally adopted him some months ago.

Ellayne put a leather marker in the book and closed it carefully. It was a big book; it had been the baron's when he was a boy and had to be handled with care. "Don't peek," she said. "You'll spoil the story." And she got up and followed her father into the house.

"It sounds like she's in trouble," Enith said. She lived next door with her grandmother and her aunt, who both worked for the baroness, and her grandmother's husband, who had a shipping business. "I wish I knew what it was!"

"It's a break from this foolishness about magic, at least," Jack said, and he and Enith drifted into an argument about the story.

Baroness Vannett was waiting for them in the parlor. She smiled at her daughter.

"Sit down here by me, Ellayne," she said. She didn't seem angry. With only a little bit of trepidation, Ellayne joined her on the couch.

"We have to make a decision about your future," Mother said. Ellayne didn't like the sound of that. "As you know, it was always my wish to send you to finishing school in Obann to learn how to be a lady: to learn how to wear nice clothes properly, and how to dance, and how to behave in gentle and refined company."

"Oh, no!" thought Ellayne. Her stomach crawled.

"But a few things have changed, haven't they?" said Father. "The city of Obann isn't what it was—Temple destroyed, palace gone—and there's no more Oligarchy."

"Which means your father will never become an oligarch," Vannett said. "He'll have to settle for being the Baron of the Eastern Marches, by appointment of the king. That's better than being an oligarch."

"And you've changed, too, my girl," said Roshay Bault. "You don't want to go to finishing school, do you?"

Ellayne shook her head, vigorously. She didn't dare speak.

"Yes, many things have changed," Vannett said. "I'm hardly the same person I used to be, if it comes to that. At any rate, we've decided not to send you to finishing school. We're both sure you would hate to go, and trying to turn you into a nice, decorative lady would simply be a waste of good material. We love you as you are."

"Which is not to say you'll be allowed to dawdle away the rest of your life," Roshay said. He sighed. "It's all your brothers can do just to keep the family lumber business going. Josek and Dib are solid young men, and we're very proud of them. But I need someone to help me in my work as baron. There's so much to do! Much more than I can hope to do myself. I have to inspect the river patrols this week, which means I won't be here to read and answer messages. And there are always so many messages! It isn't always easy to pick out the important ones."

"What your father means to say, Ellayne, is that if you're willing to help him in his work, he'll be more than glad to have you. There'll be plenty for you to do here at home, without your going off to the city to learn how to flirt."

"You're getting to an age when you can't just be a child anymore," the baron said. "I think you passed that age when you went off to climb Bell Mountain—you and Jack both. There's a lot I'll have to teach you, but only if you want to learn. Do you?"

Ellayne opened her mouth, but it took a moment for any words to come out. "Do you mean it?" she cried. Her father was not above having a little joke from time to time.

He laughed, knowing exactly what she was thinking. "Of course I mean it!" he said. "It'll be to my great gain, after all. You've already seen more of the world than I ever will and done things that I never would've dreamed of doing—and gotten out of scrapes that I don't even want to think about."

"And besides," Vannett said, "you have God's blessing on you. You have done Him mighty service—you and Jack, and Martis, too."

"As you grow up, and as he grows up, too, King Ryons will need your help," Father said. "You and Jack both. I'll be an old man by then. The king will need your wits and your pluck. You're as brave as any warrior in his army, but as your mother has said, you have God's blessing on you. Fine ladies can be had for the asking, but wise and faithful servants to a king can hardly be had at any price."

"The choice is yours, Ellayne," said Mother. By way of answer, Ellayne hugged her as hard as she could.

"You might want to let your mother breathe, Ellayne," said Roshay Bault.

———————

Martis was riding back from a visit to the mountains with an urgent report to make.

On the other side of the mountains, the Abnaks' revolt against the Thunder King had drawn the whole wrath of his empire down upon their heads. His armies swarmed around the skirts of the mountains, merciless, slaying, burning. Family by family, clan by clan, the Abnaks were being forced across the mountains. It was the only way they could save their wives and children. They retreated into Obannese territory, sparsely settled, but those who lived there knew King Thunder's hordes would someday follow the Abnaks into Obann.

"A nice mess for the baron!" Martis thought.

The information he brought was vital, and so he rode hard, following the roads that paralleled the great Imperial River, the lifeline of Obann. His wiry Wallekki horse, Dulayl, kept up the pace all day long.

As vital as it was to gather accurate information for the baron—only a fool would believe the rumors that trickled down from many miles away—Martis could never leave the baron's town of Ninneburky without some second thoughts. He'd sworn an oath to defend Jack and Ellayne with his life, and it made him anxious to be away from them. He would never forget how his former master, Lord Reesh, the First Prester, had sent him out to kill the children rather than let them ring the bell atop Bell Mountain. Lord Reesh was dead, but Martis thought there must be servants of his still at large, who would sell the children to the Thunder King. As safe as they might seem to be in the baron's house in Ninneburky, Martis knew that that was only seeming. His place was with them; it was why God had spared his life on the summit of Bell Mountain. Martis had gone up the mountain with a brown beard and come down with a white one. It was not an easy sign to ignore.

But the Abnaks couldn't be ignored, either. For a thousand years their raiding parties had stolen into Obann in search of slaves, furs, and scalps. The slaves they sold to the Wallekki; the furs they kept for themselves; and the scalps they took were the takers' pride and joy. There could soon be trouble on Obann's side of the mountains.

Trouble might have started already, if not for some scattered communities of Abnaks mixed with Obannese—persons who had come together because both were oppressed by the Thunder King while he controlled the Golden Pass and built a road down to the lowlands. Rebel Abnaks and runaway Obannese slaves had merged into a new people, living together and intermarrying. Here the Word of God had filtered into the wilderness, bringing hope where no hope was.

But the peace wouldn't last, Martis thought, unless something could be done to foil the Thunder King—if anything could be done against so great a power.

"Faster, Dulayl!" he spoke to his horse. "Faster!"

"So what was that all about?" Jack asked, when Ellayne came back out to the porch.

"You'll find out soon," she said. "They want you now, in the parlor."

"But what is it?" Enith cried.

"It's something I want to think about for a while. I have to take it all in."

"Ellayne!"

"I'm going to my room now," Ellayne said. She picked up her book and went back into the house.

"Well, I like that!" Enith said. "She didn't even say how Abombalbap got over the glass bridge, either."

"Oh, on a flying horse or something just as silly. I've got to go."

He left Enith fuming on the porch. When neither of them came back outside, after a time she went into the kitchen to help her aunt prepare the supper. Aunt Lanora often spoke of things that weren't rightly her business, but today she hadn't managed to overhear anything that Enith wanted to know.

She'd never known anyone like Jack and Ellayne for keeping secrets. Enith had been trying for months to pry those secrets out of them. "They'll see," she thought. "They'll see they can't keep their secrets forever."

CHAPTER 2

Jandra and the Book

Many miles away in Lintum Forest, where King Ryons had his throne, another child, a girl much younger than Ellayne, had her head bent over a book. This was a big book that belonged to Obst, a book of all the Scriptures in a single volume. For uncounted years it had sat unopened and unread in a book room in the Temple in the city of Obann. Obst had taken it with him when he had left the Temple to be a hermit in the forest. He'd been a young man then.

The book lay spread out on a wooden table, where the king, under Obst's guidance, had been studying it an hour earlier. The little fair-haired girl, herself not much bigger than the book, sat on the tabletop with her lips moving as she read the words. Behind her towered the ruined pile of stone that was Carbonek Castle, now the seat of Ryons' kingdom.

Here Ryons came to learn the Scriptures when the weather was nice. He came back today to play with the little girl, who loved him; Jandra was her name. Being king and having so much to learn, he had few idle hours. The Ghols of his bodyguard taught him horsemanship and archery and the fine art of knife-throwing. Helki taught him woodcraft. The other chieftains in his army, men of a dozen different Heathen lands, taught him the ways and customs of their nations. When it seemed his head would burst for all the teaching they were trying to cram into it, Helki would send him into the woods with only his hound and his hawk for company—and the horse-sized killer bird, Baby, to protect him. "Learn to love the forest, Your Majesty, and the forest will love you back," was Helki's teaching. "Every plant, every animal, every bird has something to tell you, if you can learn how to listen."

King Ryons stood beside Jandra, watching with astonishment as she read the words that so often tripped him up. She didn't seem to know he was there. When he spoke to her, she didn't answer.

"It can't be!" he said to himself.

He leaped onto a second table and waved to a woman passing by, not willing to raise his voice. She saw him and came at a run.

"Your Majesty?"

"Please—go find Obst and send him here. Hurry!" Ryons said. "And Gurun and Abgayle, too."

The woman curtseyed and sped off. There were not yet so many people settled around Carbonek that anyone lacked a chance to speak with the king. In the little time it took her to come back with Obst, a small crowd had gathered around the king and Jandra, but no one made a sound.

"My lord, what's the matter?" Obst started to say, but Ryons cut him off.

"Shh! Listen!"

Jandra read in a voice much deeper than any little girl's: "The nations bow themselves before idols of wood and stone, the work of their own hands. They bow down to trees, to birds and beasts and creeping things, the work of My hands; but they know not Me. They walk on My earth and eat My fruits and meat; I send the rain that makes their crops to thrive. They have no understanding.

"But to you, My people, I have spoken, to you have I revealed Myself. But you have shut your eyes to Me, and shut your ears, and closed your minds, and hardened your hearts. You have yourselves become like wood and stone. But I shall visit you, and you shall know that I am God: there is no other."

Jandra's head drooped, and she fell asleep on top of the open book.

Obst gnawed on his beard. "Prophet Ika," he muttered, "fifth fascicle, verses fifteen and sixteen."

"She reads better than I can," said Ryons, "and you've been teaching me for all this time."

Abgayle came and gathered Jandra into her arms. Since Helki had found the child wandering alone on the plains and had brought her to the forest, Abgayle had served as Jandra's mother.

"Abgayle, have you been teaching Jandra how to read?" Obst asked.

She laughed. "How pretty she is!" Ryons thought. "Helki ought to marry her."

"Me, Obst?" she said. "But I don't know how to read."

"Maybe it's Gurun who taught her," Ryons said.

But when Gurun joined them, she said, "No, my lords, I haven't taught her anything. It is hard for me to read the Obannese lettering." Gurun knew the Scriptures better than anyone but Obst, but she was not Obannese. She came from Fogo Island in the distant north, blown to Obann by a storm, which she accepted as God's providence. Everyone here called her a queen, which embarrassed her. She loved Ryons, but he was just a boy, much too young to have her or anyone else for a queen. At home she would have been married by now, but island girls married young. The Obannese calendar was different, so Gurun had lost track of her birthday. She was at least seventeen, she reckoned. Ryons always looked at her with admiration—tall and straight, with bright blue eyes and shining golden hair. She deserved to be a queen, he thought.

"If Jandra reads the Scriptures, and no one here has taught her," Gurun said, "then it can only be the gift of God."

Onlookers exchanged perplexed glances, but Obst nodded. "That's my thought, too," he said. Obst had seen God take a boy from Heathen slavery and make him king of Obann; He could certainly make a little girl to read. It was Jandra who had first announced God's choice of Ryons as king, and everyone recognized her as a prophetess. Since King Ozias' bell had rung from the summit of Bell Mountain, many marvelous things had happened in the world—not all of them pleasant.

———

It was a busy time at Carbonek. It was God's will that they should carry His word into Heathen lands, and the chiefs of the army were preparing their campaign. They would have to get across the mountains before the end of summer. But where should they cross, and how would they supply themselves?

"Wherever we cross, we'll have plenty of fighting," said Shaffur, chief of the Wallekki. His riders had been scouting far and wide. "Maybe more than we can handle, I think."

The First Prester was on his way to Lintum Forest to bless the king and his army, but no one knew where Helki was. He'd gone off with three of his best woodsmen to find a way across the mountains and hadn't been heard from for two weeks. "Let the chieftains get things organized," he'd said. "I'm no good at that."

Chief Buzzard wanted the army to cross into Abnak lands and help his people in their revolt against the Thunder King. "We'll have all the Abnaks fighting on our side," he said. "We'll take many scalps."

Obst hardly thought that the best way to export God's word, but he couldn't deny the army's need for allies.

"We should wait for God to speak to us," said the Fazzan chieftain, Zekelesh. "What's the use of having a prophetess among us, if we aren't going to listen to her?"

And now the prophetess had spoken—a little girl who couldn't read, reading from the Scriptures. And no one understood the message.

———————————

Along with Gurun and the old Abnak subchief, Uduqu, a boy named Fnaa had escaped from the city of Obann upon the destruction of the Palace last summer. Now he spent much of his time with King Ryons, playing and exploring the forest together. Both had Heathen blood in them. Both had been born slaves. But that wasn't all they had in common.

Fnaa was the king's double, and you could hardly tell the two of them apart—two dark-haired, dark-eyed boys, slightly undergrown. But Ryons had a red streak in his hair, a sign of his descent from King Ozias. If you covered it with charcoal, the boys were practically identical.

By the time Ryons and Fnaa got together at the supper table, the whole settlement buzzed with word of Jandra's reading. Fnaa was sorry he'd missed it.

"I did see the whole Palace go up in flames," he said, "and that ought to count as a miracle. But for Jandra to read that great big book—why, I can hardly lift it!"

"Abgayle has a little book of stories someone gave her, but she says Jandra can't read that." Ryons shook his head. "I wish Helki was here."

"What for? He can't read, either! He's out hunting bandits somewhere—unless they're hunting him."

"I don't like to think about it," Ryons said. When he was a slave, nothing ever worried him as long as he had enough to eat and escaped beating. Now he was a king, and many things worried him. "I don't know how we'd ever get along without Helki."

"Oh, he'll be all right," said Fnaa. "My mother always prays for him."

CHAPTER 3

Helki the Hunted

As the day gave way to dusk, Fnaa's mother would have
prayed harder had she been able to see what was hunting Helki even as she and the rest of Carbonek settled down
to supper.

He'd had a fleeting glimpse of it, up there in the trees, an
animal whose like he'd never seen before. Obann was full of
strange animals these days. This one looked something like
a marten, but almost the size of a grown man, and bearing
a thick coat of shaggy black fur. It stalked him from above,
waiting for a chance to spring down on him. It moved with
great care, making hardly the slightest sound. It had posi-
tioned itself upwind from him, so there was no scent to be
detected. He wouldn't have known it was there at all, but for
the shrill, scolding chirp of an unseen sparrow and the indig-
nant chattering of a squirrel as it fled out of the hunter's way.

Helki the Rod was a big man. You wouldn't think he
could make himself invisible, but he could: that was how he
stayed alive. His clothes, a mass of sewn-together patches
in every shade of green and grey and brown and yellow you
could think of, helped him to blend in to any kind of forest
background, and he was a master of the arts of silence and
stillness.

Unable to see or hear its prey, the beast now hunted by

14

scent alone. The sparrow kept on scolding, by which Helki was able to know the beast's location. It would be too bad if he had to kill it, he thought. Maybe if he remained invisible a little longer, it would give up and move on. Already it seemed to be hesitating, unsure of what to do.

Helki was alone. Yesterday he'd sent his three men back to Carbonek to report his plans. They'd raced across the plains to reach the wooded foothills of the mountains.

"We know there's an army waiting for us on the other side of Silvertown," he'd told them, "and a much bigger army hammering the Abnaks. I'm thinking we might be wise to take the long way around, by the new road the enemy made to the Golden Pass. That means we'll have to get an early start; it'll be a long march. Go back and tell the chieftains. I'll go on ahead and see what's what." He would cover much more ground without them.

The sparrow's cries got shriller; the predator was now almost directly overhead. The wind had shifted slightly, and the hunter was confused. Helki heard it snuffle, trying to pick up his scent.

A new plan suggested itself.

With a roar that made the woods ring, Helki leaped out from concealment and whirled his staff over his head with a whoosh.

"I see you!" he bellowed.

Startled and unnerved, the hunter leaped with a snarl to the next tree and went crashing off through the foliage. Helki wasn't surprised: ambush predators didn't like it when their prey could see them and seemed ready for a fight. He laughed quietly to himself.

"I win," he said aloud. There would come a time, perhaps, when he didn't win, and that would be the end of all such games. But as Obst would say, "That's in God's hands, not ours."

Helki continued on his way.

The next day he found what he'd been looking for, a small encampment of refugees, Obannese and Abnaks together, some twenty adults and a few small children. They lived in a handful of Abnak wigwams, saplings fastened into arches and covered with skins, sheets of bark, and layers of leafy boughs. He did his best to avoid startling them, but the Abnak men were annoyed with themselves for letting him get so close without their knowing it.

"Peace to all the enemies of the Thunder King!" he said, raising a palm. "I come from King Ryons. My name is Helki."

"How did you get past our hunters?" demanded an Obannese man in ragged clothes.

"Very carefully!" Helki said.

"You're lucky no one speared you," said an Abnak with a grey scalp lock. "I am Ogo, of the Cicada clan, the headman here. If you are Helki the Rod, I've heard of you. You killed the giant."

"God blessed my staff that day."

"We have heard of the Obann God, too. Hlah tells us that He is the God of Abnaks, too."

"I know Hlah—old Chief Spider's son," said Helki. "I'd like to talk to him."

"His camp is a half-day's march north of here," said Ogo. "He visits us sometimes to tell us things that come out of a book. He is the servant of this God."

"And so am I," Helki said.

He stayed the night with Ogo's people and learned what he had hoped to learn. The war with the Abnaks on the east side of the mountains had drawn off much of the Thunder King's strength—and there was no Heathen army guarding the way down from the Golden Pass.

"They fear that place," said Ogo, as they ate roasted squirrel around a campfire. "Thunder King doesn't like for anyone to see where all the snow came down and buried his golden hall. They say it's haunted by the ghosts of all the mardars who died there. Maybe it is. Some say the Thunder King himself died there, but that cannot be."

"The troops get discouraged if they see that, eh?" Helki said. "The truth is, Ogo, that the Thunder King did die in that avalanche. I was there; I saw it. But they just raised up another one and pretended it was the same man. Who can tell the difference behind a golden mask?"

Ogo and his people had never heard that news before. They filled the night with excited murmurings.

"It's good to know the Thunder King can die!" Ogo said. "If there were more of us, we would send men back to Abnak country to help in the war. But we have to hunt food for our wives and children. Most of our young men have taken Obannese wives—who would have ever thought a thing like that could happen? But everybody says that if the war goes on much longer, all the Abnak tribes will have to come over to this side of the mountains. King Thunder has too many men; Abnaks can't kill them all."

"They can try!" added a woman with a baby in her arms. And Ogo laughed at that.

Hlah, the son of Spider, had a wife and child of his own, but he wasn't thinking about the war. He was thinking about the helpless madman he'd brought up into the hills with him and then taken down again, all the way to Obann City—a starving, dirty madman who was now best known as Lord Orth, First Prester of Obann by the grace of God and election by the College of Presters. But Hlah and his wife knew him better by the name Hlah had given him: Sunfish.

"I can hardly believe it!" May said, as they discussed the matter privately. "The First Prester coming here!"

"He was here for quite a while, as Sunfish," Hlah said.

"That was different. He wasn't First Prester then. He wasn't really anybody."

By special messenger Lord Orth had sent Hlah and May a book of Scripture, one of the first of what was going to be thousands of new copies. It came with a letter from Lord Orth himself, stating his intention to visit the hill country in person late this spring. He had signed it "Sunfish."

"We ought to keep it a secret until he's almost here," said Hlah. "It might be bad if the Thunder King got wind of it."

It had been Hlah's dream to go back over the mountains and preach the God of All Nations to the Abnaks in his native land. He hadn't been able to do so; his people needed him here.

"They probably would have killed me, anyway," he said.

"Remember what Lord Orth said to you before we came home from Obann," May answered. "Carry out the work that God has given you." Which he found himself content to do.

CHAPTER 4

News from the East

Under the back porch of Baron Bault's house lived Wytt, when he wasn't living in the baron's stables or somewhere in Ellayne's bedroom. He liked it under the porch because it ran beneath the kitchen and he could smell everything that was being cooked and overhear everything that went on in the house.

Maybe you already know what kind of creature Wytt is: an Omah, a little manlike thing about the size of a squirrel, with a glossy coat of reddish fur. He was Jack and Ellayne's companion and protector on their travels.

He shared the space under the porch with an old rat that had been driven out of the stables by the younger rats. The ones in the stables were aggressive. Wytt had had to kill one, and so they learned not to be aggressive toward him. But the old rat under the porch was peacefully inclined, and he and Wytt had become friends. If the baroness had ever known she had a rat under her kitchen, she would have set a trap for it. She didn't much care for Wytt being there, either, but she didn't complain. As long as she didn't have to have anything to do with him herself, she accepted his close bond with the children. "Still," she said, "if he's your pet, Ellayne, he ought to be in a nice hutch, like a rabbit."

"Oh, Mother! That would be like putting a person in a

hutch! He's not an animal!"

The baroness couldn't quite understand that. For her daughter's sake, she put up with it.

Sometimes Wytt brought tasty tidbits from the kitchen, which he shared with the rat. It would have offended the cook to know that. On this particular evening he brought bacon scraps. Knowing that he was eating much better than the youngsters in the stables, the old rat was content.

They didn't converse—how could they?—but had they been able to, their talk might have gone something like this.

"A change is in the air," the rat would say. "I feel it in my hair and in my bones! Don't you?"

"I do," Wytt would answer. "It's almost like the way you know that spring is coming, even before you see any buds on the trees. Only spring is already here, so it must be something else. I wonder what it is."

"It's got me all excited," the rat would say, "but I don't know why."

Even had he been able to talk, here he would have run out of words. Whatever might be going to happen, it was beyond his imagination. As for Wytt, he very seldom imagined things at all. His was not a human mind, nor was it an animal's.

━━━━━━━━

Around the city, which some said was a dying city, life in Obann had begun to settle down. The remnants of the Thunder King's vast army, which Ryons on the great beast had scattered in every direction, were starved, killed, or had fled into parts unknown or gone into the service of the king of Obann. Having failed to take the city, they could never return to homelands ruled by the Thunder King. Many of them, now under Obannese officers, patrolled the roads.

So it was deemed safe for the First Prester to travel to Lintum Forest and beyond. The project of copying and distributing the Scriptures he'd left in good hands. Prester Jod in Durmurot was now the Vicar of the Temple—not the old Temple, which lay in ruins in the middle of the city, but the new one envisioned by Lord Orth, not built with human hands but with God's word and His people. And General Hennen, now Baron Hennen, governed the city in King Ryons' name.

It was a new thing for the First Prester to travel. "The people must be brought to know that God is with them," Orth said, "and it's our mission to lead them back to Him. The old Temple was in Obann, and in Obann it stayed. But the new Temple must be everywhere."

There was, of course, another New Temple—the one built by the Thunder King at Kara Karram, far out in the East in Heathen lands. "He means it as a snare and a temptation to us," Orth said. "We must not permit him to deceive us."

Orth traveled by the roads along the river in a fine coach drawn by two white horses, with an escort of twenty mounted spearmen clad in mail. People came out to see him, and he delivered sermons to them wherever he stopped. To see and hear the First Prester was a new thing in their lives and a new thing for the First Prester, too. Everywhere he spoke, he preached repentance.

"We have entered a new era in our history," he said. "God is shaking the earth, so that the things that cannot be shaken will remain. We have a king again, of the blood of King Ozias. We have rediscovered God's word. Rejoice! For you all heard Ozias' bell ring from atop Bell Mountain, far away. Rest assured that our God has heard it, too."

Before he left the city, Gallgoid advised him there was war on the east side of the mountains—"war that might spill over into Obann before you can even reach the mountains." Gallgoid ruled a network of spies, and he knew whereof he spoke. "It might be better if you didn't journey quite so far, First Prester." Gallgoid had once saved Orth from a dangerous plot and felt an attachment to him.

"I must go where I am led," said Orth.

———

Not everyone in Obann wished to enter a new era.

Ysbott the Snake, who didn't die when Ellayne had escaped from him, was one of those. He dared not return to Lintum Forest, where Helki's men continued to hunt down outlaws. He haunted the woodlands that marched along the river east of Ninneburky, recruiting desperate men with prices on their heads.

For a time Ysbott feared he might have been struck permanently blind by the flash of light that had erupted from Ellayne's hand when she overtaxed the power of a witch's spirit imprisoned in an ancient artifact. The girl herself was a witch, and Ysbott was not likely to forget it. The wound in his cheek, inflicted on him by Wytt with a sharp stick, had finally healed after a very bad infection, leaving his face disfigured by an ugly scar. And his eyes still hurt when he had to venture into the full light of day.

Although he alone was responsible for all the suffering he'd had, he lived for revenge on the victims who'd escaped him.

"Make no mistake," he told his men. "The Thunder King will come again. There'll be great rewards for those who serve him!"

He had a mixed band of Obannese outlaws and Heathen fugitives, some fifteen men all told. The baron's militia hunted them but hadn't caught them yet. They lived on what they stole from farms and villages, and left a red wake behind them wherever they went.

———————

At last Martis came home from the hills. He delivered his report at the baron's dinner table. Ordinarily Jack and Ellayne would have been dismissed, but not anymore. "If you two are going to help me in my work," Roshay said, "it's time you started learning what the work entails." Normally the baroness would have excused herself, but she'd gotten out of that habit. But Lanora the cook was sent home after she'd cleared the table.

"The Abnaks won't be able to hold their lands," Martis said. "They fight hard, but their resistance must be broken very soon. The enemy is pouring troops into their country. He knows that if the Abnak revolt succeeds, there will be many more revolts in other countries. I believe he means to exterminate the Abnaks, and he'll follow them across the mountains to do it."

Roshay frowned. "I could send maybe five hundred good spears to help the Abnaks. A thousand, if I had more time."

"Even a thousand would be too few by far," said Martis. "The enemy has emptied the Zephite lands of fighting men and sent in more from farther east. They're no match for the

Abnaks in the woods, but there are so many of them coming in, it hardly matters. And they're killing every Abnak they can get their hands on, women and children especially. The Abnaks will have no choice but to retreat across the mountains. If they try to stay in their own territory, they'll all die." Martis' face normally looked a little sad while in repose, but it seemed to Ellayne that these things had truly upset him. She could feel it.

"The end of the Abnaks!" Vannett said. "Not so long ago, everyone in Obann would have been glad to hear that news."

"Until King Thunder finished with the Abnaks and came down after us," said Martis.

Ellayne and Jack exchanged a look. Killing women and children, on purpose, was something they'd never heard of. Besides, there were quite a few Abnaks in King Ryons' army. They'd made friends with some of them and learned they weren't monsters. They'd seen old Uduqu run to the rescue of Helki when Helki slew the giant and a mob of enemy warriors charged him. Uduqu hadn't waited for anyone else to come with him. He might easily have been killed.

"Maybe the king's chieftains can do something," Roshay said. "They have at least five thousand men in Lintum Forest. I'll send a messenger tonight."

Martis rested from his journey, sitting on the porch steps with a mug of beer. Ellayne and Jack sat with him, and Wytt came out and chattered at him.

"What's he saying?" Martis asked. The children understood the Omah's natterings as if it were human speech, and Wytt understood them as if they were Omah—a gift they'd received on top of Bell Mountain.

"He says something's going to happen, but he doesn't know what," Jack said.

"Something good or something bad?"

"He doesn't know," said Ellayne. "But it's something in the air. He can feel it."

"I can, too," said Martis, "and I don't like how it feels."

CHAPTER 5

The Gold of the Golden Pass

Ryons had a letter from Lord Orth, delivered to the edge of Lintum Forest by a rider on a swift horse and through the forest to him by a pair of his Attakott scouts. No one could enter the forest without their knowing it.

It took him some time to make out the name on the letter, and then for a moment he forgot he was a king. He felt like a slave who'd come into possession of something that he shouldn't have and would probably get a whipping for it. It passed soon enough, but then he discovered that he couldn't read the great lord's handwriting. He took it to Obst, who said it was a matter for the chieftains. They assembled around their king and his makeshift throne, a piece of carved stone broken off the castle, and Obst read the letter to them. Those who couldn't yet speak Obannese heard it in their own languages, for Obst had received the gift of tongues. So had Gurun, but Obst was their teacher.

"To Ryons, King of Obann by the grace of God, from his servant Orth, First Prester by election, greetings," Obst read.

"If it please the king, be it known that the Abnak tribes,

26

pressed by a merciless enemy, will soon be forced to enter the king's lands on the west side of the mountains, or else perish. These marches are sparsely populated, and I propose to His Majesty that he grant the Abnaks leave to come into his lands and live, free of all conditions, by the king's grace under God. Let the king make this offer freely, before the Abnaks can petition him, as an act of friendship pleasing in the sight of God.

"For it is not enough to fight against a common enemy. Our nation of Obann came into being, in ancient times, when many nations joined together under the One God who rules them all and became the Tribes of the Law. It may be that the time has come, under the providence of God, for Abnaks and Obannese to become one people, so that centuries of enmity shall be washed away. Or it may be that the Abnaks, in time, will recover their own lands. But until such a time, let Your Majesty extend his hand to them. Our Lord shall bless him for it."

Silence fell, but only for a moment. Chief Buzzard broke it with a throaty laugh.

"Now that's what I call clever!" he said. "We gain a whole nation of hard fighters to our side and hardly have to lift a finger for it! This First Prester has a good head on his shoulders."

"I don't think he meant it as an act of cleverness," said Obst.

"That doesn't make it any less clever. And it's good sense, too. What do you say, King Ryons? I have to say the thought of Abnaks and Obannese as one people amuses me!"

"There are many nations in this army," Obst said, "but it's one army. Still, the decision is yours to make, O King." He bowed to Ryons.

He hated it when anyone did that. They were all training him to be a real king, training him all the time. He supposed they had to.

"I'd rather hear my chiefs speak first," he said, "all of them. How would I know what to do?" He was still a little bit in awe of these men of war who'd accepted him as their lord. These chiefs were fierce in battle; he'd seen it for himself.

"Your Majesty is king, and we have learned to be your servants," Chief Shaffur said. "But if you want my advice, I say it'd be great folly if we wound up having to fight the Thunder King and the Abnaks at the same time. By all means make friends with the Abnaks!"

Xhama, chief of the Red Regiment of the black Hosa, from a very distant country, agreed. "If we can serve you and God, let the Abnaks do the same. My men and I cannot go home again. It's too far away. The Thunder King has stolen many people's homelands, as he's stolen ours. But now let his loss be our gain. I haven't forgotten the sight of the Abnaks and the Fazzan, in this our army, storming the walls of Silvertown."

None of the chieftains spoke against the plan. Now Ryons himself would have to speak.

"Well, my lords, it sounds right to me," he said.

"Then Your Majesty must issue a proclamation, and it must be carried to the Abnaks," Obst said. "Let Chief Shaffur write it. He knows the best words for such things. And let Chief Buzzard choose two or three reliable men to carry it to the Abnaks on their side of the mountains."

"I don't think any of my men know how to read," said Buzzard, "but they can learn it by heart."

Having traveled as swiftly as only he could through wooded lands, Helki stood at last on the road down from the Golden Pass, looking up at the ruins of King Thunder's golden hall.

The snow had melted, most of it, and the gold gleamed like fire in the sun. "Someone ought to come up here and bring it down," he said to himself. "There's enough gold here to buy up everything between the mountains and the sea!" But the very fact that the gold still lay unplundered proved that no one came here. The site was haunted, people said. "All the more reason for King Ryons' army to come this way," he thought—although what some of the lads would do when they saw all that gold lying about for the taking, he didn't care to guess.

There were places in Lintum Forest that were said to be haunted—shapeless heaps of rubble that had once been castles where some great but nameless crime had been committed long ago. Omah lived there now, untroubled by the ghosts of men. Human beings stayed away.

Helki didn't believe in ghosts and had no qualms about making his camp amid the ruins. Tomorrow he'd go down a little ways on the east side to see if the pass was being guarded. He didn't expect that it was. Thanks to the Thunder King, or rather to his hosts of slaves, a road ran all the way down into the lowlands on both sides. "That's what we want," he thought, "a way to get over before King Thunder knows we're there."

Four or five thousand men invading the Thunder King's domain—sheer foolishness, Helki thought. "But that's why no one will expect it."

In the shelter of a crumpled wall he got a fire going, and there he spent the night. The wind moaned and wailed as it blew through cracks and crannies in the sprawling ruin. Sometimes it sounded like voices. You could almost make out words, but they would be words you wouldn't want to hear. And there was a dark cloud, low in the sky, for all the world like a looming head and shoulders of gigantic size. No wonder people stayed away.

Somewhere under it all lay the bones of the previous Thunder King with a golden mask on his face, and also the remains of Lord Reesh, late First Prester of Obann. If anyone were going to do any haunting, Helki thought, it'd be those two. But wouldn't it be a fine trick to play on the present Thunder King, to dig up that gold mask and confront his armies with it! They never saw their master's face; if they ever saw anything of him at all, it'd be the golden mask. The mardars taught them he was a god in human form. But what would the Heathen think if they saw that mask on someone else?

"Not a bad idea, not bad at all," thought Helki. But even he couldn't dig down through that mass of shattered timbers and heavy sheets of gold. You'd need an army of diggers for that, and it might take them all summer. Maybe even longer.

All the same, he thought, it was an idea worth holding on to.

———————

Helki wasn't the only one thinking about the gold of the Golden Pass.

Gallgoid the spy had been there as the servant of Lord Reesh, escaping after he'd learned there was no Thunder

King but only a succession of imposters. He'd fled some days before the avalanche, and on his way down the mountain passed the Griff mardar, Chillith, going up to confront the Thunder King. Ellayne had been guiding him because Chillith was blind, but he'd gotten Gallgoid to bring her down with him. Gallgoid had lost her to Jack and Martis, who were trailing Chillith, and he would have died in the snow if Helki hadn't saved him.

Even now King Thunder's secret was still not widely known in Obann. Ryons' advisers had decided not to publish the news of Lord Reesh's treason. Gallgoid would have preferred to shout it from the housetops. "Let the truth be told, for once!" he said. But Obst feared the truth would turn the people entirely against the clergy, and innocent men would suffer.

The gold was another matter. It ought to be brought down, Gallgoid thought, and converted into coins—coins that might buy off a host of Heathen chiefs wavering in their allegiance to the Thunder King. Gallgoid liked the idea of using the enemy's gold against him. "Golden spearmen might be of much more use to us than men of flesh and blood," he thought.

He discussed the matter secretly with Baron Hennen, general of all King Ryons' forces in the west.

"It'd take a lot of men and carts to bring it down," Hennen said. "And it would be even harder to keep their work a secret. We might be attacked and wiped out before we got the half of it."

"The enemy's armies are busy with the Abnaks."

"I don't have that many men to spare. There are still some fugitives from King Thunder's army to be rounded up, and towns and villages to be resettled."

"You can pick up more men as you go," said Gallgoid.

"There's always the possibility of a plot or an insurrection right here in the city. That's my chief concern."

Gallgoid nodded. Obann was full of men who thought they ought to be ruling it as oligarchs, without a king. In spite of the First Prester's preaching, there were many who wanted the Temple restored and reestablished as it had always been. There were even a few who wished to pledge themselves to the New Temple in the East, hoping it would mean peace with the Thunder King. Gallgoid's agents listened to what people were saying in the market squares, the ale houses, and on the street, and reported to him faithfully.

"Since the burning of the Palace last summer," he said, "I've detected nothing that looks like an active plot against the throne. People are trickling out of the city and not coming back. At least consider my proposal, Baron. Maybe send a hundred men. Baron Bault in Ninneburky may be able to lend you more."

"One hundred men? I might be able to send that many. I'll consider it," said Hennen. He broke into a grin. "It's only fitting that King Thunder ought to finance our war against him!"

CHAPTER 6

The Great Bridge

ost of the time when Jandra looked at Obst's big book, it was only a curiosity to her—a lot of funny markings on a page. She knew she was a prophetess because everybody said so, but she couldn't have told you what a prophetess was. They called Ryons a king, but that word had very little meaning for her, too. He was just a boy who chased her when she wanted to be chased. She was old enough now to run, and she enjoyed it.

Whatever had happened to her mother and father was lost to her memory. She was a well-loved little girl who had Abgayle to take care of her, and the scarred old Ghol Chagadai to set her on horseback and walk the horse around for her, and her own toothed bird that followed her everywhere she went—a revolting creature, most people thought, about the size of a large crow, with dirty purple plumage and a long tail like a lizard's, but covered with stiff feathers. It had claws on its wings and hissed and snapped at people who got too close to Jandra. She loved it as another child might love a playful dog.

She did understand, in a way, that the grownup people at Carbonek were in awe of her and that she was a very important person. This might have spoiled some children, but it hadn't spoiled her.

33

All she knew was that she sometimes fell asleep in the middle of whatever she was doing. They told her that while she was asleep, she prophesied—whatever that was. She couldn't remember a time when she hadn't done that, so she just accepted it.

Today she was going to meet Lord Orth, a great man who'd come all the way from Obann City to visit Ryons. They'd had to march up to a place in the northern fringes of the forest to meet him. Abgayle bathed her and washed her clothes, and men took turns carrying her piggyback through the forest. The Ghols sang to her from deep down in their throats, and sometimes King Ryons walked with her, hand in hand. All the chiefs were there, too. Jandra's bird had plenty of people to hiss at.

Orth gave a talk, with the chiefs and Obst and Gurun in a circle all around him. Jandra liked the look of him—a big, sturdy man with a black beard shot with grey and a wonderful voice like great wheels rolling. But whatever he was talking about had no meaning for her. She sat on the ground and offered little twigs to her bird, who shook them fiercely and cast them aside. She liked the way he did that.

She was surprised when Abgayle picked her up and put her in Lord Orth's arms. He beamed at her.

"'Babes and children see what is hidden from you in your foolish wisdom.' King Ozias spoke those words, preserved for us in Scripture," Orth said. "But you, my lords and brothers, have not been foolish. You have listened to this little child and done the will of God." Quietly, Obst repeated his words so that all the chiefs could understand them.

"You and your people are the Lord's first fruits among the Heathen. There will be many more to come. The spirit of the Lord goes forth as a conqueror, confined no longer to a Temple in a single city. When you carry His word across the mountains, He will bless you. For He loves you mightily, and in His service you'll do mighty deeds."

The chiefs in all their warlike finery sat silent, their eyes fixed on the speaker. But then Jandra suddenly perceived that they weren't looking at him, but at her. And that was all she knew until she woke again in Abgayle's arms, not his.

―――――――――

Lord Orth was like a man who'd been stabbed, Ryons thought. When God's words came out of Jandra's mouth, Orth's face went all pale and stony. When Jandra stopped speaking, and Abgayle came and took her, Gurun helped the First Prester to a vacant stool such as the chieftains used. He almost fell off it when he sat.

"Thank you," he gasped.

"It is hard to hear that voice come from such a little girl," Gurun said. "It doesn't happen so often that one gets used to it."

Ryons thought it was happening a bit more often, lately. The army was preparing to move, the chiefs only waiting for Helki to advise them what route to take. They expected God to advise them, too, through Jandra. God had done that before. But Ryons had never seen anyone quite so shaken up as Orth was.

"It is my sins coming back to accuse me, my lords," Orth said, after taking a deep breath. "When I was an ambitious man, I persecuted the prophets. God sent them to give our city warning, but I spoke against them. When we hanged them, I consented to their deaths. I did it out of ignorance.

I was blind; I did not see. But the Lord has opened my eyes and has forgiven me. How He was able to do that, I don't understand. But when I remember what I did, my shame is almost too great to bear."

No one answered him. Ryons was glad he had no such things on his own conscience; he hoped he never would. The man was in great pain, a kind of pain the boy had never known existed.

"And now," said Orth, "that God should speak to me, through this innocent and lovely child, face-to-face!" He sighed and shook his head.

And what was it that Jandra had said?

"You are the last of the old presters, my son, and the first of the new; and you shall bear a burden for me, too heavy for your strength. But I will lend you strength, and you shall be a bridge; and my people shall cross over you from one age of the world into the next."

What that might mean, Ryons couldn't imagine. Maybe Obst could. There was pity in his face as he looked down at Orth seated on a stool, sweating on a cool spring day under the shade of the trees. But it was Gurun who stood beside him with a hand on his shoulder, and he reached up and covered her hand with his own.

"Be comforted, my lord," she said. "The Scripture says that there is no man righteous: no, not one. But there is a seed of righteousness that God Himself has planted in us, that grows toward God's own righteousness. Did not Ozias say so, in the Sacred Songs?"

Orth nodded, but did not speak.

"My lords," said Obst, "we are all part of the great bridge God is building. For now, a bridge across the mountains, into Heathen lands. You were all Heathen once, warlords. But God has accepted you as a new people who belong to Him."

The chiefs muttered their assent. They had all seen God win battles for them.

"It's a miracle that any of us is still alive," Chief Zekelesh said, "the kind of scrapes we've been in."

Orth wanted to stand back up, and Gurun helped him.

"To meet you, and to hear you speak, has been a blessing to me, my lords," he said. "I'll remember it as I travel on to Ninneburky, and from there to the mountains. You'll all be in my prayers from now on." He turned to Ryons and bowed. "And you especially, my king. May your reign be long and glorious."

Because it seemed the right thing to do, Ryons stood up and doffed his black-feathered Wallekki headdress.

"Thank you, First Prester," he said. It was in his mind that he was in the presence of a great man deserving of honor and respect. "May your reign be long and glorious, too." He truly didn't know what else to say, but that seemed sufficient.

———

It reached the ears of Ysbott that the First Prester was coming to Ninneburky.

"If only I had a way to get this news to the Thunder King!" he said in front of his men. But they were no help. He did all their thinking for them; otherwise, they would not survive.

Ysbott made it his business to know what was happening in Ninneburky. He had two or three persons in the town who kept him informed and whom he paid with stolen money. These relayed news to a few farmers, shepherds, and river-folk outside, whom Ysbott repaid by not stealing anything from them. He'd never had to do this when he lived in Lintum Forest, but nowadays he found it necessary. He had to know, at least, in which direction the baron's mounted patrols were headed.

Someday, he was sure, the baron's daughter would come out again, and he would pay her back for using witchcraft on him and almost blinding him. No demand for ransom this time—he'd sell her into slavery and let her father know it.

He would have been interested to learn that Ellayne was getting itchy feet again, despite her eagerness to learn all she could about her father's business.

"I'd love to see Lintum Forest again," she confided to Jack, "and King Ryons and Helki, and Obst and Fnaa. I wonder what they're all doing."

"Don't you want to stay and see the First Prester when he comes?" Jack said. "He'll be here soon."

"He'd want to see us, that's for sure—if he knew we were the ones who rang King Ozias' bell and found the Lost Scrolls in the ruined Temple. Do you think anyone has told him? It's something he ought to know."

"You make me nervous when you talk like that," Jack said. They were in the space between the back of the stables and the hedge, practicing throwing Jack's penknife so it would stick in the ground. "We can't go around telling people about those things! How many times does Martis have to tell you that?"

Ellayne sighed. "It's hard to believe there's nothing more for us to do," she said. "And we're only kids."

"There'll be plenty for us to do when we grow up. The war's not over yet. The Thunder King will come again, or at least his armies will."

While the children were away on adventures, an army of Zephites once came to Ninneburky. Roshay Bault led a desperate defense of the town, and finally God drove off the Zephites with a storm of ice and snow. It had taken a long time to bury the dead bodies, people said. Even now you could still find bits of weaponry, and bulls' horns broken off the Zephite headgear, scattered around outside the palisade. Jack was thinking it would be good if such a thing never happened again, but was afraid it might.

"Wytt thinks something big is going to happen soon," said Ellayne, "and I'm beginning to think so, too. It's been quiet for too long."

"You read too much Abombalbap," Jack said. But he knew that all the quiet was too good to last.

CHAPTER 7

Who Will Go, and Who Will Stay

When he was the leader of an outlaw band in Lintum Forest, Ysbott the Snake robbed and murdered whom he pleased without fear of retribution. It was an easy life.

Now, with mounted patrols on the lookout for him and much more open, settled country around him than he liked, it forced him to do more—and better—thinking than he'd ever had to do before. His talent for crime began to blossom as it never would have done without such challenges.

One morning he shaved off his beard, cropped his long and stringy hair and darkened it—and his moustache and his eyebrows—with charcoal. He wrapped a bandana around his head, as a man might do for protection from the sun, which concealed the scar upon his cheek, and donned a hat with a broad and floppy brim.

"Waha!" said one of his men, a Wallekki straggler. "Your own mother wouldn't know you, master! But why do you do so?"

"I'm going to spend some days in Ninneburky," Ysbott said. "I want to get a good look at the First Prester when he comes and see for myself what's what."

"But it's the baron's own town!" another man objected. "Isn't it too dangerous to go there?"

"Right in the middle of Ninneburky is the last place they'd ever look for me. I'll stay with our friend, Hrapp the cobbler. He'll keep me safe—for a little money and a promise not to cut his throat."

"But what'll we do, chief, while you're gone?"

"Lie low," Ysbott said, "and don't get up to any mischief. Do nothing! Is that clear?"

"Nothing?"

"Nothing until I return." Ysbott didn't trust this bunch not to get themselves captured and hanged the moment his back was turned. They'd be small loss to him, but it would be a bother to recruit another gang.

Nor could he trust any man of them to come with him to Ninneburky, with or without a disguise. Whomever he picked, the fool would be bound to get drunk one night and say or do something that would get them both arrested.

He packed his bag with provisions, filled his waterskin, took up his walking-staff, and set out for Ninneburky, a full day's march from their camp in a wooded tract beside the river. His men looked wistful as they stood to see him off.

"Remember!" he said. "Do nothing till I'm back."

"Can we do a bit of fishing, boss?"

Ysbott glared at them, then turned and walked away.

———————

Helki's three scouts returned to Carbonek with his advice to march to the Golden Pass, and that as soon as possible. The chieftains met to consider it.

"It's the long way around," said Shaffur. "I don't like

giving the enemy that much time to prepare for us."

"But Helki's counsel has always been good counsel," said Tughrul Lomak of the Dahai. "We can cross the river at Ninneburky and go on from there—an easy journey."

"First we have to decide who goes with us and who stays here," Chagadai said. "Shall our father the king go?"

"Let the king decide for himself," said Shaffur.

"Why is it always me?" thought Ryons. But the answer to that was always, "Well, you are the king, aren't you?"

"I go where my army goes," he said; and that was the answer they wanted to hear.

"When you're a man, Your Majesty, your army will go where you go," Shaffur said.

It didn't take them long to decide to follow Helki's advice. It took them much longer to decide to leave two thousand men at Carbonek. They'd be needed, in case the Thunder King's mardars launched another attack on Silvertown.

To the Golden Pass would go those who could travel fastest—the Wallekki and the Ghols on horseback, most of the fleet-footed Attakotts, the long-striding Griffs, and the Hosa regiment, some five hundred men. "We can march all day at a run," said Hawk, the chief, "and still fight a battle at the end of it." The Obannese, the Abnaks under Chief Buzzard, the Fazzan with Chief Zekelesh, and Tughrul's kilted Dahai, would stay behind to defend Carbonek and do whatever unexpected things needed doing.

"This is hard for us to bear," said Zekelesh. "Our wolf's heads have been carried into every one of King Ryons' battles and never turned aside. We want to be with him."

"Never mind," Tughrul said. "Something will come up

that calls for fighting."

Obst, of course, would have to go. The army wouldn't move without its teacher. The chieftains wanted to leave Gurun behind, but she wouldn't hear of it.

"I should have died," she said, "when the storm caught my father's skiff and hurled it over the sea—but I didn't. The boat didn't fall to pieces until it brought me all the way to Obann, and that was God's will. My place is with King Ryons. My filgya told me so."

Some of the chieftains nodded. They knew the story of Gurun and the storm and knew that the filgya was a messenger of God. Which is not to say they understood it, but they had learned to accept such things.

Jandra would have to stay behind. She was much too young to go. But old Uduqu wouldn't stay with his fellow Abnaks, but demanded to go with the king.

"I took a shine to him when he was still a slave and he sassed me in my own tent," Uduqu said. "I almost died where I stood, that time he charged the enemy single-handed and put them to flight—a scared little boy who had all he could do just to stay on the horse." Chagadai the Ghol whistled through his teeth and shuddered. As the king's bodyguard, he would never forget that awful moment. It was the horse's fault, but Ryons got great glory from it.

Uduqu rose from his stool and flourished a great sword that took all the strength in both his hands. "Most of you were there the day I won this sword," he said. "It once belonged to Shogg the giant, King Thunder's champion, that Helki killed. I picked up this sword and cut two men in half with it, just like that. You saw me do it.

"This sword doesn't want to rust in its sheath, and nei-

ther do I. We both belong to King Ryons, and we will fight
for him again before I close my eyes for the last time."

"Hoo! Hoo!" growled the Abnaks and smacked their
palms against their thighs. This was the kind of talk they
liked. But when they were quiet again, Obst said, "Maybe
there will be more battles, maybe not. Whatever the case, we
go east as the servants of God—you and I, Uduqu, and King
Ryons, too. And every one of us."

"You have my meaning, Teacher," said Uduqu, as he sat
back down.

It was decided that Fnaa should remain at Carbonek,
too, in case any need arose for the king's double to imper-
sonate the king. He took it badly, and it fell to Obst to try to
comfort him.

"It's not fair!" Fnaa cried. "I want to ride with the army.
You're going, Obst, and you're as old as the hills. If you can
keep up, then so can I."

"You don't think I want to go, do you?" Obst answered.
"All my life I've never wanted anything but to live here in
peace, as a hermit. But I do the work that God has given
me—as must we all."

"But Gurun will be going, and she's only a girl!"

Obst smiled. "If you can think of a way to stop her, I'd
like to hear it. But think of Ryons," he said. "He never wanted
to be a king! I'd say he was more cheerful as a slave. But God
has chosen him to be a king, and he obeys. You can be sure
God had a good reason for bringing you forth as the very
likeness of the king. Stay here and do whatever work He sets
for you. Stay here and learn the Scriptures. I have a feeling

that your work is far from over—very far."

"And what about yours?" Fnaa said. "How much longer can you do it? They say it is a long way to that Golden Pass."

Obst shrugged. "No one has to tell me that I'm old, my boy. I'll just carry on for as long as I can, until the Lord releases me."

Fnaa took a long, hard look at him.

"That might take a while longer than you think," the boy said. "Did you know that a few of your hairs have turned black? I'm sure they were white in the winter, and now they're black. I've only just noticed it."

Obst couldn't help reaching up to feel his beard, which of course told him nothing.

"That's not a nice prank, Fnaa."

"It's not a prank. It's the truth. Ask someone else about it; they'll tell you. How old are you, anyway?"

"I don't know," Obst said. He paused to think, but couldn't find the answer. "I lost track of the years a long time ago." He said no more. What could it mean for black hairs to be sprouting up among the white? It troubled his spirit.

"Maybe you're getting younger instead of older," said Fnaa.

"Hush! That's foolishness!" said Obst. But he was afraid to ask anyone else about it.

CHAPTER 8

Dinner with Lord Orth

The whole town of Ninneburky, and other folk from miles around, turned out to see and hear the First Prester. There was no room for them all in Ninneburky's little chamber house, nor in any one place inside the town. The baron had carpenters erect a platform just outside the gate, and everyone gathered around it.

Martis cautioned Jack and Ellayne—especially Ellayne. "Remember," he said, "not a word about Bell Mountain! It wouldn't be safe for you, and it wouldn't be safe for the First Prester to hear it."

Martis would be the only man in town not to attend Lord Orth's sermon. "He would just recognize me as Lord Reesh's servant; he was deep in Reesh's confidence. We don't want him wondering what I'm doing here! I'll stay out of sight until he moves on."

"Why would it be unsafe for him to know about us?" Ellayne asked.

"Not all the serpents have been put out of the Temple," Martis said.

Ninneburky's own prester, Ashrof—Jack's mother's uncle and his last blood kin—had nearly been put out of the Temple for being old and useless. Now he stood beside Lord Orth on the platform to introduce him to the people. And the First Prester presented him with a new book of all the Scriptures to be read to all the people in the chamber house.

"These are God's own words to us," Orth said, "and for too long have they gone unheard. From now on, God's word shall be preached in all the chamber houses of Obann—not what men have said about it, but the word itself."

In his wonderful, deep voice that carried to the farthest fringes of the crowd, he spoke of his vision of the Temple— a new Temple, not made with human hands, but one that would be everywhere. Because people living this far east had seldom had a chance to see the great Temple in Obann, they were more receptive to the vision than the people of the city.

Every day the baroness read to Ellayne and Jack from their own copy of the Scriptures, the gift of Queen Gurun. But when Lord Orth recited Scripture, it was like thunder rolling in the hills.

"My house shall be the house of prayer for all the nations on the earth," he quoted from the Prophet Enwy. "O people, rejoice—for we shall see the beginning of the fulfillment of this prophecy. First to the Tribes of the Law, the many peoples who became one people of Obann, and then to the peoples of the mountains, and then to the peoples of the East—God's word goes forth to save, to heal, to conquer. As King Ozias wrote, 'to bring sight to the blind, and hope to the hopeless, salvation to the lost, and wisdom to the simple.' We won't live to see the end of this great thing, but we are here for the beginning."

———

Ysbott the Snake stood unnoticed in the crowd.

"Words, words, words!" he thought. "Will this fellow

never make an end of words? What's his temple and his book to me?"

Ysbott was waiting for something; he didn't know what. Once or twice since his arrival in Ninneburky, he thought he'd seen the baron's daughter in the street. He'd seen the baron several times, Roshay Bault, striding around in his own importance, who would hang him if he ever got the chance. Once Roshay passed him almost close enough to touch, but never even looked at him. Ysbott nearly laughed out loud.

"All in good time—all in good time!" he thought. Some lucky chance was bound to come his way. And then he would have his revenge, and maybe more.

———————

The First Prester had dinner at the baron's house.

It was just as well for the baroness and the cook that they didn't know Lord Orth used to be famous in Obann for the sumptuousness of his table, second only to Lord Reesh in that respect. As it was, Lanora outdid herself to produce a feast: leek soup, leg of lamb, fresh fish from the river, with sweet iced cakes for dessert and the baron's best beer to wash it down. Vannett fluttered in and out of the kitchen all afternoon, trying to make sure everything was perfect. "Oh me, I'm trying, I'm trying!" wailed Lanora. They didn't know First Prester Orth was now famous for the simplicity of his meals and for always having places at his table for the city's poor. More than a few of Obann's needy citizens could say they'd had supper with the First Prester of the Temple.

He was a nice man, Ellayne thought, and certainly a noble-looking one. Enith, she knew, would have given her eyeteeth to have been there; she was bound to ask a hundred questions about what the First Prester said, and did, and what he ate, and how he liked it. Ellayne wished she could tell him all about the climbing of Bell Mountain and impress him. Jack must have read her mind, the way he kept shooting warning looks at her.

When the meal was mostly finished, and everyone was just filling in the corners with dessert, Roshay Bault launched into more serious talk. But first he cautioned his daughter.

"You're going to need to know about these things, Ellayne, if you're going to be a help to me," he said. "You, too, Jack. But even more, you'll have to learn to keep such matters to yourselves. If you can't, you'll be no use to me." He looked sternly at Ellayne. "And then you might as well go off to finishing school! I hope that's understood."

Ellayne just nodded. She knew when her father was in no mood to be teased.

"My lord First Prester," Roshay said, "I understand you intend to visit the people in the mountains. I can see why you wish to do that—but is it wise? There's no telling when war might break out up there. It won't be safe for you to be there when it does."

"It's necessary, my lord Baron," said the First Prester. "Someday soon we must build chamber houses in that country, where the people can go to hear God's word. They've been neglected much too long. Abnaks will be coming in, more and more of them, and they will need to hear it, too. The king has given them leave to cross over."

"I'm not looking forward to having to ride up there with my troops to rescue you."

"I wouldn't want you to. They'll be needed to defend the towns along the river."

Roshay told him of the Zephite army that came down and almost captured Ninneburky.

"There's no doubt in my mind that God Himself saved us, when we were at the end of our strength," he said. "But for that, this town would be nothing but a heap of charred timbers today and all the people killed or sold into Heathen slavery. You'd understand if you had seen it, my lord. As for me, I pray I'll never again see anything like it."

"Baron, you cannot contain the spirit of God. He has heard the bell ring on Bell Mountain. He has restored to us the Lost Book of Ozias. He has done away with the old Temple to make place for the new. His spirit is on the move, and we cannot hold it back. We'd be very wrong to try. And very foolish, too."

Under the table, Jack squeezed Ellayne's hand good and hard. The way the First Prester spoke, you could understand that these were great matters, to be taken seriously. "If we hadn't climbed Bell Mountain," Jack thought, "someone else would have. God would have called someone else because it was time." And now was not the time for a couple of kids to be bragging about themselves! But of course Ellayne had more sense than that and said nothing at all.

"It will be the spirit of the Lord, and not our armies, that decides the events of this age," Orth said. "He honors and He blesses us by letting us take part in them, but the work is the work of His hands."

Baron Bault sighed, but did not speak. Even Ellayne looked solemn.

"Well," said Vannett, breaking the silence, "I hope you'll be careful, my lord First Prester! Obann can ill afford to lose you."

Orth gave her such a look that made Jack wonder; you'd think he had been stabbed.

"Thank you, Lady Bault," Orth said, "but I am the least of God's servants. He will raise up a better man in my place. But I will be careful, and I have friends in the mountains who will always take good care of me. Have no fear on my account."

———————

Lord Orth set out for the mountains the very next day. He and his escort crossed the river on the baron's ferry, with the townsfolk cheering on the riverbank. Off in the east loomed the mountains, waiting for him.

Ninneburky then went back to its everyday business, and Ellayne answered questions from Enith until she could have gagged the girl. And you had to be careful when you were answering Enith's questions: she knew her friends were part of something secret, and she never gave up trying to tease the secret out of them.

"I have an idea," Jack interrupted. "Why don't you read us more of that story about Abombalbap and the glass bridge?" He turned to Enith. "Unless you don't care about it anymore."

"Don't care?" Enith said. "I've been wondering about it all this time!"

Ellayne ran off to get the book, and they settled down with it behind the stables. Wytt found them there and climbed onto Ellayne's shoulder.

"He doesn't understand those stories—does he?" Enith wondered.

"He doesn't see any point to them," Ellayne said, as she

opened the book and found her place. "He just likes to listen." She began to read.

"Abombalbap sat long pondering how he might get across the bridge. By no means, he thought, could he ride across on his horse; and surely, if he went on foot, the weight of his armor would be the ruin of him. Forsooth, he said, a man might hardly run over that bridge naked, but it would shatter under him.

"And as he pondered, there came another knight on a black horse, having a red shield. Sir, he said, I would joust with you for the honor of being first across yon bridge, to save the damsel from her prison. But Abombalbap said, Nay, I will not joust with you: for it seems to me that no knight may cross that bridge, however valiant he might be.

"Well, said Brandyle, for that was the knight's name, I am no dastard, to hang back when brave deeds beckon. It seems to me that speed and courage will carry a good knight across any bridge in this world, and I will essay the adventure.

"I would not, if I were you, said Abombalbap, for this is no bridge of any worldly kind. It is a bridge magical and sorcerous and may not be crossed by dint of any speed of horse or hardihood of man. But Brandyle laughed him to scorn and said, Fie, you sluggard knight! You shall see me achieve what you durst not attempt.

"Then Brandyle drew his sword and set spurs to his horse, and cried a great cry, and galloped with all possible speed upon the bridge. But before he could advance the length of the horse's body, the bridge shattered into a thousand thousand shining shards that glistened in the sun like specks of ice and flew away in all directions; and man and horse cried out grievously in great despair as together they fell. Long time they cried before Abombalbap could hear them cry no more.

"Poor Brandyle! he said and stood up to see if there were aught that he might do. And no sooner was he on his feet than, in the blink of an eye, the glass bridge once again spanned the gulf between him and the island of the castle: for it was replenished in an instant by a mighty magic, and it was as whole again as ever it was before."

Here Ellayne replaced the marker and closed the book.

"You're not stopping!" cried Enith.

"It's a long story," Ellayne said, "and you'll like it better if you don't get it all at once."

"But how is Abombalbap ever going to rescue the princess if he can't get across the bridge?" The story had gone to Enith's heart.

"Nobody could ever make a glass bridge, anyhow," Jack said. And yet it seemed to him, for no reason he could think of, that Lord Orth, of all people, would have liked this story and would have had something shrewd to say about it. Obst always said there was no such thing as magic, and Jack agreed with him. But Orth surely would have said something that the children never would have thought of by themselves. "Too bad we didn't get a chance to read it to him," Jack thought.

CHAPTER 9

The Army on the March

Taking his time about it, Helki wended his way back from the Golden Pass.

The forest that clung to the skirts of the mountains was not like Lintum Forest, and Helki wished to know it better. Its trees weren't as tall as the trees of Lintum Forest, but there were more of them, packed more densely together. It was an older forest, dark, disorderly. In olden time noblemen had castles in Lintum, and little villages sprang up around them. That had never happened here. Hunters and trappers came, but left no mark on the country. No one could farm the rocky ground, and no one wanted to live so close to the Abnaks. The few settlements that had been lately founded here, in the wake of the Thunder King's invasion, lived close to the bone indeed. Game was plentiful enough, if you had the skill to catch it, and there were wild berries, edible mushrooms—and some that had better not be eaten—and roots to be collected. The settlers wouldn't starve, but they would never know abundance.

From Hlah, on his way back from the pass, Helki learned that the king had opened the country to the Abnaks—not that any power in Obann could have kept them out.

"I hope they'll behave themselves," Helki said. "Old habits die hard."

"The men will settle their women and children," Hlah said, "and then go back across the mountains to take scalps. My people will never surrender their own country to the Thunder King. If they have to stay here for seven generations, they'll never stop fighting."

"What I want to know," said Helki, "is whether the Thunder King has any scouts this side of the mountains."

Hlah shook his head. "None that ever come back to him alive," he said.

So that was good, thought Helki. The mountains would conceal the movements of King Ryons' army. He hoped the king's advisers would find a way to convince the enemy that the army was still in Lintum Forest, poised to rescue Silvertown, should the Heathen attack it again. But everyone was saying they were too busy with the Abnaks.

"We should get to the Golden Pass without much trouble," he thought. "But what we're going to do when we come down, God only knows."

With little more than half his army, King Ryons was on the march. They were out of Lintum Forest and making good time across the plains, bound for Ninneburky and the river.

They sang as they marched. The Ghols made music deep down in their throats and sounded hardly human. The Hosa chanted songs of war, beating time with spear on shield. Wallekki riders sang epic tales of ancient feuds, breaking into endless verses on the genealogy of heroes. But from time to time they all came together to sing the army's anthem.

"His mercy endureth forever!"

This was the best part of the adventure, Ryons thought—hearing his men praise God in their triumphal discord of unrelated languages. Some who knew no better might have thought they were stirring themselves up for a riot, but Ryons by now was used to it. If you listened carefully, you might pick up a subtle melody that unified the chaos. Ryons sang along with them, sometimes trying (and failing) to imitate his Ghols, but mostly singing in the Wallekki dialect he'd learned growing up as a slave in their camps. He'd had no mother then, no father.

The verses of the anthem came and went, made up on the march by men as words came to them.

"We washed our spears at Silvertown!" rumbled the Hosa. "O-hoo, o-hoo! God lent us might! We march all day and camp at night, under the stars of heaven!"

And the Griffs sang this:

"The Great Man took away our gods—

"Weep no more, O Griffs!

"The Father of Gods has made you strong:

"You're men again, not children—

"Weep no more, O Griffs!"

Alongside Ryons' horse trotted Cavall, grinning, with his red tongue hanging out. Overhead flew his hawk, Angel, honored by the Hosa as the hero of the Battle of the Brickbats, when they captured Silvertown. And behind him, led by Perkin the wanderer, stalked Baby—raised by Perkin from a chick that sat on the palm of his hand, but now grown taller than a man, with a beak that could crush a horse's skull in a single bite. Baby had grown accustomed to the army and no longer snapped at men and horses.

"Is it not good, Father, to be out under the open sky again?" said Chagadai, who rode at Ryons' right hand. Ryons was young enough to be his grandson, but it was the Ghols' custom to call him their father. "Lintum Forest has been good to us, but it's still no place for horsemen."

Ryons was thinking how happy he'd be to go back to the forest when all of this business was over and done with, but he didn't say so. "It won't be so good, once we get into a battle," he answered.

"Bah! Is that any way to talk, for the king who routed single-handed a whole host of enemies at the very gates of Obann?"

"It wasn't me. It was that great beast that picked me up and put me on its back."

Chagadai laughed. "If you were my child," he said, "I wouldn't let you anywhere near a battle—not at your age! But God has made you king, and we have to make the best of it."

A little ways off rode Gurun, sitting tall and straight in the saddle, fair and noble in a gown of bluest blue, her mind concentrated on the task of not falling off the horse. Around her trotted eighteen Blays, stout little men, expert slingers from a country even farther east than the Ghols'—all that remained of three or four hundred that had marched into Obann for the Thunder King. They didn't look like tireless runners, but they were.

"Look at that girl, there," said Chagadai. "She's not afraid of battle! And I'm sure she's never seen one."

"That's why she's not afraid," thought Ryons. But he doubted Gurun was afraid of anything.

Not being human himself, it never entered Wytt's mind to look down on humans' shortcomings. He accepted it as their nature to be practically blind, deaf, without a sense of smell, and almost as helpless as a newborn Omah, pink and hairless. If Wytt had had the habit of wondering about such things, he might have speculated endlessly on what humans were like when they were born.

Wytt knew that Ysbott the Snake was nearby—not that he knew the man's name or cared to know it. Nor had his eyes seen through Ysbott's disguise, because to an Omah, one adult male human being looks as much like another as any pair of starlings would look to a human. But Ysbott's scent was in the air, just the faintest whiff of it, and Wytt remembered it as the scent of an enemy. It belonged to the man who'd kidnapped Jack, not so long ago, and whom Wytt had stabbed in the cheek while he was sleeping. Wytt found a house where that scent was particularly strong, but didn't go in because there was an unfriendly cat on the premises.

You might have thought he would immediately tell Ellayne and Jack what he'd discovered, so that Whiteface—Martis—could deal with the man, but he didn't. He fully intended to, but his kind takes little notice of the passage of time. Having to live inside a colony of Big People made him more cautious than he would be otherwise. But he did share the news with the old rat under the porch.

The rat was not happy that an enemy was in town. He had a tolerant view of human beings. None had ever chased or screamed at him, and they were, after all, the source of those delicious tidbits from the kitchen. To learn that some of those large, two-legged creatures could be dangerous unsettled him.

"Whiteface and I, we will kill him someday soon," Wytt said.

The rat shivered. Rats fought and killed each other, occasionally. He was just barely able to imagine a kind of rat-fight involving human beings, and he didn't like it.

"We kill him somewhere else, not here," Wytt promised. And the rat was reassured.

———

Back in Lintum Forest, Fnaa suffered from a sense of being left out of important doings.

Some of the adults at Carbonek teased him by calling him "Your Majesty," as if being the king's double were a joke. He'd enjoyed himself in Obann, holding the king's place until Ryons should turn up again; but at the same time, he'd understood that he was doing something tremendously important, and that if he didn't do it well, there would be trouble like he couldn't imagine. But now the few people who'd appreciated his work—Queen Gurun and Uduqu and Obst—had all marched off with Ryons. And he missed the king especially, who'd become the best friend he'd ever had.

Do what is in your heart, Jandra had told him, back in Obann: for God is with you.

"When are you going to do some more prophecy?" he asked her, the morning after the army set out from Carbonek. Jandra only giggled and didn't know what he was talking about. She was just a little girl and didn't even understand the word "prophecy." She just did it sometimes, and didn't know she did it.

"That's as it should be," Obst always said. "She is pure. She's not old enough to make up any of the things she says.

By this we can be sure it's God's spirit speaking through her."

"They shouldn't have left me behind," Fnaa said. But Jandra just said, "Look at bugs!" She pointed to some ants going around in circles.

Fnaa sighed, but he couldn't help looking. Someone who knew about ants might have told them that these had somehow lost their scent trail and couldn't find their way back to the anthill. "Ants are supposed to know what they're doing," Fnaa said, "but these don't. What's the matter with them?"

Jandra's toothed bird squawked, and she got up and merrily chased after it. She didn't toddle anymore, Fnaa noticed. She'd learned how to walk properly. When had that happened?

From the castle wall, a cardinal chirped to its mate. City-born and bred, Fnaa enjoyed listening to the birds in the forest. But just now he ignored it.

"There's nothing for me to do around here," he grumbled to himself. "And if anything happens to Ryons, and he doesn't come back, I can't just keep on pretending to be him for the rest of my life!" He was sure God would not be pleased with that.

"I can at least go as far as Ninneburky," he thought. He wanted to see Jack and Ellayne again, even if he couldn't catch up to Ryons and the army. "Yes—I'll go."

CHAPTER 10

The Chieftains and the Gold

All the city of Obann was agog. A couple of trappers had come down from the north and set up an exhibit in a corner of High Market Square—three sets of gigantic antlers, impossibly huge, mounted on a wooden frame atop a cart. For a penny they would let you touch the antlers and see that they were real. And for the coins people tossed into their oaken bucket, the trappers told wonderful stories.

Gallgoid went to see for himself. They weren't ordinary antlers, from ordinary deer. Venison used to appear often enough on Lord Reesh's table for Gallgoid to recognize the difference. These antlers were flattened, spread out almost like moose antlers, but their points were long and sharp. The deer that carried them must have been as big as houses. Gallgoid paid his penny and ran his fingers over them. They were real, all right.

"Well, no, the critters aren't as big as you might think," said one of the trappers, a squat, grey-bearded man. "They're bigger than your regular deer, sure, but not that much. When you see one, you wonder how he can hold his head off the ground with all that artillery up there. But he does—

61

and heaven help you if you get too close! They move like lightning."

Gallgoid dropped a silver coin in the bucket, and the younger man took up the tale. But it wasn't animal stories that captured Gallgoid's interest.

"Oh, yes," the trapper said, "Lord Chutt has pretty much straightened things out, up north." Chutt was the only survivor of the old High Council of the Oligarchy. He ran away from Obann City when the Heathen armies came. "He's got the people organized, you see." Indeed, Chutt had raised his own militia, swelling its numbers by taking into his service fugitives from the Thunder King's scattered horde.

Gallgoid went on to bear this news to Baron Hennen, but Hennen had already heard it.

"I'm going to have to march up there with at least two thousand men," he said, "and see if I can make Lord Chutt swear allegiance to the king. It sounds to me like he has ideas of setting up his own kingdom in the north. That might be a danger to us."

"I should know more about this," Gallgoid said. "I'm afraid I've neglected the north."

"I thought Chutt was dead, like all the others. I'm sorry, Gallgoid, but I can't spare any men for the Golden Pass."

Gallgoid nodded. It couldn't be helped. But at least the city itself was quiet. His agents had assured him of that.

He returned to his office. He had a feeling Hennen didn't quite believe in the great store of gold that lay unguarded at the pass. Gallgoid was the only man in Obann who'd seen it with his own eyes.

"It's going to breed trouble, all that gold," he thought.

Helki made his way quickly down the river and arrived in time to join the king's army while it camped outside Ninneburky. After paying his respects to the king, he visited Jack and Ellayne.

It seemed strange to have him in the baron's parlor. He was as out of place there as a wild boar would be, and he felt it, too.

"Believe it or not," he told the family, "this is the first time I've ever been inside any place that could properly be called a house." But the children were overjoyed to see him again, and he them. "You've grown, the pair of you," he said. "I wouldn't be surprised if the next time I saw you, you were all grown up."

"You haven't changed a bit," said Ellayne, "and the king and queen and Obst had supper here last night! Oh, how I wish we were going with them when they leave tomorrow!"

Her father flashed her a stern look. "Watch out for these two, Helki," he said. "Their adventuring days are over, but sometimes I don't think they know it yet."

"We know it!" Jack said with a smile.

"We have to have a pow-wow, Baron—you and me and all the chieftains," Helki said. "Tonight, I mean. In the chiefs' black tent, with no one else."

"Bad news?"

"Oh, I wouldn't say that!" Helki grinned. "Might even be good news, if we can find the right thing to do about it. We'll talk about it later." He turned to Ellayne. "How about Wytt? Is he still with you?"

"Come on," Ellayne said, "we'll find him."

Now gold has a way of making itself known even when

people try to keep it a secret. And it was gold that Helki wished to discuss with the chieftains. Except for Roshay Bault himself, no one else from Ninneburky was invited to the chiefs' big tent that evening, nor any soldier in the army.

This was the tent they'd brought with them when they'd invaded Obann in the service of King Thunder. It had room in it for a good two hundred men and women, but Gurun was the only woman there tonight, and most of the space was empty. The chieftains posted guards at the entrance, two of Helki's own most trusted Griffs. Obst was there, of course, but the king had been sent to spend the night at the baron's house.

"There's more gold at the top of the Golden Pass," Helki began, "than any of you have seen in all your lives. It's lying there for the taking. No one's guarding it. The hill-folk are sure the place is haunted, and the Thunder King sends no one near it because he doesn't want anyone to see what happened to that hall and the king who built it. You've never seen such a ruin in your lives, either. And the former Thunder King lies dead there, under a mountain of gold."

The chieftains muttered excitedly—they knew what gold could buy—but Obst shook his head.

"We have not been called by God to gather gold," he said, "but to go down into Heathen land and proclaim Him in countries where He has not been known. What good is all that gold to us? The previous Thunder King owned all of it, and you see what good it did him."

Helki shrugged. "As for me, I've never held a gold coin in my hand for as long as I've lived," he said. "But you ought to decide what to do, before your men see all that gold and make some decisions of their own. Some of them might have a powerful hunger for it. They might not want to come down from the mountain without it."

Hawk stood up. He and his brothers were the first Hosa men to join King Ryons' army. By now he'd learned to speak good Obannese.

"What do we care for gold!" he said. "The Thunder King sent his mardars into our country. They poisoned our springs. They made our cattle cast their young. Our own babies were born dead. They forced us to march far away, to make war on people who had never done us any harm, in countries we had never even heard of. They made us slaves! But the God of Obann made us free again. We will never turn aside, not to the right nor to the left, until there is no more Thunder King at all."

When the applause died down, Chief Shaffur said, "Everyone knows my people have a lust for gold. It buys good things. Why else do you suppose Wallekki traders cross the desert and risk their lives in savage and uncouth countries?" For some reason, that made Helki smile to himself. "When my men see that gold," said Shaffur, "they'll desire it with all their hearts. As will I!" He paused to glare at the other chiefs. "But we will ride right past it, every single one of us. You have my word."

Attakotts had no use for gold, said their chosen leader, Looth, and the Griffs said they could do without it, too. Then it was Roshay's turn to speak.

"If the gold is there," he said, "we ought to have it. With it we can raise and equip new armies, which we'll need. We can repair the damage the enemy has done to our towns and farms. We can fortify towns and build new chamber houses. We ought to bring it down before the Thunder King can find a way to get it back."

"You haven't seen the place," said Helki. "It'd take this army the whole summer to carry it down the mountain."

"Maybe my people could do it," Roshay said, "while this army marches into Heathen lands."

"We had hopes you might march with us," Shaffur said. "How many spears could you add to our force?"

"A thousand, at the most. I'd have to hold back at least that many for defense."

"A blade of grass," said Tiliqua, the Griff, "compared to the tens of thousands commanded by the Thunder King."

"Warlords!" cried Obst. "Please put out of your minds any thought of conquering the Thunder King's dominions with this tiny army! Our enterprise is in God's hands, not our own. It makes no difference whether we march east with three thousand men or three hundred thousand. It will be by God's power whether we stand or fall."

So it was decided that Roshay and his militia should stay behind and do what he thought best. He thought it might be possible for him to come up after the king's army and haul the gold back down to Ninneburky. But even that, said Shaffur, would be dangerous.

"You'll find it a hard thing to maintain your men's discipline, Baron," he said. "I know the people of Obann. They're as bad as we are when it comes to gold. Your men will want to keep it for themselves."

"Even that would be better than letting the Thunder King get his hands on it again," Roshay answered.

———————

The army marched the next morning, with King Ryons at its head and Jack and Ellayne waving to him in the crowd that assembled to see him off.

How can gold be kept a secret? By the end of the day, everyone in Ninneburky knew there was a treasure waiting for anyone who'd come and take it. Even before the baron could send out riders to call up his militia from all along the river, Ysbott the Snake had heard the rumor.

As yet it was only a rumor, a garbled tale of gold and jewels somewhere in the mountains. Ysbott had never heard of the Thunder King's golden hall and its destruction by an avalanche. Having lived all his life in Lintum Forest, where immense wealth is unknown, he had only a vague idea of what a treasure could buy. But the very vagueness of his ideas set his mind on fire. If he had gold, he thought, he could hire every outlaw in Obann and have a bigger army than the king. He would live in a palace and sit on a throne. He could buy Helki's scalp to decorate his belt. He, Ysbott, would be the lord of Lintum Forest. And while he was at it, he would avenge himself on Baron Roshay Bault and all his family.

But Ysbott was not such a fool as to think he could do this all by himself.

"Send word to my men," he told the cobbler, who was his uneasy host. "Tell them that I won't be coming back for quite a while yet. Tell them they can now do as they please—I want them to enjoy themselves. Tell them the country is going to be emptied of militia soon and that they must feel free to help themselves to whatever they can get."

The silly beggars, he thought, were sure to go on a rampage and just as surely would be caught. Ysbott didn't care. If they were all caught and hanged, the baron would think he'd solved his bandit problem. Ysbott needed better men than these, if he hoped to gain a treasure.

"Will you be staying here for very long?" asked the cobbler.

"Much healthier for you if you don't know," said Ysbott. And after that there were no more questions.

CHAPTER 11

How the Army Climbed the Pass

Ryons' army had to cross the plain between the Imperial and Chariot rivers. Where the sources of the Chariot tumbled down from the hills, they would strike the Thunder King's road leading up to the Golden Pass. This they accomplished in good time.

The passage of invading armies had driven out the shepherds and cattle drovers who normally made use of the plain and left it a lonely country. To the west lay King Oziah's Wood, upon whose borders the Thunder King's host fell into disunion and the Abnaks mutinied. Ryons would have liked to visit this small forest, which had once sheltered his ancestor, King Ozias, from his enemies. Here Ozias had met the prophet, Penda, who'd assured him that if he erected a bell atop Bell Mountain, God would hear it when it rang. But many generations had passed before that happened.

Scouting for miles ahead of and around the army, Looth's Attakotts found no sign of enemies. But they did find game, and plenty of it. Their poisoned arrows brought down beasts that no one had ever seen before.

There was a big, clumsy grass-eater that gathered in

small groups around the springs and waterholes: so big that they had to cut one into many pieces before they could bring the meat back to the army. It had a divided lip, like a rabbit's, but stood as tall as a horse on legs like tree trunks.

"Is it safe to eat when you kill it with poisoned arrows?" Obst wondered.

"Safe and good," said Looth, "if you drain out all the blood and don't eat the liver."

There were great hunting birds, like Baby, and smaller kinds that ran but didn't fly; these made good eating. Once Looth brought back a kind of antelope with three forked antlers on its head instead of two. The wiry little Attakotts sang the praises of the country as a hunters' paradise. They didn't know it had never been like that until quite recently.

"Maybe someday we would like to live here," Looth said, "if the king will give us the land."

"I don't see why not," Ryons said.

Soon enough they reached the road, a bare swath that stretched up into the hills as far as the eye could see. At the top was the Golden Pass.

"It's not much of a road," Helki said, "but you'd never get the wagons up without it. These hills bear the thickest woods I ever saw." He'd gone ahead, scouting the road, and just returned.

"That road was built to bring armies down into Obann," Shaffur said. "The Thunder King never thought it would bring armies into his lands. It's a good joke on him!"

Uduqu looked up at it and said, "It's a long way to walk."

━━━━━━━━━

One of the Abnaks caught Fnaa trying to run away to

Ninneburky and brought him back to Chief Buzzard.

"And where were you off to, Your Majesty?"

Fnaa and Uduqu had become friends in Obann, so the boy had no fear of Abnaks. Besides, he suspected they didn't like being left behind at Carbonek any better than he did. So he answered, "I was just looking for something to do that's a little more fun than hanging around here, watching the moss grow on the stones. I was on my way to Ninneburky to visit my friends, if that's what you want to know."

"Oh, sassy!" said a warrior. "That's just the way King Ryons used to talk to us before he was a king."

"So I've heard," said Buzzard. "This is a boy who will give some grey hairs to his mother. Someone go fetch her!"

That made Fnaa squirm. "Chief," he said, "the prophetess told me to do anything that was in my heart to do, and it was in my heart to go to Ninneburky."

"Without your mother's leave?" Buzzard said. For all their ferocious ways, Abnaks loved their own children and took good care of them. Boys were expected to stand up to warriors—it showed the right kind of spirit—but never to their mothers.

Fnaa's mother, Dakl, had been a slave all her life. Now she was free. While Fnaa impersonated the king, she'd pretended to be his servant and a handmaid to the queen. That took courage, Gurun used to say, and Fnaa believed her. It was Dakl who had taught him to play the fool so that he wouldn't be sold away from her. So Fnaa knew his mother was anything but a timid, silly woman. While Chief Buzzard told her what her son had tried to do, Fnaa wished he could crawl into a hole and hide.

"You would have gone away and not even told me?" she

said. She'd come at a run and had to keep brushing a loose lock of hair from her eyes.

"Mother, you sent me to Ninneburky once before, all by myself." Fnaa thought it needful to remind her of this.

"That was different!" Dakl said. "King Ryons was in danger and that was the only thing we could do to help him. And I worried myself to sleep the whole time you were gone!"

"I thought you'd say no, this time," Fnaa said. "But Jandra said I should do what's in my heart to do. That's why, when I was holding the king's place for him, I made believe I was a daft king. It came into my heart to do it, and so that's what I did."

"God speaks through that little girl, sometimes," Buzzard said. "That's how Ryons was made king. We set great store by those words! I don't know—maybe God means for this boy to go to Ninneburky instead of staying here. But one thing I do know—he would have gotten lost before he came even close to finding his way out of this forest."

"A fine figure you would have cut, blundering around the woods until you could be rescued!" Dakl said. Fnaa's face burned because he knew Buzzard was right: he would have surely gotten lost.

"If you like," the chief said to Dakl, "I'll send someone with him to see he gets to Ninneburky safely."

"And back again?"

"And back again, for sure."

"Then I will let him go," said Dakl. "I don't know much about the God of Obann. I am Fazzan by birth, but I never knew my people's gods. Chief Zekelesh says they weren't worth knowing. But I do know that God spoke to my son once, back in Obann City, through the little girl." And to

Fnaa, "If you had a father, he would fetch you a good, hard clout for trying to sneak off without a word to me. But we were slaves, and you were all I had. I have always been too soft with you."

"I'll clout him, if you like," said Buzzard. For a moment Fnaa had a scare that did him good. But Dakl said, "The next time he has earned a whipping, I'll bring him straight to you. But this time he shall do as he pleases. I don't like to go against the words of the prophetess."

————————————

Using the road, it took King Ryons' army not quite three days to get to the top of the pass. And then they stood there marveling at the wreckage of King Thunder's hall and the gold that shone like fire.

"It's like the sun has fallen to the earth!" said Chagadai. "It hurts my eyes to look at it."

Uduqu was almost too weary to spare it a glance. The uphill march was the hardest thing he'd ever done in his life. With a great sigh, he found a convenient boulder and sat on it. Obst stood beside him, tall and straight.

"Ah, my legs!" Uduqu said. "It feels like every year I've lived is wrapped around my ankles! If I tried to climb another step, my feet would stick to the ground. I'm glad the rest of the way is all downhill!"

"We got here, though," Obst said. "I never thought I'd ever climb these mountains again."

"Oh, but look at you!" Uduqu looked him up and down. "Aren't you bone-tired? You've walked all the way, and yet there you stand, as fresh as a young warrior courting a girl who smiled at him! Old man, how do you do it?"

The question troubled Obst. "I don't know," he said. "When I climbed Bell Mountain with the children, I foundered before I reached the top. I nearly died. Maybe I did die, for a little while. But when I heard the bell, I got right up and nearly skipped back down the mountain! It was the gift of God—along with the gift of tongues, which I discovered later.

"But it's true, Uduqu—I ought to be exhausted, and I'm not. I feel no more tired than if I'd done an ordinary day's work around my cabin."

"Ha! I see it now," Uduqu said. "You're getting younger instead of older."

Obst shuddered. "Don't say that!" he said. "Someone else said the same thing to me, not long ago—Fnaa, I think it was. But it was just a foolish thing to say. But now you've said it, too."

"By the time we're done with all our work," said Uduqu, "you'll be a beardless boy again."

"I hope not," Obst said. "I was an awful fool when I was young."

Up in front of the army, on her horse beside the king, Gurun felt a shiver—not that it was cold.

"This is an evil place, my lord," she said. "I am not going to be happy until we leave it far behind. I wish we didn't have to spend the night here."

"Why do you say that, Gurun? I wish you wouldn't!"

"Wicked men died here. They died in their sins, smitten by the hand of God. Do you see those heavy timbers? Those were no protection! And all that gold? I can't help wondering how much evil they did to acquire so much gold. They must have robbed whole nations—and I think robbery was probably the least of their crimes."

Chief Shaffur raised his voice so that everyone could hear.

"Behold the Thunder King's treasure!" he cried. "And he lies buried underneath it! Let any man who wishes a share in the curse lay his hands on this gold!"

No one moved. However they might lust for gold, the Wallekki were a superstitious people.

Helki broke the spell. "I reckon I'll take some of my boys and scout a little ways downhill," he said. "Make your camp here, Chieftains, and set a strong guard over it. We don't know who might be coming up this pass from the other side." He twirled his staff over his head and walked off with his Griffs. Looth whistled and the Attakotts followed, each with an arrow nocked to his bow.

The army got busy making camp. The Hosa had taught the others their custom of each man carrying a stake sharpened at both ends, which could be thrust into the ground to make a palisade of sorts. It would at least stop an attack by cavalry. In the middle of the camp, the Wallekki set up lines for the horses. The Hosa took the side facing the east end of the pass, with the Wallekki on the flanks and the others facing west. It was a far cry, thought Ryons, from the way the army used to set up camp—in no particular order at all. They'd all learned a few things, since then.

By the time the sun set, they were all having their supper. And the Ghols were singing to keep off the spirits of the dead.

CHAPTER 12

The Lure of Gold

When the excitement over the king's visit had died down, Enith pressed Ellayne for the rest of the story of Abombalbap and the glass bridge.

"Let's go down to the river instead," Jack said, but he was overruled. Ellayne brought the book out to the porch and picked up reading where she'd left off.

"After Brandyle came a young knight named Gwydd, eager to try the adventure of the bridge. Abombalbap told him how Brandyle and his horse had fallen into the abyss, but Gwydd said, He was a foolish knight to think he could cross over on his horse.

"Then Gwydd alit from his horse and stripped off all his armor and laid his shield aside; he was clad only in his undergarment with his sword in hand. Abombalbap said, In God's name, sir, what do you mean to do? For I much fear for you. But Gwydd laughed and said, Now, Sir Faintheart, you shall see what one who is both brave and fleet of foot can do! And he ran out onto the bridge so swiftly that he left behind his shadow; but before he was halfway across, the bridge broke into a thousand thousand flying splinters; and with a great cry, Gwydd fell headlong into the abyss, and his shadow dived in after him. And when he was gone, the bridge restored itself by magic. God save us! said Abombalbap.

"And so knights came from far and wide, each of them seeking to rescue the princess from the crystal castle; and one by one, all those knights fell to their deaths. Abombalbap sorely grieved them, but he knew not whether to go from that place or stay.

"Then there came a strong knight named Aristomar, who greeted Abombalbap with good cheer and spoke to him. I have long pondered this adventure, said he, and it seems to me that all those knights were ill-prepared for it. But I went to the chamber house for thirty days in a row, and each day made a donation to the house, and each day prevailed on the prester to say a prayer for my good enterprise. Furthermore, on each of those days, I cut a page from a book of Holy Scriptures and burned it, and mixed the ashes into my wine, and drank it down.

"God defend us, said Abombalbap, think you to compel the Lord to do your bidding? I pray you, Sir Knight, not to hazard yourself upon this bridge: for I perceive now that it is a temptation. But Aristomar laughed him to scorn and said, Now by the power vested in me I will deliver the damsel! And he walked out onto the bridge, and as soon as he set foot on it, the bridge broke into a thousand thousand pieces, and Aristomar fell."

Ellayne closed the book.

"No wonder Obst says those are foolish stories," Jack said.

"Foolish?" cried Enith. "It's a marvelous story! Read us the rest of it, Ellayne!"

But Ellayne was beginning to get an uneasy feeling about the story. There was nothing like it in the Scriptures that her mother read to her every day, although the Old Books were full of stories. She'd read this story of Abombalbap before, and always enjoyed it, but now there seemed more to it than there used to be. Something made her wonder if it was a good story or a bad one. Could Obst be right about these stories? Or was there something in them that he'd failed to see?

"I wonder why Aristomar fell," Ellayne said. She'd never wondered about it before; she'd just accepted it. But now it seemed the story was trying to tell her something that she didn't understand.

"He fell because he was so cocksure of himself, that's why," Jack said. "Anyone can see that."

"But what about the prayers and the donations?" asked Enith. "And he even ate pages from the Scriptures!"

"I'm pretty sure you're not supposed to do that," said Ellayne. But she couldn't explain why.

———

It would take many days to assemble a thousand men of the militia. How many, the baron didn't know. "It's a good thing for us to find out now," he said, "rather than wait for war to come upon us. We need to know how long it takes to muster men for battle." He kept Ellayne busy writing summonses to captains and sergeants up and down the river, and Jack making sure the summonses went out.

But already the whole town had heard the whisper of gold as a whisper in the air. It was the Thunder King's gold. It was up on top of this mountain, or that mountain, and belonged to anyone who'd go and take it. The rumor put out other branches, too. King Ryons had gone up to get the gold, but the baron was planning to take it away from him and make himself king. It was piled up in bars and ingots. No, it was a heap of golden coins, or a great cave stuffed with golden crowns and necklaces and other gorgeously beautiful things. No guard stood over it. It was guarded by barbarians. It was guarded by ghosts.

Here Ysbott the Snake saw his opportunity.

"Why should a boy king have all that gold or those foreign Heathen in his following? Why should Roshay Bault have it all to himself? You have just as much a right to it! Whose farms were stripped, whose herds were driven off, when the Thunder King's hordes came down the mountain? Not the king's! Not the baron's. Why should they get fat on treasure, while you stay lean? Just two pockets full of that gold would make any of us rich for life."

Ysbott knew that those who heard him would repeat his words to others, until the whole town heard them. Very soon, what he meant to happen began to happen. One by one, two by two, men began to steal out of Ninneburky and on up toward the hills, following the river. Only then did he speak of his plans to Hrapp the cobbler.

"Make ready to close your shop," he said. "I want you to come with me up the mountain."

"Are we going for the gold?" Hrapp said. He'd heard about this from several of his customers. He was a timid man, but greedy: easy for Ysbott to handle. "It looks like nearly everyone in town will be heading for the hills."

"The more who go, the safer it'll be for us," said Ysbott. All he really wanted was for Hrapp not to stay behind while he went on. The cobbler might say something that he shouldn't say. "With enough people swarming all over the countryside, the baron won't know what to do. Among so much confusion, we'll have our best chance to do well for ourselves."

"I've never been up to the hills," Hrapp said.

"I wouldn't dream of leaving you behind! And you'll go because I've asked you nicely—won't you?"

Hrapp was more afraid of Ysbott than he was of any dangers that might be lurking in the hills, so of course he agreed to go—as Ysbott knew he would.

———————

How many of his townspeople had already left before he noticed they were leaving, the baron couldn't even guess. And as yet only some two hundred of the militia had reported for duty.

"Why don't you send some riders after the people to tell them to come back?" said the baroness. "I should have known something like this was happening when Lanora went to Stenn's bakery the other day and found a sign on the door that said 'Closed Until Further Notice.'"

"They won't come back because my riders tell them to," Roshay said. "They've heard about the gold—and it was supposed to be a secret! I don't know what to do." He ground his teeth because he hated not knowing what to do; it wasn't a position in which he often found himself. "At this rate, the whole town will be deserted before I can muster the militia. Silly fools—and I'm responsible for them!"

"Can't you just shut the gates and not let anybody leave?"

"I can try."

———————

That was the same day the king's army made ready to descend the pass. The chieftains put the men in marching order, but first Obst had something to say to them.

"Warriors!" His voice carried well in the crisp mountain air. "Today marks the first time in all of history that a king of Obann will cross the mountains with an army.

"Once, long ago, after he had lost his kingdom, Ozias came this way, alone but for a few loyal servants. Later, but still a thousand years ago, the Empire sent many armies into the East and conquered it, all the way out to the Great Lakes. But that was done in pride and lust for power, and the Empire perished in the Day of Fire.

"We, behind our king who is a descendant of Ozias, now embark on quite another mission, and in a spirit of humility, knowing that our enemy is stronger than we are and that our lives are in God's hands. We make this crossing in obedience to Him—not to conquer for ourselves, but to proclaim the lordship of our God to peoples who have never known Him.

"To your peoples, my brothers! Not to take from them, but to give; not to enslave them, but to set them free. For the law of our God is the law of liberty."

And all those warriors, who were born Heathen but now belonged to God, sent up a cheer that made the mountains ring.

"Well, then," said Uduqu, "what are we waiting for? Let's go down! It's bound to be easier than going up."

Behind their tribal standards flapping in the wind, King Ryons' small army invaded the vast dominions of the Thunder King.

CHAPTER 13

How Helki Left the Army

Accompanied by an Abnak named Trout, one of Chief
Uduqu's men, Fnaa enjoyed an easy crossing of the
plain. Trout had been that way before. Along the way, he
taught Fnaa how to find edible birds' eggs in unlikely places
and edible roots in even more unlikely places. He did not
succeed in teaching Fnaa to eat grasshoppers and certain
beetle larvae much prized by the Abnaks.

"You'll always be a city boy," he said. "You don't know
what's good."

Once they were stalked by one of the enormous birds—
like Baby, only wild—that had come to haunt the plains in
recent years. Trout eventually decided it was getting too
close, so he unlimbered his stone axe and advanced on it,
shouting insults. The bird trotted off the way it came, and
Trout stood his ground until it was out of sight.

"That was brave!" said Fnaa.

Trout laughed. "Learn to know about animals," he said.
"Hunters, like that bird, they don't like prey that wants to
fight. They might get hurt, and then they starve."

"But that bird could have killed us!"

"Not worth it to him, if first I hit him with my axe."

In a matter of days they made the crossing and found
all of Ninneburky in an uproar. Fnaa knew the way to the

82

baron's house, and it took some minutes for Ellayne and Jack to get over their surprise at seeing him.

"It's a mess," Ellayne said. "Half the men in this town have gone running after gold—the Thunder King's gold, away up in the mountains."

Vannett had them sit in the parlor and brought them lemonade. Trout stood in the middle of the room, marveling at the walls, the windows, the carpet, and the furniture. He didn't know what to do with himself in such strange surroundings. Vannett took him by the arm and made him sit in the baron's own stuffed chair.

"I'm sure you're the first Abnak who has ever come under the roof of this house," she said. "Not so long ago, I would have been terrified at the sight of you! But things change. Be at ease, Mr. Trout, as much as you can. You're among friends."

Trout, for the time being, was speechless. But Jack and Ellayne wanted all the news from Lintum Forest, and the baroness could hardly take her eyes off Fnaa.

"Now that I've met King Ryons, I doubt I could ever tell the two of you apart," she said.

"Ryons has a red streak in his hair," Fnaa said.

"Maybe," said Ellayne, "but you fooled everyone in Obann City for a long time."

Fnaa wanted to hear about the gold. It was very far from being a secret anymore, and the baron's family felt free to speak of it. Vannett also decided that he and Trout should be her guests for as long as they wished to stay in Ninneburky.

"And how long will that be?" Ellayne asked.

"Oh, I don't know," Fnaa said. He couldn't stop thinking about the gold. City-bred, he knew what gold could do.

It could make a man a slave or buy his freedom. It made people who would otherwise ignore you listen when you spoke. If so many people from Ninneburky had gone after it, he thought, maybe he and Trout ought to have a go at it, too. But he didn't think it would be wise to say that to the baroness.

———————

As many of the men in Ryons' army knew, at the bottom of the pass began the Griffs' country—well-watered grasslands, gently rolling hills. North of it lived the Zeph, and north of them stretched mile after mile of swamps that hardly anybody ever entered, and few of them, it was said, ever came out again. The way to the Great Lakes, long ago the boundary of Obann's Empire, lay straight through Griffland.

"But the Great Lakes are a long way off," said Tiliqua, chief of the dozen Griffs who followed Helki. "To get there, you must pass through countries populated by very barbarous people. Beyond the lakes rise the red cliffs of Kara Karram and the fortress of the Thunder King. But who can say we'll ever get that far?"

The Griffs in their homeland were still the subjects of the Thunder King, but most of their fighting men, Tiliqua said, would have been sent south to make war on the Abnaks. "Unless the Zeph have kept an army somewhere to the north, we shouldn't see much trouble—for a while."

Helki had gone on ahead, but early in the afternoon came back to report that the way was clear, all the way down the mountain. "We're the only people on this road, just now," he told the chieftains. "Whoever lives at the bottom of the pass in good times, they're not there now. The war has sucked all the people out of this country. And that being so, for the time being, I'll leave you to it."

"What do you mean, you'll leave us to it?" Shaffur demanded.

"Well, you won't need me to scout. The Griffs in the army know their own country a lot better than I do, and I'll leave Tiliqua and his lads with you. But I have a feeling that I ought to go back up the pass and see what's what. I'm uneasy about it. I'll catch up to you later."

Ryons heard this with some misgivings, although he didn't speak up. Helki made you feel safe. There was no one else like him. But the chieftains all seemed to accept his decision.

"Someone ought to be watching over that gold until Baron Bault comes to get it," Shaffur said. "Do what seems best to you, Helki."

Helki trekked back up the road and the army continued on down. He couldn't say what troubled him. He remembered the story Gallgoid told, when he'd helped him down the mountain in the winter. Somewhere under those ruins lay the dead body of a Thunder King with a golden mask on its face. "If I were as superstitious as our Wallekki," he thought, "I'd almost think the ghost was putting a hoodoo on me—calling me back to dig up the corpse so it could walk again. But that's all fiddle-faddle."

He hadn't brought up the subject when the chiefs conferred in Ninneburky, but maybe it was something he ought to mention to the baron when he got there.

"Can't just leave it lying about!" he thought. "The man is dead, but the mask might still be dangerous."

CHAPTER 14

A Surprise for Lord Orth

Some distance to the south of the Golden Pass, in the hills that led the way up to Bell Mountain itself, the First Prester of Obann spoke to an audience whose like had never before been addressed by any minister of the Temple. But Orth was speaking not as a prester of the Temple, but as an ambassador of God.

Gathered around him, perhaps a thousand strong, were Abnaks—the men tattooed and shaven-headed, except for the scalp lock that hung down one side, and many Abnak women in doeskin, with their long black hair in braids, and many children with them, too. For the Abnaks were bringing their families over the mountains, out of reach of the Thunder King—for now.

Hlah had sent out messengers inviting them to come and hear the First Prester. People who'd known Orth when he'd been among them as a simple man named Sunfish, and loved him, remembered how he used to recite the Scriptures to them and teach them. They rejoiced at his return and were eager to hear him again. Word of him had spread throughout all the new settlements in the hills and aroused the Abnaks' curiosity.

"Wait'll you hear him," said a chief named Ootoo, who'd founded his own settlement in the hills. "He's the best kind of madman. His God speaks to him every day."

Now Orth was speaking to the Abnaks, standing on a big stump in the middle of a clearing, with Hlah standing before him to translate.

"For a thousand years, your people and mine have been enemies," he said. "But we are both God's people. You have not known him, but He knows you. He created you and gave you your own country that you love, full of good things that sustain your lives. Although you worshipped other gods, He forgave you because you did it out of ignorance.

"But the time has come for you to know Him! The Bell atop Bell Mountain has been rung, and you have heard it. God has begun to gather to Himself all the peoples of the world, that they might love Him as He loves them and that He might protect them from their enemies."

As he translated, Hlah studied the faces of his people. They were listening attentively, he thought. The very trees of the forest were listening. Orth's voice compelled it.

"How will this God of yours protect us?" a chief called out. There was a deep murmur of agreement.

"By the strength of His hand, which created the heavens and the earth," said Orth, "and by His righteousness. You don't know Him, but He knows you. Your very names, each and every one, are written on His palms.

"The Thunder King invaded Obann with the greatest army the world has ever seen, and inside the city, there was treachery to help him. I know it, to my shame, for I was one of those who betrayed the city to him. I was one of those who opened the secret gates and let his warriors in. They burned down the Temple, of which I was one of the chief men. They forced open the great gates of the city.

"But God sent a young child to deliver Obann and sat him on a great beast that was like a mountain walking, and by this means God scattered that great host and saved the city. Neither force nor treachery could prevail against Him.

"If you put your trust in Him and call upon His name, He will hear you. And He will deliver your country, too, and restore it to you, its rightful owners."

"And what will He want in return?" cried the chief. "Our gods are little gods. For a pot of beer, they would give you good hunting. But they couldn't protect us from the Thunder King! He took them away from us and told us that from then on, he would be our only god.

"It seems to me that your God will want more than pots of beer! What sacrifices must we make to Him? How much of our flesh and blood will He require?"

Orth smiled. It calmed the crowd, which had begun to get excited.

"He doesn't want your beer," he said, "and He doesn't want your flesh and blood. He wants your love. He wants to be your Father. He wants your hearts and your obedience. And He wants you to be able to live in peace, enjoying the good things He has given you."

"How can we live in peace," said the chief, "when we're at war? The Thunder King has promised to exterminate us. Will this God take away the Thunder King?"

"Oh, He most assuredly will!" Orth said. "The Thunder King and all his works will be like dried grass for the fire. Of that you may be absolutely certain."

There were other translators scattered amid the crowd, so it only took some moments for Orth's words to be understood. And suddenly a cheer broke out—at first a ripple, and then a mighty roar, and then a chorus of high-pitched war cries. Warriors raised their weapons, brandished them over their heads. Women made a shrill, trilling sound, as of birds. Children jumped up and down. They had heard, all right, thought Hlah—and understood.

A great chief stepped out from the midst of the crowd—the people made way for him—and stood in front of Orth, demanding to be heard.

"You all know me—Foxblood, of the Centipede Clan. Chief Spider was my cousin, so this young warrior is my kin by blood." He nodded to Hlah, who was Spider's son. "This is a great day for us! I am ready to follow the Obann God, of whom we have heard so many good things. I will follow this man, His servant." He looked up at Orth with a fierce grin. "This is the man to lead us against the Thunder King. He can speak to God for us.

"What are we waiting for? Let's take him back with us across the mountains, and put his God to the test against the Thunder King! This man will have honor among us if we win, and he can die with us if we lose."

This needed no translation. The hills rang with wild whoops and cheering. But Hlah felt sick with dread.

"No, no, no!" he cried. "This is the First Prester, and his place is in Obann! You can't just carry him off!" But Orth held up his hands for silence, and when he got it, spoke again.

"Be of good cheer, Hlah," he said. "God's ways are often strange to us. But if we have faith in Him, we obey. When He calls, we go."

He looked around at all the Abnaks.

"I will go with you," he said, "although it's not what I expected. I am no man of war, but my master is the Lord of Hosts. If you become His people, surely He will fight for you. If it's His will that you conquer, no enemy will withstand you."

"Please, my lord!" cried Hlah, speaking in Obannese. "You don't know my people. They're not ready for this! Like as not, the first time anything goes wrong, they'll slay you where you stand. But Obann needs you!"

"Obann is in God's hands, as are we all," said Orth. "Besides, there are Prester Jod in Durmurot and Preceptor Constan in the city, and others elsewhere, who are better men than I have ever been.

"All my life, I did what it pleased me to do and hoped to gain from it. You saw where that got me—I was a witless madman starving in the marshes when you found me. So now I will do what God calls me to do. It's only right."

Hlah's eyes filled with tears. But his people, once they understood how Orth had answered them, exulted.

"Be sure to tell everyone that I went of my own free will," the First Prester said.

———

Roshay Bault couldn't wait for a thousand men to be collected. It was taking too much time, and meanwhile too many men from Ninneburky had run off seeking gold, and he was afraid they would fall into mischief. When he had some four hundred men assembled with their horses, he decided to set out for the Golden Pass.

"Organize the others into troops when they get here and have them follow me," he told the captains he'd left behind for that purpose. "And make sure there is a guard for Master Harfydd's barges."

Harfydd, who'd been a rich man in Obann City before the fire that destroyed the palace burned down several of his warehouses, had married Enith's grandmother and now made his home in Ninneburky. He'd offered to send his barges up the river as far as they would go to aid in transporting the gold.

To Ellayne—and to Jack, too—her father gave stern warning.

"I expect you both to be here when I get back," he said. "No running off on adventures of your own! If the gold can draw honest men out of Ninneburky, it'll have no trouble luring outlaws, too."

"Can't we come with you?" Ellayne asked.

"Not on your life."

Along with the rest of the town, Jack, Ellayne, and Fnaa saw the baron off when he set out with the militia that afternoon. All were on horseback, although some were yet a ways from being riders.

"Everybody thinks riding a horse is easy, but it's not," Fnaa said. "I had to ride the king's horse, Dandelion, so the people could all see me. I'm glad I don't have to do it anymore!"

So the baron rode out from Ninneburky and wasn't there when Hlah came looking for him in the evening at his house.

Hlah had been there before, when he and May had brought Sunfish back to Obann. He'd hurried with all speed back from the gathering of the Abnaks—straight down the river in a borrowed canoe, paddling for all he was worth, day and night. When he turned up at the baron's door just after supper, he looked every inch a man who'd made a long journey in a short time. Jack, answering the door, hardly recognized him. Ellayne called for her mother.

"Hlah! Why, what's the matter? You look terrible!" Vannett took his arm. "Come and sit down, before you fall down. Find him something to eat, Ellayne." She led him into the parlor, and there he told his tale. Before he'd finished, Fnaa and Trout appeared in the doorway, where they listened.

"My people have forced the First Prester to go back across the mountains with them to fight the Thunder King. He has commanded me to tell the baron that he goes of his own free will and not to send a rescue expedition after him."

"It seems I'm not the first Abnak to have been a guest here, after all," Trout interrupted. At the sight of him, Hlah stopped short.

"I didn't count Hlah," Vannett said. "He's married to an Obannese girl. Hlah, this is Trout, my guest. He came from Lintum Forest with this boy, Fnaa. Please do go on with your news!"

"My friend, Chief Ootoo, knows Chief Foxblood," Hlah said. "Foxblood is a good man, Ootoo says. He'll take good care of Lord Orth."

"That's so," Trout said. "Foxblood is a famous chief. He's lifted many scalps." Vannett did not find that as comforting as it was intended to be.

"Abnak country, in a time of war, is no place for the First Prester of Obann!" Hlah said. "My people honor their shamans, but a shaman who makes prayers that aren't answered or prophecies that don't come true, they kill. And what will become of all his work, if Lord Orth isn't here to do it? But he just says it's all God's will."

"Maybe it is," Vannett said softly.

Ellayne spoke up. "Jack and I will go and tell Father. Wytt and Martis can come with us, so we'll be safe enough. And you, Mother, must send messages to Lintum Forest and to Prester Jod. They've got to be told about this!"

"I'll go, too!" Fnaa put in quickly. "And Trout, too, to help watch over us."

It would have been the easiest thing in the world for Vannett to say, "No, absolutely not," and she almost did. It was what her husband would have wanted. But it came to her that her daughter and adopted son had done many harder journeys in God's service. And if Martis, Trout, and Wytt couldn't protect them, who could? Besides, she could hardly leave it up to Ellayne to write the letters. It wasn't every day that the First Prester of the Temple got whisked off into another country. Indeed, it had never happened before. Those letters would take a lot of thought.

When she spoke again, she spoke more as a baroness than as a growing child's mother.

"Hlah, you must stay a little while and help me write the letters," she said. "Ellayne, Jack, and Fnaa, you must promise to do everything that Martis and Trout tell you to do, and not stray out of their sight. Give me your word on it!"

All the children promised. Vannett didn't know Fnaa, but she supposed that if he could be trusted to masquerade as the king and hold his place for him, he could be trusted in this, too. As for her own children—well, they weren't just little children anymore. In truth, they both knew more about these things than she did.

"Very well," she said, "I'll let you go, all three of you. Ellayne, find Martis and bring him to me. You'd better set out first thing in the morning."

"I ought to go, too," Hlah said. "It was I who gathered the Abnaks to hear Lord Orth speak. I fear for him."

"Naturally," said Vannett, "but you're all done in and not fit to undertake another journey until you rest. Oh, I knew this would happen! Or something very like it."

CHAPTER 15

A Treasure Trove That Guards Itself

Ysbott and Hrapp made their way swiftly across the plain between the rivers, following the trail of Ryons' army. Even Hrapp could have followed that trail, had he thought of it. But some of the men of Ninneburky hadn't thought of it, and so far Ysbott and Hrapp had overtaken no one on their trek.

"I wonder where they all went," Hrapp said.

"Most of them left before we did, and we haven't caught up to any of them yet," Ysbott said. "But I'm afraid some of them just took off in various directions, all wrong. Too bad for them."

Still, by the time they came to the first upturning of the hills, the end of the plain and the beginning of the wooded country, they had overtaken half a dozen gold seekers out of Ninneburky. Ysbott gathered them into a group and made himself their chief. He'd always been a leader of outlaws, never a follower. It came naturally to him, and these townsmen responded to it.

"We ought to stick together," he said, "in case there's any danger on the way. And six men can carry away much more gold than one or two." Lying came to him even more naturally than leadership. "I'm just an ordinary fellow like the rest of you. For the past few years, I've been a trapper and a fisherman, up and down the great river, so I know a thing or two about living off the land. My name is Tobb."

Not that Ysbott's name was well known in Ninneburky, but he deemed it best to be careful. He had already warned Hrapp never to speak the name of Ysbott.

"Don't worry—I won't," said the cobbler, not needing to mention his firm belief that Ysbott would stick a knife between his ribs if he crossed him in any way.

Ysbott urged his new followers to speed. Soon they found the Thunder King's road and were on their way to the Golden Pass.

———

Roshay Bault's progress was slow. He had to keep sending out patrols, some of them all the way to the banks of both rivers, to round up any of his townspeople who'd gotten lost. Before he was even halfway across the plain, his riders had brought in a good fifty of them.

"You cusset fools and butterheads!" the baron growled at them, when they all stood sheepishly before him, under guard. "Half of you would have wandered here and there until you starved, and the rest would have found more original ways of coming to a bad end. For your own protection, I'll have to force you to come with me and make yourselves useful."

One man, bolder than the rest, objected.

"We're not slaves, Baron! I remember when you were only the chief councilor. Who are you to forbid any man from trying to better himself? Why should you have all that gold—eh?"

Under their breath, the townsmen murmured their agreement. But Roshay turned such a fierce look on them, they subsided almost instantly. His rages had long been known in Ninneburky as something to avoid.

"I know you, Donn Decker—once a troublemaker, always a troublemaker! It was a bad day for me when I let you out of the stocks—and with only half a flogging, too." The baron's face was getting red. With an effort anyone could see, he swallowed his wrath.

"That gold belongs to King Ryons and to all the nation of Obann," he said. "We have to get it so that the Thunder King will never get it back. It's not for me—and it's cuss't well not for you, either! It's for rebuilding towns that were ravaged in the war, and houses, barns, and boatyards. It's for equipping more soldiers to defend us, because the Thunder King will come again. Strong walls and deep ditches: every town will need them. Or would you rather the Zephites came and took you while you were gambling away the last of your riches behind the nearest ale-house?"

One of the gold seekers forgot himself and raised a cheer, and all the rest joined in. Donn Decker was silenced. And when the cheers died down, the baron spoke again.

"It's going to be mighty hard work, bringing all that gold down from the mountain. Naturally, every man who helps to carry it will get a share of it, paid enough to make it worth his while." He looked down from horseback at the men he'd rescued from their folly. "Even you ninnies," he added, "if you don't blunder off and get lost again."

That night Helki sat alone by the ruins of the hall, listening to the wind make ghost noises. In the distance some animal cried out—once, twice, and then no more. It was the cry of no beast that Helki knew, and he knew them all. Maybe it was that creature that hunted in the trees, the one that had stalked him once before.

No other living thing came anywhere near the site.

Sooner or later, according to the plan, Roshay Bault would arrive to take the gold. Helki had explored the heaped ruins. "It'll be a tricky job," he said to himself. It was snow that had destroyed the place—flattened it, disarranged it, choked it. When the snow melted, it left gaps and cavities among the heaped-up stones and timbers, and left many pieces precariously balanced, one atop another. One false step, Helki reckoned, and there would be another dead body lying crushed amid the rubble. As it was, you didn't have to probe very deeply to find human bones. Even with no one touching the pile, you would occasionally hear a low rumble, a high-pitched creak, or even an explosive snap as the ruin shifted under the pressure of its own weight. Had Helki grown up in a house with toys to play with, he might have likened it to a gigantic game of pick-up sticks—devilish hard to remove one stick without jiggling the others and losing the game.

Some of the gaps and cavities were big enough to admit him, should he try to crawl in and explore further. Those lightless spaces tempted him: no telling what secrets they might hold. That was by far more tempting to him than the gold, but he resisted. "Not worth getting buried alive for," he thought.

As the night wore on, he decided not to wait for Roshay

Bault. The baron had a good head on his shoulders—no need to warn him that this place was dangerous. "It needs no guard," Helki thought, "because it guards itself." Much better, he decided, to move on, southward, and see if there was anything happening among the settlements that King Ryons ought to know about.

CHAPTER 16

A Witness in the Heathen Land

Wytt was happy.

Perched atop the pack on the back of Ham, the children's donkey, he drank in the smells and birdcalls of the early morning. Ham was happy to be on the trail again, with Jack leading him and Ellayne treating him to pieces of an apple. Ham and Wytt had climbed Bell Mountain together, almost to the top, and visited the ruins of the Old City of Obann when the children and Martis found the lost scrolls of King Ozias.

Martis rode ahead on his Wallekki horse, Dulayl, with Trout striding beside him, following the plain trail of Ryons' army and the baron's militia. Martis and the children had been to the Golden Pass before and had seen the avalanche bury the golden hall. None of them would have liked to go there in the winter ever again.

Fnaa scampered here and there, occasionally getting pointers from the men on how to read a trail.

"But anyone could read this one," Trout said. "All those horses make a mess."

"The baron isn't making very good time," Martis said.

"At this rate we'll catch him before he's halfway up the road. I wonder why he goes so slowly." They didn't know the baron was busy rounding up gold-hungry townsmen. "It's just as well. We'll save him from chasing off after the First Prester."

"Chief Foxblood will keep him safe, if he can," said Trout. A horse would have been provided for him, but he'd never ridden one before and didn't want to start learning now. Martis led a spare horse for the children, should it be needed.

"I'd rather walk," Ellayne said. "The time I rode to Obann, I got saddle sores."

———

Ahead of the baron, and now with eight men in his following, Ysbott found the road he'd heard about.

"No lollygagging!" he warned the others. "We want to get there first."

"It won't do us much good to be there, once the baron gets there, too," said one of them.

"We'll still have time to take some for ourselves—enough to make us rich," Ysbott said. "The more time we have up there by ourselves, the more time I'll have to think of something."

"Tobb's a thinker; you can count on that," Hrapp said. Ysbott favored him with an indulgent smile.

"They said it'd take an army of men to bring down all that gold," said someone else, "and there are only ten of us."

"If you want to turn back, Gwawl, there's no one stopping you."

None of them wanted to turn back. They were tired of working for pennies, all their lives, and the occasional silver.

Visions of wealth danced through their heads, unimpeded by any practical considerations. This one wanted a town-house in Obann with servants to call him "my lord"; that one wanted a beautiful young wife who wore mink stoles.

As for Ysbott, he hadn't thought of something yet. His thoughts were like a swimmer plunged suddenly into cold, dark water without knowing the location of the shore. But the shore had to be somewhere, and it was up to him to find it. He no sooner hatched one plan than he had to discard it as unworkable and come up with another.

"Can't you march any faster?" he goaded the men. "Anyone would think you were going to a funeral." Spurred on by faith in him and dreams of sudden wealth, they did indeed march faster, despite its being all uphill.

At the very least, Ysbott thought, these men could carry off more gold than he could ever have hoped to obtain in all his life, if he lived a hundred years and robbed a new victim every other day. It would be easy enough to have all of it to himself. These town-bred chickens wouldn't know how to protect themselves from his cunning mind, his smooth speech, or his knife.

But there also had to be some way to hurt the baron— Roshay Bault, who'd hunted him, Ysbott, like a terrier hunts a rat, and whose daughter had nearly blinded him with witch-craft. There had to be a way to make the baron suffer, and his accursed daughter.

"I'll find it!" Ysbott swore to himself.

═══════════

The Abnaks wasted no time in spiriting Orth over the mountains, out of Obann and into their country. Abnaks travel swiftly in the mountains and the woods, knowing all the paths by heart and expert at collecting food on the run. They broke up into many smaller bands and filtered across the mountains, where war awaited them. The swiftest warriors went first to spread the news: the Obann God would help the Abnaks, and Obann's greatest holy man had joined them.

Chief Foxblood took charge of the First Prester, who didn't speak a word of any language but Obannese, both classical and modern, and had never borne a weapon in his life. But Foxblood spoke good Obannese and Tribe-talk and passable Wallekki.

"There'll always be a few of us on hand who will understand your speech, First Prester—have no fear of that," he said. "And I must say, you're a lot less trouble than I thought you'd be. Hlah told me they used to call you Sunfish. Do you mind if we call you that? It's 'Et-taa-naa-qiqu' in our language—much easier to say than 'Orth.'"

Orth smiled at him. "Those were the happiest days of my life, when I had that name," he said. "I'd be glad to have it again."

"You're able to eat things that no dainty Westman can eat, not any that I've ever heard of." Hlah had fed Orth on many things that Abnaks eat when pressed for speed: various roots, fungi, beetle larvae, and other treats that would never have appeared on Lord Orth's table in the city. "Hlah taught you well."

"I owe Hlah my life," said Orth. "And he was the means by which God restored my soul."

On the other side of the mountains the Abnaks gathered again, a great gathering, all of them eager to see the great Obannese holy man, rumored to be a shaman without peer. With Foxblood translating, Orth addressed them.

"Children of God—new children, who have not yet known their father—the Lord of All has been a long time waiting for you," he said. "You do not know it yet, but He has plans for you.

"For the Lord means to build a new Temple, not like the Temple in Obann, which perished. The first Temple, built by great King Kai in ancient days; the greatest of the Temples, the second, built in the days of Obann's Empire and perished in the Day of Fire; and the third, in the new city of Obann on the north bank of the river, which the Thunder King destroyed—all three, the work of human hands, have perished. But this will be a new kind of temple that cannot be destroyed: a temple not of wood and stone and gold, but a temple of the human heart, whose floor will be God's earth and whose roof, God's sky. It will be a temple not just for Obann, but a house of prayer for all the peoples under the sun. The work has already begun. Men and women and children of the Abnaks, you will be as stones built into a glorious temple of the heart—"

At this the crowd grew noisily excited.

"They want to know," said Foxblood, "if God is going to turn them into stones. Don't be afraid, Et-taa-naa-qiqu. They're not angry, not a bit. They just don't understand. But it is the kind of talk they like to hear from a holy man."

That put Orth off his stride, but only for a moment.

"Don't be afraid!" he cried, raising his hands for silence. "You won't be turned to stone. There won't be any stone in this new Temple. It is God's will that you should live in peace, enjoying your own land and all the good things that God has given you. All He asks is that you learn to know Him and love Him and trust Him and honor Him, as He loves and cares for you. For it is not His will that you should be as prey to the Thunder King."

The Abnaks, when Foxblood had translated those words, broke out into cheers and dancing.

"They're doing a scalp dance without the scalps," Foxblood explained, "although they expect to get some, rather soon. They like your words, Sunfish. But of course there's first the little matter of a war we have to win. But now they want you to bless their axes for them and their spears."

So Lord Orth, a man of peace and the greatest scholar in Obann, invoked blessings on the barbarians and their weapons—not entirely sure that he was in the right for doing so, but praying silently that God would make it right in the end. "Give me the words you wish me to speak to these people, O Lord," he prayed, "and lead me well, because I don't know where I'm going."

———

At the bottom of King Thunder's road, in the country of the Heathen, Obst bid the men of the army to gather stones, as many as they could, and heap them into a great pile: "Something that will not be easily removed," he said.

"Why?" said Shaffur. "What do we want with a great pile of stones?"

"Please, my lord—you'll see."

The Wallekki warriors grumbled, but went about the work as hard as any of the others. "Once we would have refused to do this," Shaffur said to Ryons. The boy king nodded, knowing very well that Wallekki males reserved all such work to slaves. He'd been one of those slaves, not so long ago.

"Why do you do it now, Chief?" he asked.

"Because we are sworn to serve God, but we don't know how we are to serve Him unless our teacher tells us." Shaffur scowled, but suddenly his scowl gave way to a smile. "We would all be dead men many times over, had God not saved us. Better to pile up stones for God, than to be buried under stones by the Thunder King."

Gurun came up alongside Ryons while the men were working.

"This is from the Scriptures," she said. "When Osper led the Tribes of the Law across the great river, to the land that God gave them so they could live in peace, he had them pile stones beside the riverbank so that, when they saw it, they would remember what God did for them."

Ryons looked up at her, but did not speak. There was something solemn about this labor. The men performed it very quietly.

At last, toward the end of the afternoon, Obst said the pile was big enough and assembled the army before it. He raised his hands in blessing.

"Let us pray," he said. "O Father, may these stones be a witness, for all ages to come, that we came here and proclaimed your name in Heathen country, in obedience to your will. And let this be a Heathen land no more."

He lowered his hands. "Sing aloud, you people of the Lord! For you will be the first to praise God in this land—but not the last."

The warriors sang their anthem, in all their different languages: "His mercy endureth forever!" Around them in all directions stretched a grassy plain with no sign of human habitation, but now it seemed less empty than before. Ryons felt a prickle up and down his spine. His ancestor, King Ozias, seemed to be there, somewhere—as if you could see him, if only you knew where to look.

Around Gurun stood her little bodyguard of Blays, all eighteen of them, brandishing short spears and whirling slings above their heads. Around Ryons, on horseback, sang his fifty Ghols. Many times in the past had Ghols raided the Blays' country for slaves and booty. Now they stood together. Shingis, the chief of the Blays, exchanged grins with Chaga-dai, the captain of the Ghols.

They sang until the sun set, and then they pitched their camp.

"What do we do next?" Ryons asked Obst.

"We go a little farther," the old man said. Beyond that, who could say? All the way out to the Thunder King's castle at Kara Karram, maybe. "But how many of us will have to go that far," he said, "I can't imagine."

CHAPTER 17

Ysbott Shows His Temper

A special messenger, the fastest rider left in Ninneburky, carried Vannett's letters to Obann. But before he could arrive, another messenger came down to the city from the north: one of Baron Hennen's most trusted aides, in search of Gallgoid. Even with Hennen's instructions, it took the young man all day to find the chief of spies. And such were Gallgoid's precautions, that the messenger didn't know his real name and didn't know he was a spy. Gallgoid thanked him and dismissed him, and only opened the letter when he was alone again. It was in a cipher known only to the general and the spy, and this is what it said.

"Hennen to Gallgoid, greetings—

"I've not yet met with Chutt, who is a day's march away in Market City, but already I smell treason. Depend on it, that it's Chutt's desire to restore the Oligarchy and make himself master of the city. There can be no other reason for the great number of troops he has mustered to himself, far more than he needs to pacify the north. If it comes to fighting, my two thousand spears will be insufficient."

Chutt had recruited all the Heathen he could find, remnants of the Thunder King's host that had fled into the north, Hennen wrote.

"You know the man better than I do, but he has an evil

108

reputation. He is said to be a coward, but I think the numbers he has behind him now will make him bold.

"To turn back to the city before I have secured his oath would be a disservice to my king. I will press on and see what I can do. In the meantime it must be your task to prepare the city for defense. Do whatever you can. I'll return as soon as possible, God willing. Hennen."

Gallgoid folded the letter and tucked it into a secret compartment in his belt. Lord Reesh, he well recalled, despised Chutt as the weakest of the High Council, a man thoroughly unreliable, who'd acquired his position by flattery. "One of these days, I'll have you poison him," Reesh used to say, but he'd never gotten around to it. And when the Thunder King's army came, Lord Chutt ran away—the only member of the High Council besides Lord Reesh, who did not die in defense of the city.

Hennen had left another two thousand men behind him in Obann to defend it and deal with unexpected needs. The rest were scattered all over the country on both sides of the river in twenty-man patrols. There were still Heathen freebooters for them to hunt down and local militia for them to train.

"There's no one here who understands military matters—including me," Gallgoid mused. In Hennen's absence, the highest authority in the city was the mayor, a wool merchant named Istrigg. "So we have two thousand men," thought Gallgoid, "but no one who will know how to use them properly." The deputy commander left in charge by Hennen was a mere legate not yet forty years old. King Thunder's invasion had badly mauled the armed force of Obann, and the losses had yet to be made good.

With misgivings he could not easily dismiss, Gallgoid sent for the legate.

————————

Helki roamed the foothills south of the Golden Pass and so learned that the First Prester had gone across the mountains with the Abnaks. A lone trapper told him so.

"News travels fast in these parts," said the trapper, one of the few Obannese who'd lived in the hills all his life. He had a wife in one of the new settlements, he said. "Now most of the Abnaks who live here are itching to go east and join the war. But it'll go hard with the rest of the folk, if they're not here when winter comes. A lot of the people will starve without them." It was the Abnak hunters who kept the settlers fed.

"I reckon Lord Orth didn't dare say he wouldn't go," Helki said.

"Oh, they say he went of his own accord, because they asked him." The trapper shook his head. "If he thinks he's going to make the Abnaks get religion, he's in for a disappointment. There never was much religion around here, even before the Abnaks came. Most of us have never even seen a chamber house, let alone been in one."

"Times are changing," Helki said.

He decided he ought to talk to Hlah again. Hlah could tell him more than this trapper. It would mean another few days away from Ryons' army, but this was news that Obst and the chieftains needed to know.

Helki wondered what had made Orth go with the Abnaks. Well, the First Prester was an unusual man, not quite like anybody else. You'd never be able to guess his reasons for it, Helki thought. They were bound to be surprising.

━━━━━━━━━

With his militiamen behind him, and now some sixty less-than-happy gold seekers in tow, Roshay Bault led the way up the Thunder King's road. He'd come that way once before, albeit not all the way up to the Golden Pass. He didn't know his daughter and his adopted son were only a day's march behind him, with tidings that would startle him.

Martis drove them hard, but not too hard. These were youngsters who'd already walked more miles than most Obannese men would walk in all their lives. They could almost keep up with grown men, and could keep going for a lot longer than some adults he knew. Even so, he didn't want to overtax them.

"Your father has picked up a little speed, now that he's struck the road," he told Ellayne. "It's all uphill from here. Are you sure you wouldn't rather ride than walk? Dulayl has carried you and Jack before."

"Not yet, thanks!" Ellayne said.

Fnaa was riding the spare horse. He kept teasing Trout to try it, but Trout only said, "An Abnak on a horse is like a beaver up a tree."

Jack was enjoying the trip. It was like old times, only without the fear of being captured by outlaws. "I guess the baron might as well let us go all the way up the mountain with him," he said. "I can't see him sending us back the way we came."

"Easy to enjoy a long walk when the weather's good," Trout said. "But it's going to rain soon, no more than two days from now—and then see how you like it."

"Rain? There's not a cloud in the sky!" Ellayne said. "How do you know it's going to rain?"

Trout shrugged. "I know," he said.

———————

Ysbott's men were exhausted, almost too worn-out to ravish their eyes with the gold. But they were at the top of the pass before anyone else, and as one of them said, that had to count for something.

"Look at it!" said Hrapp the cobbler, whose whole business, shop and all, might have been sold for two gold pieces. "I never knew there was so much gold in all the world."

"It'd take a thousand men and a thousand carts to carry it," panted Gwawl.

Ysbott, who hadn't spent his life puttering around a small town and barely stretching his legs, didn't share their fatigue. But at the moment he was stunned by the vastness of the treasure. It was as if the sun itself had fallen out of the sky and landed on the pass. How many gold coins could be minted out of just one of those big sheets of gold? Enough to fill a hefty strongbox! Enough to make him rich for all his days. But could ten men even carry one?

"Let's see how hard it is for us to lift one of those sheets and carry it," he said.

Two or three men actually groaned. All they wanted was to sit and let their sweat dry.

"Get up, you lazy dogs! A little hard work won't do you any harm." Not that Ysbott had ever done an honest day's work in his life. But Hrapp knew him well enough to stand up right away, and the others soon followed.

"Let's find a loose one and see if we can shift it."

He soon discovered that a lot of the big pieces shifted all by themselves as soon as you tried to approach them. It was a tricky business, trying to maneuver among that jumble of timbers and gold sheets. They were like jaws waiting to snap shut on your shins.

"How about this one, Tobb?"

It was a loose sheet, not attached to anything else, lying at an angle upon a mass of broken beams. Ysbott, Hrapp, and Gwawl grabbed it by one end and tried to drag it clear. It slid easily enough: indeed, it suddenly slid down and almost took their fingers off. With just a little more labor they had it free from the pile.

It was as long as Ysbott was tall, but not so wide as his outstretched arms. It was beaten thin, as thin as birchbark, with its edges twisted and crumpled this way and that, and many dents in it.

"Everyone get a grip, and see if we can lift it," Ysbott said. "It looks like this must have been nailed to the wood as a covering. See, there's a rusty nail still in it."

At his count of three they raised it from the ground. It was heavy, but not too heavy, not at all. Four or five men ought to be able to carry it. He put a man at each corner and they carried it some yards away, then put it down.

"That wasn't so bad," he said.

"But there must be hundreds of them!" a man said.

"I don't fancy having to lug these through the woods," said Gwawl. Ysbott shoved him backward to the ground; he landed hard.

"I won't stand for any more complaining," he said. "You'll do as I say, or else. Give these lads some good advice, Hrapp."

"Better do as he says, men." The cobbler made a valiant effort not to stutter. "Tobb's got a temper."

But one thing Ysbott didn't have yet was a plan, and that was not good for his temper.

CHAPTER 18

How Someone Crossed the Bridge

So Ellayne and Jack were off again, as if they were already all grown up, and here sat Enith, left behind, with no one to talk to or play with.

What was the secret of those two? Enith had collected tantalizing bits of it from other children. Everyone in Ninneburky knew that Jack and Ellayne had run away from home two years ago and were gone for months and months, no one knew where. They ran away to Obann once, too, and the baron gnashed his teeth but didn't do anything about it. No one knew why those two seemed to be such privileged characters. People said they were King Ryons' friends. How could that have happened? And who was that boy, Fnaa, who came out of nowhere with a big, fierce Abnak at his side?

"I know you miss your friends, Enith," said the baroness, "but they'll be back before too long. I miss them, too. So maybe you and I can keep each other company."

"I'd like that, Baroness!" Enith answered. "I wonder—would you mind reading me the rest of a story in that book about Abombalbap? Ellayne never finished it."

Vannett involuntarily made a face, and Enith remembered Ellayne saying that her mother didn't altogether approve of those stories. But the baroness surprised her by saying, "All right. Go get us a couple of honey-cakes from the kitchen, and I'll fetch the book."

They settled down in the parlor. Vannett opened the big book—it barely fit on her lap—to where Ellayne had left the leather bookmark, and began to read.

"So there sat Abombalbap, and he saw the princess praying in the crystal castle and wiping tears from her eyes; but he knew of no way that he might deliver her, where all those other knights had failed.

"And in the morning came walking up to that place a common churl, little more than a boy, with no shoes on his feet and a smudge of dirt on his cheek. And the boy said, Sir Knight, who is that poor lady yonder, who prays and makes such tearful cry? Abombalbap said, She is a prisoner by means of enchantment in that crystal castle, and no knight, be he ever so hardy, is able to deliver her. Many a knight has essayed the adventure, only to fall into the pit because the glass bridge shatters when he dares set foot on it; and then, by a magician's evil art, the bridge is made whole again. May God defend me, but I have found no means that I might cross that bridge without being cast into the abyss with all the others.

"But the boy said, I will cross the bridge, if God wills it. Do you please pray for me, Sir Knight.

"As the Lord lives, cried Abombalbap, you must not! For even the life of a slave is precious in His sight. But the boy paid him no heed; and Abombalbap rose up to lay hands on him and hold him back, but before he could reach him, the lad stepped onto the bridge.

"And even as Abombalbap prayed for him, for there was nothing else he could do, the boy walked straight across the bridge. With every step he took, the bridge of glass became a sturdy bridge of wood, and the boy passed over the abyss and reached the castle. And when he came to the castle, he went in, and the damsel seeing him rose from her knees. The boy came to her and took her hand and led her out of the castle, which, when they had passed through all the doors and were come outside again, shimmered like snow struck by the noonday sun, and in the twinkling of an eye, dissolved into the air and was no more. And the boy led the lady safely across the wooden bridge.

"Abombalbap cried, God be praised for this miracle! But the lady made a graceful curtsy to the boy and thanked him. As you are the man who has delivered me, said she, when all those strong knights failed, my father shall give you my hand in marriage, and you shall be his son afterwards, a prince, and rule his kingdom after him.

"And Abombalbap did homage to the both of them and mounted on his horse and went his way. And it became known all throughout the land that, at the very moment that the young man and the princess crossed the bridge, the magician in his tower gave a great cry and threw himself from the highest balcony and was dashed against the earth and so died. And the country was freed from his sorceries forever."

Vannett closed the book.

"My father told me that story when I was a little girl," she said. "It always rather scared me, but I hope you enjoyed it."

"Oh, yes—I did!" said Enith.

Word came quickly to Lintum Forest that Abnaks had abducted the First Prester to bring him into their war against the Thunder King. But it was also said that he'd gone willingly. The chiefs that had been left behind at Carbonek called a council.

"This is a fine bunch of worms in the stew meat, and no mistake," said Tughrul Lomak, of the Dahai. With Obst absent, they all had to speak in Tribe-talk. "Our king has marched into the enemy's country; this First Prester has gone across the mountains—and here we are, growing moss on our backs. What use are we to anyone?"

"If Abnaks meant to harm the First Prester, they would have just scalped him on the spot. They wouldn't have taken him home with them," Chief Buzzard said. "You know why we stay here, Tughrul. If something happens here or at Silvertown or anywhere else, there's only us to deal with it. We defend the king's people while he's gone."

"What—with half an army?" Tughrul said.

"What do you want to do, Tughrul?" said Zekelesh, chief of the Fazzan.

"No one will praise us for staying here while Lord Orth dies in Abnak country. We ought to go and bring him back. And then I'd like to help the Abnaks with their war! There are yet two thousand of us. We might be able to achieve something."

"God knows I would like to be there with my people," Buzzard said. "My sons' sons must be warriors by now. I'd like to see them again before I die. But we've given our word to remain here, and I do not lightly break my word."

"I liked that First Prester," Zekelesh said. "He struck me

as a great man." He took off his wolf's-head cap and fiddled with it. "Maybe we ought to ask the prophetess what God wants us to do."

"You know she only speaks when God would have her speak," Tughrul said. "She's just a little child, otherwise."

"It won't hurt to ask," said Zekelesh.

They sent for Abgayle, who came leading Jandra by the hand. In her other hand she carried a book of Scripture—not Obst's volume of the Old Books, but a present given to King Ryons by Lord Orth: one of the first copies of the Lost Book of Ozias. Jandra's toothed bird stalked after them, glaring at the chieftains.

"Abgayle, we would ask—" Zekelesh started to say, but she held up her hand and didn't let him finish.

"Read to the men what you read to me," she said to Jandra, and handed her the book.

Jandra sat on the ground and opened the book. The chiefs fell silent. They'd seen her like this before, grave and solemn as no child of her age could ever be. She was going to prophesy, after all. God was going to speak to them. It made them feel like Jandra was the adult, a great and famous woman, and they were the children. Not one of them would dare to speak or stir—not now.

Jandra turned the pages slowly, one by one, found the page she wanted, and began to read. Her voice was not the voice of a child.

"The Lord said to me, I have established your seed forever, and it will not fail. It shall sleep sometimes, but it shall never die.

"If your sons and your daughters forget me and turn away from me, I shall prune the tree of its unfruitful branches and cast them away; but not the root, for I have planted it, and it shall live.

"And I shall raise up your throne again, and bless it, and endow you with mighty men to be your servants. They shall go out when you bid them to go out to war, and come in when you bid them to come in, and they shall stand still when you bid them to stand still. And my blessing shall be upon all of them that serve you faithfully, and I will hold them dear, as my servants."

Jandra closed the book, then closed her eyes and fell asleep sitting up. Abgayle gathered her into her arms.

"There, Chieftains," she said. "I don't know what your question was, but now you have your answer."

When she went away to put Jandra to bed, Zekelesh sighed and put his cap back on.

"Well," he said, "I guess we stay."

Tughrul nodded. "At least for now," he said. "Until King Ryons calls for us. I think he will, before the end."

———

Enith couldn't help asking the baroness, "But how was that common farm boy able to cross the bridge, but not the knights? It doesn't make sense!"

For the same reason, Vannett thought, that Ellayne and Jack had been able to climb Bell Mountain. But that wasn't something she could say to Enith.

"Why do you think he could do it?" she said.

"I don't know! I thought Abombalbap was going to do it, or some other knight."

"God doesn't see as we see, Enith. He saw something in that boy that he didn't see in any of the knights. And we know from the Scriptures that He likes using the weak to defeat the strong, and He likes to exalt humble things, and humble people, over things and people that we think are grand and important. And I'm afraid," said Vannett, "that's all I know about it."

CHAPTER 19

A Heap of Stones in Griff-land

Trout's prediction came true, and it rained heavily the very next day. He and Martis made a camp beside the road with shelters that kept out the rain, or at least most of it. There could be no more traveling until the rain stopped.

Halfway up the mountain, Roshay Bault tried to continue his march, but could not. There were muddy places in the road where the horses slipped dangerously, and the men were miserable. That was when everyone realized they hadn't brought tents. Roshay could only command that they all get to work constructing lean-tos and whatever other kinds of shelters they might devise, nowhere near as good as the ones Trout and Martis made. The baron set a good example, hacking at saplings with his sword and arranging them as best he could. When the men saw he was no better off than they were, they thought the more of him. Sergeant Kadmel and two troopers offered to improve his lean-to for him, but he wouldn't allow it.

"See to your own shelters," he said. "I hate it, but I don't suppose this cusset rain will kill me."

Fnaa kept his companions entertained with stories

of the capers he'd cut while he pretended to be the king in Obann. "I had to make out that poor King Ryons had gone all simpleminded," he said. "Queen Gurun thought I'd be safer if those men on the council thought the king was just a fool. But they didn't like it when I threw the tax money to the people in the street! How they scrambled for it! I enjoyed it."

There was no such amusement in the baron's camp—only wet clothes, cold rations, and short tempers. All of those men had much to learn about campaigning as soldiers.

But on top of the mountain at the Golden Pass, things were quite different.

"This rain is the best stroke of luck we've had yet," Ysbott told his men. As an outlaw in the forest all his life, he was used to rough living. "Roshay Bault will have to stay put until the sun comes out again, but we won't." By now they were all too afraid of him to do anything but obey.

Having done it many times before, Ysbott made himself a snug little shelter that kept out the rain. "Just do as I do," he told the men, but gave them no more help than that. What they built was only a little better than nothing.

"While the baron sits idle, we'll be able to move some of this gold a mile or so down the mountain and stash it in the woods. They'll march right past it, and whatever else may happen, that gold will be ours—enough to make us all rich for as long as we live."

So Ysbott explained his plan, as far as it went, and the townsmen thought it was a good one. Some of the gold sheets were thin enough for several men to carry. Just one would be enough for all ten of them to live comfortably from then on. "Imagine what ten sheets would do!" they encouraged one another. Nothing else would have ever gotten them to toil up and down the mountain in that pouring rain.

"How will we find it again?" Gwawl asked, as they buried the first of the sheets under leaf litter, deeply enough so that no glint of gold could escape.

"I'm a woodsman. You can leave it to me," Ysbott said. These town chickens would lose the gold and then get lost themselves, if you gave them half a chance, he thought. At best, they'd know enough to follow the road back down to the plain—empty-handed and half-starved.

Up and down they toiled in the rain, lugging sheets of gold, manhandling them through stubborn trees that showered still more water on them. It took all day to transport and cache four sheets. "When we've got the mountain to ourselves again," Ysbott said, "we can bring a cart up here to carry our gold the rest of the way down."

By the time they stopped for the day, they were thoroughly exhausted and even more thoroughly soaked. Ysbott was the only one who could get a campfire going, having taken the precaution, before it started raining hard, of collecting dry firewood and stowing it in his shelter. The others had to do without, although he let them take turns sitting by his fire. Otherwise they'd be useless in the morning. As it was, it took them all the next day to move and cache three sheets. By evening, the rain began to let up.

"I've never worked so hard in my life!" Hrapp said. "But once we're safely home with all this gold, none of us will ever have to work again."

———

It rained on Griff-land, too, but not so heavily. King Ryons' army, having advanced another day's march eastward, erected another cairn to bear witness to God's name.

They had just finished it when they had visitors, a band of Griffs from a nearby encampment—women, children, and a few old men. All the warriors, they said, had gone south to fight the Abnaks. They were afraid of the army, but their curiosity outweighed their fear. Obst received them as welcome guests, although they cast uneasy glances at Ryons, Gurun, and the chieftains.

"We can't defend ourselves from you," an elder said, "but we have nothing worth taking. We have barely enough food to keep ourselves alive. Some Zephites passed through here a week ago and ate up most of that."

"We won't take anything that's yours," Obst said, "nor will we harm a hair of your heads."

"What means this heap of stones you've made?" a woman asked. "It seems a strange thing for anyone to do, to pile stones like that."

"Tell her, Tiliqua," said Obst. He thought they might be more receptive to the message if they heard it from a fellow Griff.

"We come in the name of the only true God, who has made us His children," Tiliqua said, speaking to them in Griffish. "This is the God of Obann, and now our God, too. These cairns we have made so that everyone who sees them will know that we came here in His name."

"But why have you come?" asked the elder.

"To set you free," said Tiliqua.

"Ask them about those Zephites," Shaffur said.

"My men will go out and find them," Looth said.

"The Zeph had a poor harvest last year, so now they come down and raid us for food," the elder said. "They'll give you a hard fight if you meet up with them. We and they alike are subjects of the Thunder King, but he doesn't protect us from the Zeph. He has taken away our fighting men, and we cannot defend ourselves. The Zeph could kill us all, if they wished to."

"Our God will take away the Thunder King," Tiliqua said. "Your young men will come home."

"Will you make this boy our king? Is that why you've come?"

Obst spoke up. "This is Ryons, King of Obann by the grace of God. He seeks nothing that is yours, neither lands nor people."

"I crossed the mountains westward with the Thunder King's great army," Tiliqua said. "God destroyed that army. Surely you have heard the news."

But they hadn't heard. No man of that army had ever returned, until now.

"Don't you know," Tiliqua said, "that the Thunder King himself went up to the Golden Pass and perished there?" He pointed to the mountains in the west, dyed purple by a setting sun. "We came down by the same road that he built. There was no one there to stop us."

They remembered the cavalcades of wagons bringing gold and provisions and other supplies up the mountain, and the great show made by the Thunder King and his mardars when they passed through Griff-land. He never came back down, but they had never heard that he had died.

"How else do you think we could have come down King Thunder's road?" Tiliqua said.

"But he couldn't have died! Not him!" said a woman.

"He is as dead as any man can be. The power of God

destroyed him and the great golden hall he'd built up there. No army of ours came anywhere near him. God smashed him and his hall under an avalanche of ice and stone."

"How could they not know these things?" Ryons wondered, after Obst had translated. Well, the mardars certainly would not have told them. There couldn't have been any survivors in that avalanche. And no one could have survived the avalanche and come down.

"Some of you may have known a man named Chillith, who became a mardar among the Griffs," Obst said. "He lost the sight of his eyes and became a servant of God. Alone and blind, he climbed the mountain in the winter, and in that golden hall, pronounced God's judgment on the Thunder King. And judgment came. But there are more judgments yet to come."

The Griffs needed time to take this in, discussing it excitedly among themselves. Tiliqua translated for the chiefs.

"A few of these did know Chillith," he said. "They remember the day he cut off all his hair and became a mardar." That, of course, was a shocking thing for a man of the Griffs to do: they are famous for the attention they lavish on their hair. "They're afraid, hearing all this news about the disasters that befell the Thunder King. You'd think it would make them glad! But all they know is that there is still a Thunder King in Kara Karram, and if he died in the avalanche, how can he still be alive in his castle, far away?"

By nightfall the Griffs at least understood that Ryons' army meant them no harm. The warriors gave them rations—Looth's hunters and foragers never came back empty-handed—and made friends with them. The Griffs gathered around Ryons, marveling that a boy should lead an army. They were even more interested in Gurun and could hardly take their eyes off her.

"How is it that such a maid as this dares to go against the Thunder King?" the elder said. "Is she magical? Are there spells woven around her?"

"Please—there is no magic in me!" Gurun said, blushing. "God sent me to Obann from a faraway country that you've never heard of to stand beside King Ryons. My people are fishermen and farmers."

"We've never seen your like," said an old woman. "The Thunder King took our Griff gods away from us, said he would be our only god from now on. He took our goddess, too. We had a maiden goddess named Lucalla. And yet now you come, a girl, and your king is just a boy. There is something about this that we don't understand! How can the likes of you bring destruction to the Thunder King, when our gods themselves could not?"

"It is not by us that he will be destroyed," said Gurun.

"People of the Griff," Obst said, "we will move on from here tomorrow, and you'll return to your own village. Tell everyone, in all the Griffs' encampments, what you've seen and heard today."

"We will tell them," said the elder. "And sometime soon we'll come back to this place and stand before this heap of stones that you've made to your God. We must wisely consider all these things."

"If there's any wisdom left in us," the old woman added, "after all that's happened."

In the seminary of Obann, in an office whose window

looked out on the charred ruins of the Palace, Preceptor Constan read Baroness Vannett's letter. You might have thought he was reading a list of supplies for the scriptorium, for all the reaction he showed. His students and assistants complained that you never knew what the preceptor was thinking until he spoke his mind—if you could stand to wait that long.

When he'd finished reading, he sat perfectly still for a while. You might have thought he was asleep, but he was thinking. Constan thought slowly, because he thought most thoroughly. Eventually he wrote a brief note and sealed it in an envelope, then summoned a student to deliver it at once to a certain housemaid in a certain house, who would see that a certain other person would get it without delay. That person was Gallgoid, who came to the preceptor's house that evening after supper. Constan had sent his two servants out on errands, time-consuming but of no great importance, so that he would be alone when Gallgoid came.

"Read this," Constan said. "It's from the baroness in Ninneburky." They were seated in his study with the door shut and the curtains drawn.

Anyone else might have burst out with an exclamation at the news that was in the letter. Gallgoid thought highly of Lord Orth, but didn't show it.

"I don't see what we can do about this," he said.

"I'm thinking we had better keep this to ourselves," Constan said. "She's sent a letter to Prester Jod, too. I've invited him to come and see us."

"Good." Gallgoid paused, then added, "She says Lord Orth went with the Abnaks willingly. That's to be considered. Did you know King Ryons is across the mountains, too—or should be, by now?"

"I didn't know. But I suppose Baron Hennen has been informed of that."

"That's another difficulty." For a tiny moment, a half-smile crossed Gallgoid's lips. "I haven't heard from Hennen for some days. He feared some treachery on the part of Lord Chutt."

That news made no more impression on Constan than it would have on a boulder. But that was only outwardly. Knowing Constan's ways, Gallgoid waited patiently for him to speak.

"My concern must be solely that the work of copying and distributing God's word continues without interruption," he finally said. "That I will do, as much as it lies within my power. But with Lord Orth and Hennen both out of the city, and King Ryons himself gone into Heathen lands, and none of them likely to come back any time soon, if ever, someone must take command here. Who should it be?"

"Prester Jod—if he can get here in time," said Gallgoid. "No one else has the prestige to do it. But the people will obey him, I think."

"I believe Hennen left a legate named Ullun in charge of the troops," Constan said. "It's a far cry from Lord Gwyll." It was Lord Gwyll who had led the defense against the Thunder King, but he'd died in the battle. "Our city is not what it once was."

"There will be worse in store for it," Gallgoid said, "if the people think they've lost both their First Prester and their king. We need Prester Jod."

"He will come," Constan said. "But let us pray for the others."

Gallgoid would soon learn that Hennen was a prisoner in Market City. But Hennen's officers were under orders not to fight except in self-defense and, if it could be safely done, to march back to Obann without him.

"I won't have Chutt come into possession of my troops!" he told them. "I don't think he's well-enough organized to attack you, if you retreat promptly. Get back to the city and make ready to defend it."

So Hennen went into Market City to parley with Lord Chutt, who invited him to dine with him, saw there was no budging the general from his allegiance to the king, and so had ruffians bind him and lock him in a cellar. But by then Hennen had already seen and heard enough to convince him Chutt was a fool.

Chutt had six thousand men, more than half of them stragglers from the Thunder King's defeated armies. These had joined him because they had nowhere else to go, and he was feeding them on stores that would soon run out. He would have to move them south, where they would be able to pillage farms and towns. Hennen doubted Chutt would be able to control them then. In the meantime, the man was putting on airs.

"I am the last of the High Council of the Oligarchy," he said over dinner. "Obann hasn't had a king for a thousand years, or two thousand—it doesn't matter which. But there wouldn't even be an Obann for this boy king of yours to pretend to rule, if it weren't for the oligarchs.

"We put this shattered nation back together. We reunited all the petty lords and fiefdoms. For three hundred years, sir, the oligarchs have governed. It's truly the only way to govern such a large country. Kings are all right in fairy tales, but this is the real world."

Hennen saw no point in arguing with him. He would have returned to camp that evening and led his troops home the next morning, confident that Chutt would prove to be his own worst enemy, but Chutt had him thrown into a cellar before he'd finished his dessert.

"And you can sit in the dark," Chutt said, from the top of the stairs, "until you decide to join me and do what's best for your country."

"You can't afford to wait that long," said Hennen.

CHAPTER 20

Ysbott's Plan

O mah don't live in the mountains, and although Wytt had climbed Bell Mountain and ascended the Golden Pass—the only one of his kind ever to do such things—the novelty of the environment appealed to him and tempted him to go exploring. While his human companions huddled in their shelters, Wytt went out alone, traveling under the thick brush and not caring much about the rain.

Around his neck he wore a lock of Ellayne's hair. He couldn't have told you why: only that it was "sunshine hair," which to him seemed reason enough to cherish it. Many other Omah would have felt the same.

Probing a rotting log for tasty grubs, he nearly lost his head when a pair of strong jaws suddenly snapped shut at him, just missing his face. His reflexes saved him, but he didn't know what to think of the strange creature to which the jaws belonged.

Jack would have said it was a salamander—but what a salamander! It was as big as a boy's arm, glossy black with flaming red stripes up and down its body, and a head the size of a man's fist. The salamanders Jack knew were no bigger than his finger.

From a safe distance Wytt chattered at it, brandishing his sharp stick and hurling insults. "Son of a snake! Legless vermin!" In truth the beast had legs, but they were so disproportionately small, they hardly counted. "Come and fight—I'll pin your flat head to the ground!" But the salamander only stared unblinkingly, having defended its hunting ground. Wytt was forced to move on.

Above him, in the trees, there was some other creature hunting in the rain, bigger and more dangerous than any salamander, and a lot hungrier. Wytt stayed keenly alert. He couldn't see this hunter, but he could hear it whenever it stirred, no matter how stealthily. His nostrils wrinkled at a scent he'd never known before. As rich as it was in grubs and edible tubers, and even purple berries that were as sweet as anything he'd ever tasted, this was a country full of hidden dangers—to all of which the humans were oblivious. They were big and strong, but all but useless in the wilderness. Wytt thought he would be hard put to protect them.

———

As the rain began to slacken, Ysbott the Snake moved camp.

"We don't want the baron to find us here, do we?" he said. "We'll find a place close to the gold we've brought down and sit tight while he marches right past us."

Half a mile from the road, they set up a new camp in a small clearing. Ysbott expected to be there when Roshay Bault came back down the mountain. There were sure to be stragglers. Maybe there would be a chance to grab more gold.

Not surprisingly, Ysbott's men were nearly at the end of their strength. He didn't want them collapsing just yet, so this time he helped them put up shelters. But everything was too wet for a fire.

"We're almost out of food, Tobb," the cobbler said. "What I wouldn't give for hot roast beef!"

"You can buy all the roast beef in Ninneburky when we get back home," Ysbott answered, "and the best Durmurot wine to wash it down. Meanwhile, get what rest you can. We can't work while the baron's up there."

———————

The Abnaks wanted to show the holy man that they could fight. A few dozen of them went out one night and came back two days later with a gory haul of Wallekki scalps.

"Fifty! We slew at least fifty of them!" exulted the leader of the raid. "And we burned their camp down when we were done. Look at all the horsemeat!" For Abnaks prize horsemeat as a delicacy, especially when taken from an enemy.

Orth didn't mind their feasting on horsemeat, although it would be frowned upon in Obann, but he had to look away from the warriors' scalp dance. "God help me," he prayed silently, "what kind of people are these? And what am I to do among them?" He could hardly ask them to abandon all their customs.

The chiefs and subchiefs had retired into a long house sheathed with bark—the closest Abnaks ever came to erecting a permanent habitation. Now they came out, while the dance was still in progress, and Orth startled when Foxblood came up behind him and laid a hand on his shoulder.

"Don't like it, do you?" the chief said. "Well, I didn't think you would. But it's an ancient custom of ours, a way of great rejoicing. If you could understand what they're singing, you would know they were thanking the God of Obann for giving them this victory. Besides, the men who used to own those scalps are well past taking any further harm."

"My own ancestors used to do things like this," said Orth. "But that was a very long time ago."

"There's a great camp of the Zephites further down the hill," Foxblood said, "a wooden wall with five hundred warriors inside it. That'll be the next place we attack. They're not used to seeing us come in great numbers. I'm telling you this because this time you'll be coming with us to the battle."

"I won't be any use to you," Orth said.

"Our people think otherwise. We want you to pray for us, and keep on praying until we win."

"I am a man of peace, Chief Foxblood."

"That we all know, Prester. I don't hold it against you."

"To think of men killing one another distresses me," said Orth. "To see it would distress me more! But who am I to try to be holier than God? He is a God who is mighty in battle. Your people fight to stay alive and to keep the land that God has given them for their own. Furthermore, the Abnaks have called upon His name, even if only through me, His servant. What do I matter, after all? Your people have a righteous cause, and I believe that God will bless it. Of course I'll come with you to this battle. I only hope I don't faint while I'm praying for your victory."

Foxblood took Orth's forearms in his hands and looked long into his eyes. Orth didn't know that this, which would have been poor manners in Obann, was how the Abnaks showed respect. He didn't avert his eyes from that searching look. Once upon a time in his life, it would have made him much more uncomfortable than it did today.

"There is no man like you among all the Abnaks," Foxblood said, "nor has there ever been a God like yours among us. I can't tell whether it's love or fear that makes you obey Him, when I can easily see you'd rather not. Probably a lot of both—eh? I would despise a son of mine who fainted at the sight of blood. But you agree to do things that terrify you. If you faint, Et-taa-naa-qiqu, I'll tell the people it was because your spirit left your body to commune with God. They'll understand that."

Orth's eyes brimmed with tears, but he smiled. From that day on, he and the Abnak chief were friends.

The rain stopped. With all his men tired and wet and complaining, and a dull ache in the small of his back that wasn't there before, Roshay Bault resumed his march to the Golden Pass—at a brisk pace, too, to make up for lost time.

They marched right past Ysbott's hiding place, with Ysbott and his men watching, unseen and unsuspected. And as he watched, a plan took form in Ysbott's mind.

"I now know what we must do," he told his men. "We'll rest another day, and then move up close to them without being seen or heard. At night I'll steal into their camp as just another fool from Ninneburky. I'll sit with them round their fire, and I'll tell them stories—about the Thunder King and all those men of his that died there and how their ghosts hover over the place, guarding their gold. With the kinds of noises the wind makes up there, it won't be hard to scare those people. You would have been scared, yourselves, if it hadn't been raining so hard."

Ysbott knew what he was talking about. The baron's daughter had escaped, when he had her, by terrifying his men with stories of witches and the like, so that when she finally performed an act of witchcraft on them, they ran off in every conceivable direction. Ysbott himself would have run away, if the cuss't girl hadn't struck him blind. Ysbott couldn't perform any magic, but he imagined how he might do something just as effective.

"When the moon goes down," he said, "you lads will be hiding in the woods—not too close, but close enough for them to hear you. I want you to start screeching and wailing and caterwauling as loud as you can.

"No words, mind you—just nonsense. Like this: Yibba nan-ibba kamassi! It's just drivel; it has no meaning. But I'll say it's a Heathen language, and it means they're warning us off, threatening to take revenge if we take their gold. Heathen ghosts, you see! Two or three nights of that ought to break their spirit—that, and maybe a few men found with their throats cut, ear to ear. But that part you can leave to me."

Had they never seen the gold, and been bewitched by it, those Ninneburky townsmen would never have agreed to such a thing. They probably wouldn't have believed Ysbott, would've thought he was just trying to impress them with big talk, but they had learned to be afraid of him. Having spent this much time under his leadership, they were not at their best anymore.

"Can you really do it, Tobb?" asked Hrapp. "It sounds mighty risky."

"Of course I can do it! Just give me a loud enough chorus of moans and shrieks and gibberish, and I'll do the rest. I can't wait to see the look on Bault's face when all his men desert him! And it'll mean a lot more gold for you and me."

"But we already have a lot of gold," said Gwawl.

Before he could say another word, Ysbott knocked him down, sprang onto his chest, and had a sharp knife glinting just a hair's breadth from his eyes.

"I think you will obey me, Gwawl," he said. "There's no backing out of this business. Do you understand that now?"

"Yes, Tobb! Yes!"

By and by Ysbott let him up. "You'll all obey me, won't you?"

The townsmen were strangers to violence; and a man like Ysbott, who used it without a second's hesitation, seemed to them unnatural—not a man, but some kind of wild beast, dangerous and deadly. They didn't know how to respond.

So they all promised to obey, and Ysbott was content.

CHAPTER 21

In the Shadow
of the Tower

Looth's scouts found the Zeph. They weren't far away and had made camp at an unusual location.

"Everyone knows that place," said Tiliqua, when the Attakotts made their report. "It's the Tower of Griff-land, at the exact center of our country."

"I never heard the Griffs built towers," Uduqu said.

"We didn't. It's always been there, since before we first settled in this land. There used to be a god living in it, but the Thunder King took the god away."

"A relic of ancient times, I suppose," Perkin said, standing with his arm across Baby's back. "Obann's full of them."

"The Zeph are less than half our number," Looth said. "No men with horses, no archers—we can easily destroy them. The Griffs would thank us for it."

"We haven't come here to destroy!" Obst said.

They'd destroyed a Zephite army once before, in Obann. The Thunder King had sent that army to wipe them out because they'd thrown off their allegiance to him. "The Zephites are to have their freedom, too," Obst said.

"If they want it," Shaffur added.

The chieftains arranged the army with the Hosa in the center and the Griffs right behind them, with the Attakotts to go before them as skirmishers with poisoned arrows and Wallekki horsemen on the wings. The center would fix the enemy in place while the cavalry would envelop them on two sides. "This is how we do battle whenever we have numbers," explained Xhama, chief of the Red Regiment of the Hosa, "only our wings are on foot instead of horseback. It has always served us well." The chiefs saw the advantages of the plan and at once adopted it.

"Maybe the king's brave little hawk will fly overhead and start the battle for us," Xhama added, "as she did when we took Silvertown." The Hosa honored Angel for that, but for the time being she seemed content to perch on Ryons' shoulder.

Ryons and Gurun, with the Ghols and Blays around them, were to ride behind the main body of the infantry. Should the need arise, the Ghols and Blays would function as a small but powerful reserve.

"Our place is to guard our father the king," said Chaga-dai. "But we do hate to be idle while our brothers fight!"

"There's to be no fighting, if it can possibly be avoided," Obst said. "I'll speak to the Zephites and tell them why we're here. It'd be foolish of them to try to give us battle."

"Who ever heard of Zephites not fighting when they had an opportunity?" Shaffur said.

Gurun didn't trust herself to speak. She rode beside Ryons, tall and upright in the saddle. What had she to do with battles? There were no battles on Fogo Island. Sometimes a blood feud would break out and groups of men would fight each other, but the only battles her people knew of were the ones they read of in the Scriptures—battles long ago and far away. That masses of men should clash in arms was something no islander had ever seen.

"You're calm!" King Ryons said to her. "I wish I could be so brave."

"Calm? I'm frozen!" Gurun thought. But the boy's anxious young face sent a little wave of tenderness through her and made her laugh softly.

"I suppose you have been in many battles, Your Majesty," she said.

"Enough so that I'd be happy to skip one, if I got the chance! But maybe the Zeph will listen to Obst and not want to fight."

"Our father is too modest, honeysuckle," Chagadai said. "When he was even littler than he is now, he charged an enemy force singlehanded and put them all to flight."

"That was an accident!" Ryons cried. "My horse bolted, and I couldn't make him stop."

"And it was the worst two minutes of my life," the Ghol said. "But, oh, you should have seen him—a little boy like that! But he won great glory that day."

Perkin, walking after them with Baby, said, "Don't be afraid, Your Majesties. Wherever you go, Baby will go with you. Between him and this ferocious hound of yours, I don't think anyone would be fool enough to stand before you."

Cavall barked, as if he understood.

———

They saw the Tower before they saw the Zeph.

No one, except for the Griffs in the army and a few of the Wallekki who'd been that way with trading caravans,

had ever seen anything like it. Maybe the tall brick smoke-
stacks at the old refinery in Silvertown had once resembled
it, before the Thunder King's troops knocked them down.
But this was taller and more massive, much more. It stood
all alone, with a few black holes in it that were like dead eyes
staring out at the landscape.

When you got closer, you could see it was built of white
stone blocks, maybe granite, cut precisely, joined so closely,
that the tower might have grown out of the earth like a living
thing. But it was deeply scorched and blackened, from top to
bottom. Not even a thousand years of sun and rain and ice
and wind could wipe away the scars left by the Day of Fire.

"It would not have been nice to be inside that tower on
that day," said Perkin.

Now they saw the Zeph, in their bulls'-horned headgear. The Zeph camp wasn't fortified—no sense trying to
defend it. They stood in battle array, two dense ranks. Somehow they'd gotten wind that another army was approaching.
They must have good scouts, able to elude detection by the
Attakotts.

Ryons' chieftains halted the army a little distance from
the Zephites. "Let them see that we outnumber them," Shaffur said. But first the Hosa made way for Obst to come out,
on foot, and speak to the enemy. Behind him rode Ryons and
Gurun, so the Zeph could see them.

"Men of the Zeph!" said Obst—and they heard him in
their own language because that was God's gift to him. "We
call on you to depart in peace from Griff-land. We have no
quarrel with you."

A big man stepped out in front of the Zeph. He had no
paint on his face; he was an ordinary chieftain, not one of the

Thunder King's mardars.

"Who are you," he demanded in a deep voice, "to tell us to go or stay or get out of your way?"

"We follow Ryons, King of Obann by the grace of God, and we come here in the name of God—the living God who made the heavens and the earth."

"We know of no such god. Our gods are dead. There is only the Thunder King."

"God has judged the Thunder King and numbered his days. We are here to proclaim His judgment and to proclaim deliverance to all nations: for God will set you free. Go back to your own country in peace, and rejoice. For God will deliver you from the Thunder King."

The big man bellowed out a laugh. "Ha! What nonsense! I am Jiharr, a bull among bulls. I will not go away! I'll stand right here and fight—if there's anyone among you who will dare to fight me, man to man. If he can kill me, then my people will go home. But if I kill him—and I will!—then you turn around and go back the way you came."

"He knows they can't win a battle," Shaffur said. "He's trying to get off cheaply."

Once it became understood what Jiharr had proposed, there were a hundred volunteers to fight him. He stood there with his brawny arms folded across his powerful chest, laughing at them.

"Your Majesty must decide," said Shaffur. "Who is to have the honor of fighting this fellow? If they keep his word, it'll save us a battle."

Ryons had never felt more helpless in his life. How could he choose a man to fight this monster? It made him feel sick. Gurun watched him, not knowing how to help.

Uduqu made a loud noise and forced everyone to listen to him.

"Pipe down, all of you! It's my right to fight this fight. I've been with King Ryons longer than any of you, except for Obst—and I don't think our teacher ought to try it."

"You're too old!" Shaffur growled. "That Zephite is a warrior in his prime."

Uduqu unlimbered the great sword that had belonged to Shogg the giant, slain by Helki. Even a strong man like Uduqu needed both hands to lift it.

"Yes, I'm old," he said, "and my legs are tired of walking—but I've got a few more fights left in me. We've wasted enough time jawing about it."

Ryons couldn't think of any way to stop Uduqu. He would have, if he could. He felt like he'd known the Abnak subchief all his life. But he didn't know what to do. Maybe no one knew how to turn Uduqu aside, once he'd set his will on something. Ryons could only sit still and let it happen, as if he were watching from a distance. He didn't notice when Gurun pressed his hand.

Jiharr, when he saw the giant's sword, called for a great wooden club studded with sharp chips of volcanic glass. He and Uduqu advanced to meet each other in the space between the armies. At that moment Angel chose to launch herself from Ryons' shoulder, and with a shrill cry, circled overhead. Cavall let out an angry bark, but then fell silent.

Showing off his agility, his footwork, and the skill of his hands, Jiharr danced around, brandished the club, and baited Uduqu in Tribe-talk.

"Were you the best they could do for a champion—a played-out old crock like you? Do you think that ridiculous big sword will help you, when you can hardly raise it off the ground? Why, man, you're old enough to be my father!"

But his dancing took him one step too close, and with an effort that tore a scream from his lungs, Uduqu swung the sword with both hands in a vicious arc. Jiharr tried to throw himself out of its path: few men would have been able to react quickly enough even to try. So a blow that would have otherwise cut him right in half chopped a deep gash in his side and felled him bleeding to the earth. He lay still, in the shadow of the Tower.

"You ought to respect your father," Uduqu said.

———

Gurun had never seen anything so horrible. By the sound he made when he swung the sword, she was sure Uduqu's heart had burst. She loved the old warrior. He'd been her companion in Obann, in Durmurot, and back in Obann when they'd escaped the destruction of the Palace: she and Uduqu and Fnaa.

Before she quite knew what she was doing, she was out of the saddle, racing to Uduqu's side. No one had a chance to hold her back. Uduqu's face seemed deathly pale, under his tattoos. He bent all his strength to not letting the sword slip from his hands.

She stopped short when he grinned at her.

"Easy, girl—I'm all right. Just a little winded."

She heard the crowd of Zephites muttering. It made her look at Jiharr.

"Is there any chance he will live?" she asked.

"Not likely."

A bubble forced its way out between the fallen man's

lips. It moved Gurun to pity such as she'd never known before. Why, she couldn't say.

"Poor fool!" she said. "There was no need for this to happen."

She dropped down to one knee. She wanted to try to comfort him, if there was any life left in him. The fighting men on both sides had fallen silent. Gurun could hear the last few breaths the Zephite took. She picked up his hand and held it between her two hands.

And then Jiharr opened his eyes and saw her and tried to smile.

"Who are you?" he whispered.

"My name is Gurun."

"Your champion has won the fight."

"I am sorry that it came to this," she said.

With a gasp and a groan, Jiharr sat up. She was so startled that she dropped his hand. There were loud yelps of amazement from everyone who saw this.

His bleeding had stopped. He looked down at the deep wound in his side, touched it with his fingers, and winced. "I'll need some stitching up!" he said. And to Uduqu, looking up at him, "Give me your hand, old warrior, and help me up! I want no one but you to help me to stand. You beat me in a fair fight, and we will keep our word and go away."

"By my scalp! Are you alive?" Uduqu cried. Loud exclamations broke out everywhere. All these men were warriors. They knew a fatal wound when they saw one.

"He lives!" cried some man among the Zeph. "The maiden has healed him! She put her hands on him, and he was healed!"

Only then did Gurun realize that something had happened that should not have happened—and in front of all these men, too. Jiharr should have died. Now he wanted to stand up. And everyone was saying she had performed a miracle.

"Hail, hail, the lady of Obann!" the Zephites roared. "Our goddess has come back to us!"

This horrified her more than anything. Gurun sprang to her feet, backing away from Jiharr. She didn't know that the Zeph, before the Thunder King took away their gods and made them worship him, had had a goddess that they worshipped, and to whom they made offerings when they were sick. All she understood was that suddenly they were calling her a goddess, and it made her blood run cold.

When they perceived that she was trying frantically to speak to them, the men went quiet.

"Please! You don't know what you're saying!" Gurun cried. "It wasn't me—I didn't do anything! I'm just the same as you: no goddess, but only flesh and blood. I am only a girl!

"What you have seen was God's doing, not mine! Give Him the glory, not me. Give Him your thanks! You will not see something like this every day."

Uduqu helped Jiharr to his feet. He reeled a little, but not too much. His leather leggings were bathed in blood, but the wound itself bled no more.

"Is it true, what the lady says?" he asked Uduqu.

"Oh, it's the truest thing you'll ever hear—no two ways about it. If you knew of only half the things God has done for us since first we heard His name, you wouldn't have been too surprised to see another miracle."

"But it's not my miracle—not anything by me!" Now tears flowed from Gurun's eyes. "Don't say that anymore!

You must try to understand!" It shocked the men of Ryons' army to see her weeping. But Obst came forth and took her into his arms.

The Zeph were men of war. They knew Jiharr's wound should have killed him on the spot. For him to be alive and on his feet, and not bleeding anymore, took all the fight out of them. They sat down and ate and drank with Ryons' army.

They wished to crowd around Gurun and marvel at her, but she wouldn't let them. Obst and Uduqu made them leave her alone. She withdrew to the edge of the camp and wouldn't let anyone come near her but Ryons and Shingis, the chief of her Blays.

She sat on the grass and wept. Ryons had never seen her like this, and it frightened him.

"Why you so sad?" said Shingis, who had learned to speak a little Obannese. "You do a good thing."

"I didn't do anything!" she said. "I want to go home. I want my father and my mother. I even want my brothers!"

"Please don't cry, Gurun!" Ryons said.

Shingis reverted to his own language, because he couldn't find the words he wanted in any other. But Gurun, like Obst, had the gift of understanding all languages spoken by men and of being understood.

"Listen to King Ryons, my lady. He makes good sense! You've told us many times how God brought you to Obann from far across the sea. Well, think of what God did to Ryons—made him the king of a great nation. He didn't want to be a king; he's just a boy.

"But he must do his best—and so must you. He needs

you. My men and I need you—what would become of us without you? Please think! You have taught us to believe in God. The Lord is mighty, and it's foolish to resist Him. It was God who healed Jiharr, even as you've said. You should not be ashamed that He used your touch to do it."

She stopped crying. For a moment that seemed long to them, she simply looked at Ryons and Shingis. But then she suddenly kissed them both.

"Thank you!" she said. "I'll be all right now, once I get some sleep."

CHAPTER 22

Ysbott's Campfire Tales

Roshay Bault was the first to see the gold gleaming in the noonday sun, and when his men saw it, too, they came on faster. At last they gained the top of the Golden Pass and halted before the ruins of the golden hall.

Roshay was the richest man in Ninneburky, and he knew the value of gold. If he sold his house, his logging business, and everything he owned, he would get only an infinitesimal fraction of the wealth that lay before him here. It was just possible, he thought, that there was more wealth here than in the entire city of Obann.

"I never imagined there would be so much," he said. "I would need a thousand men to load it onto carts and bring it down the mountain."

"How do we even begin?" Sergeant Kadmel wondered. "My lord Baron, this is more than anyone expected!"

"It's enough to make a fortress of every town in Obann," Roshay said. "Well, we'll just have to get started as best we can. But first make camp."

While the men busied themselves with that, Roshay and his captains dismounted and explored the edges of the ruin.

"We'll have to work from the outside in," he said, "and very carefully, at that. This will be like trying to take apart a blowdown. Those heavy timbers are all tangled up and resting on each other. I don't want anyone trying to climb around on top of it."

"There'll be dead bodies under it," someone said.

"They won't do us any harm," the baron answered.

———————

Helki had to wait for Hlah to come home from Ninneburky. He finally arrived on a mule that the baroness had insisted he ride.

"I suppose it would have taken twice as long, if I'd walked," Hlah said. "But I think my seat would be the better for it."

He told Helki how Lord Orth had spoken to the Abnaks and how they'd taken him away with them.

"Maybe I ought to go after him," Helki said.

"He doesn't want to be rescued."

"How are the Abnaks doing in their war against the Thunder King?"

Hlah shrugged. "There's been no word since Lord Orth left. I don't think any more Abnaks will be coming over to this side of the mountains for a while. Now that they have the First Prester with them, this will be their supreme effort. They'll either win the war, or die."

"I hate those supreme efforts," Helki said, frowning. "It's always better to back off and try something else when things aren't going well."

"That's not Chief Foxblood's way," said Hlah. "It's not the Abnak way, either. You know that."

Helki sighed. "I do. I do," he said. You could kill an Abnak, he thought, but you could never force him to serve you.

Trout slipped on a loose stone and turned his ankle.

"It wouldn't have happened if you'd been riding the horse," Fnaa said. No one thought that was funny.

Trout grimaced, trying his best not to show pain. It must really hurt, thought Jack, for him to make a face like that. Martis examined the ankle.

"You'll have to ride, now," he said. "It's not broken, but it's going to be sore and swollen for some days. You'd be a fool to try to walk on it."

"At home I'd be expected to fight on it," Trout said.

"We're at least halfway up the pass by now," Ellayne said. "My father will be at the top with all his men. You can have a good rest when we get there, Trout."

"Cut me a strong stick to lean on, and I'll walk."

"You can have a stick," Martis said, "but you're still going to have to ride. We'll go slowly, so you don't fall off."

"If I fall off the horse and land on this ankle, it's going to snap like a dry twig!"

Wytt looked to Jack and chattered at him.

"He doesn't like us stopping here," Jack reported. "He says it's not safe: bad men have been this way."

"But they're the baron's men," Martis said, but Wytt growled at him.

"He doesn't mean the baron's men," Jack said. "These passed this way ahead of the baron. There's hardly any of their scent left, but Wytt doesn't like what he's picked up of it."

"They'll be sorry when my father catches up with them," said Ellayne.

"It wouldn't surprise me if there were outlaws in the

neighborhood," Martis said. "The gold will draw them like spoiled meat draws flies. I had hoped to catch up to your father before we ran into any of them."

"But we don't have anything that outlaws would bother to steal," Fnaa said. Trout gave him a stern look.

"We have two horses," he said, "and three children. There's many an outlaw who'd kill for that much. And a few Abnaks that I know of, too."

———

By nightfall Roshay had come around to the idea that it would be best to remain at the top of the Golden Pass with a strong force to guard the gold and send some of his captains back down the mountain for more men and more carts. "Scare up as many as you can," he said. "I'm amazed the Thunder King hasn't sent an army to retrieve his gold. But sooner or later he will."

While the baron conferred with his captains, and the militiamen enjoyed their rations and rested by their camp-fires, Ysbott found it easy to infiltrate the camp and take a seat among the townsmen. He soon found someone he knew—Donn Decker, who was surprised to see him.

He opened his mouth to speak, but Ysbott did not let him. He pulled Donn close and whispered in his ear, "Call me Tobb! That's my name from now on."

Donn said, "I didn't know you were with us. When did they pick you up?"

Ysbott shrugged. "A few days ago, just before we struck the road. I was sick from something I ate and had to lie up for a while. Otherwise I would have been here first."

"I never noticed you," Donn said.

"I wasn't feeling all that well. Besides, I thought it best to just be quiet and see what I could see and hear what I could hear. Nobody paid much attention to me. We're all just slaves, I guess—or little better."

"We'll be paid for our work, though," another man said.

"So they say. But will we be paid enough?" said Ysbott. "I've heard a few things about this place that I don't like. Do you know what's under all that gold?"

"More gold!" Donn said, grinning.

"Oh, I don't doubt that. But I was thinking of something else, not so nice as gold." He had their attention now. "Everybody knows that hall was flattened by an avalanche. They say the Thunder King himself was caught in there, along with a lot of his mardars. Do you know what a mardar is?"

"Some kind of Heathen chief," said Donn.

"They are more than that!" said Ysbott. "They're the Thunder King's magicians. They're witches, all of them. They have terrible powers, and the Heathen are scared of them—as well they should be. It's the mardars who put hexes on their water and curse their cattle and their women to make them barren. How else do you think King Thunder conquered all those nations? How else do you suppose he keeps them conquered? They know what the mardars can do to them if they don't obey."

A few more townsmen came to sit by Donn Decker's campfire. Ysbott continued.

"I thought I could come up here and take just a little bit of gold for myself, whatever I could carry—just enough to set me up," he said. "But not for all the gold that's up here would I dig up one of those dead witches!

"What's more, I think they know we're here. I think

they're getting restless in their grave. Listen! Be quiet for a minute, and just listen."

Ysbott knew what they would hear. Behind the homey, ordinary sounds of men talking and fires crackling, you could hear the great pile shift and creak and softer sounds of voices moaning, whispering, sighing.

"Oh, that's just the wind!" Donn Decker said.

"Do you think so?" Ysbott said. "I'm not so sure. I've traveled in these hills before. I've been over the mountains once or twice, too. I've learned to speak a little Zeph, and Griffish. Some of what I hear sounds like words in those languages. Of course, the mardars would speak in all kinds of Heathen languages that nobody here can understand. All I'm saying is, those dead witches don't rest quietly. And you know how devilish hard it is to kill a witch! The Abnaks say you have to toss a witch's body into a peat bog and weigh it down with heavy stones—and drive a stake of willow wood through it, too, for good measure—to keep it from walking. Otherwise they just don't stay put. Ask anyone who knows the Abnak customs. They'll tell you the same."

Donn tried to laugh at that, but no one else joined in. There were more men around the campfire than there were a few minutes ago. A young trooper noticed and came over to join them.

"What's all this talk?" he said.

"Nothing much," Ysbott answered. "We were just saying how the wind makes noises that sound like a lot of Heathen whispering together."

"Tobb's been telling us bedtime stories," Donn Decker added.

"Don't be scaring yourselves so you can't sleep tonight,"

the trooper said. He looked like he might be a little scared, himself, Ysbott thought. "There'll be a lot of work to do tomorrow." And he went back to his own fire, not wanting to sit with a lot of chickenhearted townsmen.

Ysbott fed his audience on more Heathen lore he'd made up out of his own imagination, mixing it with some of the more lurid superstitions prevalent in Lintum Forest. By and by the moon went down, and much of the camp went to sleep. At least they tried to sleep. Ysbott lay down and pretended.

That was when the howling started.

Everyone sat up. Only Ysbott knew it was his own men hiding in the forest, moaning and wailing like tormented spirits, shouting gibberish, which he quickly identified as various Heathen languages. No one seemed to doubt him.

Following his instructions, his men kept it up for a good half hour, then abruptly stopped. Roshay Bault stalked all around the camp, cursing, giving orders, trying to force his men to get some rest. The camp finally subsided, after he threatened a few sharp floggings for the worst offenders.

But in the morning the young trooper from the other campfire lay sprawled on the ground, dead.

CHAPTER 23

A Creature
Not Worth Noticing

ord came to Gallgoid that Baron Hennen's force—
without Hennen—was retreating back to Obann under the command of Hennen's senior captain, a man named
Joah.

"I know him," Preceptor Constan said, when Gallgoid,
in the guise of a servant, came to see him at his private office
at the seminary. "His son was one of my students. Joah is
an old soldier. He won the title of First Spear, serving under
Lord Gwyll. If we have him to manage the defense of the city,
we'll be well off. And Prester Jod will be here in another day
or two."

"The people are beginning to wonder why they have
no news of Lord Orth," Gallgoid said. Constan shrugged.
Gallgoid understood it only meant he had nothing to say.
"They'll be less troubled by that, once Jod is here," the spy
added. "But it may be necessary to invent a reassuring message from the First Prester."

No one else would have dared suggest such a thing to
Constan. The preceptor blinked. He had probably never in
his life invented a message and said it came from someone

else. But he spoke no word of disapproval.

"The king is away, our First Prester's been abducted, and our chief general has been imprisoned by a traitor," Gallgoid said. "None of it's the kind of news you want circulating all around the city."

Constan didn't answer.

———

No one at the Golden Pass had the skill to explain how the young trooper had died. Roshay had his most experienced men examine the body, but they found no wound on it.

That was because Ysbott, when he killed the man, hadn't left a wound. He did the deed in silence, then stole into the forest. Donn Decker noticed that Tobb was nowhere to be seen in camp that morning, but didn't mention it to any of the officers. If Tobb chose to make himself scarce, that was his business; Donn would have done the same, if only he'd thought of it. But it never entered his mind that the man he knew as Tobb was capable of murder.

"The witches' curse got that young fellow—no doubt of it," someone said. And soon many men were saying it.

"The camp's in an uproar, sir," Sergeant Kadmel told the baron.

"I can see that for myself. Superstitious rabble!" Kadmel was used to Roshay Bault's outbursts, and didn't flinch. Roshay took a deep breath and got himself under control. "Very well," he said, "let's work them until they're just too tired to be afraid of witches. Don't be afraid to knock some heads together."

For the time being, he sent no one down the mountain. Roshay put everyone to work wrestling sheets of gold loose from the pile and stacking them neatly. He stripped off his shirt and lent his own hands to the work, pulling, pushing, and carrying. His logging men would have told you that was his way: "No one works harder than the boss." It had been some time since he'd visited a logging camp, but he hadn't lost his knack for toil. Nor had he forgotten how to give orders.

"You, there—lever that timber to the right! No, no, leave that one alone; it's not safe to disturb it. Here, give me that! You'll only smash your shins if you handle it like that." By the early afternoon there wasn't a man who wasn't drenched with sweat, aching, and untroubled by any fear of witches.

Roshay paused to survey the work accomplished so far. Although they'd stacked enough gold for everyone in Ninneburky to live on comfortably for the next ten years, the whole ruin looked like they'd hardly touched it. "What must it have been like, before it was destroyed!" he wondered. Ellayne and Jack and Martis had seen it, moments before the avalanche came down. He must remember to ask them about it, now that he had an appreciation for the vastness of the place.

Ellayne and her companions were hiking up the road even as he thought of them. "Tomorrow we'll be there," Martis said. They'd have arrived much sooner if it hadn't been for Trout's bad ankle. Martis had to help him on and off the horse. On the ground, with the help of a stick, he hobbled.

"It looks terrible," Fnaa said, fascinated by the swollen mass of black and blue.

"Where's Wytt got to?" Ellayne asked.

They hadn't seen much of Wytt all day. The children knew from long experience that it was his way to scout ahead or off to one side or another, and they were glad he did. "No telling what trouble we might stumble into, if he didn't," Martis said. His right hand jumped to his weapons with every little noise. You might have thought that he was making too much of the calls of birds and squirrels, but he'd learned from Helki that birds and squirrels had much to tell a traveler. He hadn't yet learned how to interpret their calls.

But Wytt understood them and busied himself investigating the information. Birds and squirrels were saying there were men nearby—not the great crowd of men at the top of the pass, but just a few, not far away. Birds didn't often see men in those woods, and kept a close watch on them. So did the squirrels and some other creatures who objected to the intruders' presence.

Wytt had come close enough to Ysbott's camp to pick up Ysbott's scent—the scent of an old enemy. A squirrel perched on a tree right above the camp and noisily let all the other squirrels know precisely where it was. That made it easy for Wytt to find it.

Ysbott, who'd been up all night, was sleeping. Nine men sat around, idle. They had no fire: Ysbott feared the baron's men might see the smoke. Wytt crept up close enough to study them.

Hrapp the cobbler, and a few of the others, he recognized from Ninneburky. Their scent told Wytt they were tired and hungry, and more than a little uneasy. It seemed undesirable to him that they should rest in peace, so he let out a blood-curdling screech that jerked them all to their feet—even Ysbott.

"Carrion-eaters! Robbers of babies in the nest! I am Omah—I kill!" It sounded to the men like nothing but a lot of animal screeching and chattering—but not like any animal they'd ever heard before.

"What's that? What is it?" they cried, turning around and around in frantic circles, seeing nothing. Ysbott stood still and only sneered at them.

"Pipe down!" he said. "It's only a rabbit getting eaten by a wildcat, or some such thing. Grown men carrying on like a lot of giddy girls because of animals making a ruckus in the woods! You ought to be ashamed."

Wytt added a few unflattering remarks about their mothers' mating habits. The men looked sheepishly at Ysbott, still too rattled to be suitably embarrassed. Ysbott had lived in forests all his life and never heard anything quite like the sounds Wytt made. But it had to be an animal, he thought— just some mindless little creature not worth noticing.

Finally Gwawl said, "Shouldn't we put up some kind of barricade?"

"What for?" Ysbott said. "There's no kind of animal around here that can hurt us."

"But what about a bear, Tobb—" Hrapp started to say, but Ysbott wouldn't let him finish.

"There are no bears this high up in the hills. Get hold of yourselves! You couldn't be safer if you were in your own beds back in town. Even if there was a bear, it wouldn't bother a group of ten men."

By and by he got them to sit down again. He stretched himself out and tried to go back to sleep. Wytt decided to be quiet for the time being and to remain close by to watch. A human scout might have returned immediately, to tell his companions what he'd seen, but not Wytt.

His sharp little stick wanted another bite of Ysbott's sleeping face.

CHAPTER 24

A Battle in the Hills

Helki decided to go back to the Golden Pass to see the baron, and then rejoin the king.

"I don't reckon there'll be much I can do for Ryons, down in Heathen lands where I don't know my way around," he said to Hlah, "but he'll worry if I don't come back to him like I said I would. Besides, what can I do for the First Prester? The Abnaks won't give him up just because I ask them to. It's out of my hands."

"Sunfish is a man of God," said Hlah. "I was afraid for him, but now I believe he has better protection than either you or I can give him."

———

As for the First Prester, events were moving so rapidly that he had no time to wonder whether God was protecting him or not.

Two thousand Abnak warriors—an unprecedented number, Foxblood said—swarmed down the mountain to attack Zephites who had advanced high into the hills and put up a fortified camp. Their stockade of timbers, with five hundred battle-tested fighters to defend it, never had a chance.

Foxblood, not following his people's usual practice,

launched the attack by night, with torches, ladders, and clay firepots full of burning pitch. These his men slung over the walls, and wherever they fell and broke apart, they started a fire. Unprepared for a night attack, the Zeph had to fight when they expected to rest. So many Abnak warriors had never been known to obey a single chieftain, but now they did.

"It's because we have you with us," Foxblood explained to Orth, "and they want to show their bravery to you and to the Obann God. They're excited to think that God is with them."

He had Orth stand on a hastily erected platform over-looking the battle, so that the Abnaks could see him praying for them. Orth prayed, but even his mighty voice could not be heard above the tumult of two thousand men bellowing battle cries and calling on their ancestors to be witness to their courage.

Orth was glad of the night: he couldn't see much of the actual bloodletting. The first Abnaks over the wall tore open the gate, and hundreds of men with stone tomahawks burst into the camp. In what seemed a very long time to Orth, but which was really much less than an hour, it was over. Foxblood came limping back to the platform to tell Orth to come down.

"You're hurt," said Orth.

"Just a stray spear-thrust—missed the tendon, missed the vein. I'll be all right. But come down," Foxblood said. "The men want to thank you and to thank your God."

Orth followed the chief down to the ruin of the camp. The fires were already going out. The dead, mostly Zeph-ites, littered the ground. Some of the Abnaks were already engaged in impromptu scalp dances, flourishing their gory trophies. A large number of enemy prisoners, disarmed, stood under guard. Dread was written on their faces. Their mardar's head, cheeks painted black and red, stood on a spear thrust into the earth.

A great cheer went up for Orth. The Abnaks stopped dancing. They saluted him with their weapons and all spoke at once, as loudly as they could.

"They're praising you and your prayers and your God, who has given us this victory," Foxblood translated. "They wish to know if your God will be pleased if they sacrifice the prisoners to Him."

Orth cried out in dismay. The men stopped cheering and looked confused.

"Men and brethren! Please, I beg you, listen!" Orth cried. Foxblood repeated his words in Abnak.

"My brothers," Orth said, "God has accepted you and fought for you. He is not only my God, or the God of Obann. He is your God, too.

"He does not want sacrifices! He fights for you to give you peace. All He asks in return is that you love Him and keep His commandments and be good to one another. He has heard your praise of Him and your thanks, and He is greatly pleased. He will give you more victories, and more, until your land is free of enemies and the Thunder King is no more."

They listened attentively. Orth continued.

"These prisoners are helpless now," he said, "as you were helpless when the Thunder King invaded the homeland that God gave you. Our Lord is a defender of the helpless. He raises up the needy and casts down the cruel, the proud, the arrogant. So He will not be pleased—He will not, I say!—if you deal with your prisoners as the Thunder King would deal with you.

"If you wish to please God, do as He would do. Send these beaten men away, back to their own country: for God will destroy the Thunder King, and they must not serve him anymore. Let them leave here with their lives. That's the kind of offering that pleases God."

A chief shook his head in amazement.

"No sacrifices?" he called out. "Why, any other god would jump for joy to receive these Zephites as a sacrifice!"

But Orth said, "There is no other God. There is only one true God, the God who fought for you this night. And He would not be pleased if you sacrificed these prisoners. I tell you the truth, whether it's what you like to hear or not."

"You're a brave man, Et-taa-naa-qiqu!" Foxblood muttered, so that only Orth could hear him. But aloud, to his warriors: "You've heard the holy man! Be grateful to God, and do as he says. Why should God fight for us again, if now we refuse to do what pleases Him?"

After a long moment of silence, the Abnaks began to shout again. Foxblood turned and grinned at Orth.

"It shall be as you say, First Prester!" he said. "My people are eager to please God, even if what He wants seems strange to them."

Orth's knees buckled from sheer relief. And so the prisoners were spared.

———

It took all of Ysbott's skill to sneak into the baron's camp that evening. Roshay Bault had put more guards on duty. "Keep your eyes and ears open!" he said. "Anyone caught falling asleep on sentry duty will earn a flogging." And to the whole camp: "I heard the voices in the night, same as all the rest of you. Well, wherever there are voices, there are men—not ghosts! But I'm not such a fool as to order any of you to blunder around the woods, trying to catch them. Whoever they are, if they were strong enough to attack us, they would've done it by now. That they haven't shown themselves means only one thing—they're too weak to risk a fight."

Ysbott heard that speech. He had to admit it was a shrewd one. He would have to be careful not to underestimate the baron.

He soon found Donn Decker and some other malcontents and joined them by their campfire.

"It must be the Thunder King's scouts out there," Donn said. "It stands to reason that he wouldn't leave all this gold unguarded, even if it looks that way. If you ask me, the whole setup is probably a trap."

"That's a thought, my friend!" said Ysbott. "I wouldn't be surprised if they've already made short work of our boy king and his puny army and were on their way up here in numbers that will swamp us.

"But the one danger doesn't rule out the other, does it? I still believe there's deadly magic at work here. Can't you feel it? And the more gold we take off the pile, the more wreckage we pull out of the way, the easier it'll be for the dead to walk."

As soon as it was full dark, Ysbott's men in the woods started shrieking and gabbling for all they were worth. He'd decided it would be best if they didn't perform at the same hour every night, so tonight they were early.

Roshay Bault was furious. He stalked about the camp, growling at his troopers.

"Hold on to your nerves! No one can hurt you just by making noises in the night!" But Ysbott could see they were hard put to keep their courage. Roshay saw it, too, but he couldn't order men not to be afraid.

Suddenly the noise stopped, just as Ysbott had commanded earlier. It left a lot of jangled nerves in its wake.

"I wonder why they stopped," Donn said.

"Just be ready to flee for your life when the first shriveled claw starts groping its way out of that pile!" Ysbott whispered. He didn't want the guards to overhear him. "I don't know about you, but when that happens, gold or no gold, I'll be running down the mountain as fast as my legs can carry me."

"Me, too!" someone said.

There were no more disturbances. Ysbott would have liked to murder another sentry, but there were too many guards on duty now, and they were too alert. It was all he could do to sneak out of the camp an hour short of daybreak.

CHAPTER 25

A Quiet Killing

Led by Jiharr, who walked without assistance, albeit slowly and gingerly, the Zeph departed for their own country to spread the good news of the Thunder King's impending fall. But first they saluted the king of Obann and his chieftains, and Jiharr knelt before Gurun and kissed her hand.

"I kiss the hand of my healer."

"It was God who healed you," Gurun answered, blushing.

"Then God is mightier than the sword that struck me down," Jiharr said.

"See that you remember it," said Obst.

The army resumed its eastward trek. They had no maps; there were no roads. East beyond Griff-land, said Tiliqua, lay a country much disputed between the Griffs and the Zephites, with settlers from the land of the Dahai also trying to establish a foothold in it. Beyond that, at some ill-defined distance, lay the westernmost of the Great Lakes. In ancient times, all these lands were part of Obann's Empire, but no Obannese army had come this way for a thousand years. The Griffs seldom went as far east as the lakes, so there was little that Tiliqua could tell them about what lay ahead.

Looth's Attakotts scouted far and wide, many miles ahead of the army, and Shaffur kept his riders busy on the flanks, both north and south.

"Some of the lands conquered by the Thunder King have been depopulated," the Wallekki chieftain said. "The Quadi-Quai used to live around these parts, but no more. He made them as if they never were."

"It seems strange that he has sent out no great army against us," said Hawk, the Hosa. "Can it be that he's run out of armies?"

"He will never run out of armies," Chagadai said. "He has all the vast lands of the East to draw from. Kara Karram, on the other side of the Great Lakes, is only the center of his power. There is more behind it in the East than there is before it in the West."

"A long way to walk!" Uduqu sighed.

———————

Not long at all was the rest of the way to the top of the Golden Pass, and Ellayne and her companions got there just after noon. Her father's face began to redden as soon as he clapped eyes on her.

"I told you to stay home," he began to say.

"Please, Father—we bring important news!" Ellayne said. "Martis and Jack and I came because we already knew the way."

"What news is it?"

"My lord," said Martis, "we came as quickly as we could, lest some rumor reach you first and you be misinformed." He related the news of the First Prester's abduction by the Abnaks. "Lord Orth greatly feared that you would try to rescue him and so put many lives in danger. It's his desire that no such attempt be made. We have this from Hlah, who had it from Lord Orth himself. The baroness was afraid you might hear some other version of the matter and be led to make a bad decision."

"That's putting it diplomatically!" Roshay said. "I remember Hlah—a sound young man. If he says Lord Orth has asked not to be rescued, we can believe his word." He sighed and shook his head. "And anyhow, what could I do with just a few hundred militia? But I suppose Vannett was right. I might have been tempted to try."

A little later, when the children and Trout were settled, Roshay took Martis aside to show him the body of the young trooper who had died.

"We've had some trouble, these past two nights," the baron said, and explained the situation. The body lay under a horse blanket. Roshay exposed it.

"I want you to examine him, Martis. Maybe you can tell me how he died." The baron knew that Martis had long served Lord Reesh as an assassin. Martis had long ago confessed it to him. "We found no wound on him—but a young, healthy man doesn't just fall down dead without a cause."

Martis nodded and knelt beside the body. Somewhere up above, an invisible insect began to drone. Somehow, he thought, that particular noise enhanced a kind of stillness. The noises of the camp seemed to come from far away.

Gently he removed the dead man's shirt, delicately pried open the eyelids, and saw what he already expected to see.

"This man was killed by someone who has much experience in killing," Martis said. "He was attacked from behind and a powerful hold put on his neck. But not across the windpipe—which would have left marks for you to see."

Martis pantomimed the action. The baron nodded, understanding. "It would have taken two minutes to make the kill, but only seconds to render the victim unconscious. It would have been a quiet killing, leaving no marks but for these bloodshot eyes. And if you look closely, here, you can just make out a little bruising."

"So someone came into our camp the other night and murdered him," Roshay said.

"Unless it was someone who has been in the camp all along," Martis said.

"Either way, it's murder. Please don't speak of this to anyone else."

A change of expression passed over Martis' face, like a small, dark cloud drifting briefly across the sun. "He is ashamed of the things he used to do," Roshay thought. He reached for Martis' shoulder and squeezed it. "Thank you for bringing my children safely up the mountain," he said.

As the men toiled under the hot sun, Jack, Ellayne, and Fnaa wandered here and there, watching them. Jack and Ellayne had seen the golden hall in all its glory, and seen the avalanche crash down on it like the fist of God. Fnaa listened to their tale with awe.

"Is the Thunder King buried under all that?" he asked. "But he must be!"

"No one got out except for a great big cat that ran right past us," Jack said, "and that man, Gallgoid. But he got out a few days before the avalanche."

"Chillith's in there, too," said Ellayne. She remembered him, the Griff mardar who became God's servant, with a pang of loss. "He was a good man, and here he lies with all those evil men."

"Obst says it doesn't matter," Jack said. "Chillith is in heaven, with God."

"What's heaven?" asked Fnaa.

"Don't you know?" Ellayne said. "It's where your soul goes after you die. Didn't your mother teach you that?"

"We never went to the chamber house. My mother didn't know the Obann God, and she said the Fazzan gods were too far away to do us any good."

"Obst says it's been a long time since anyone learned anything important in a chamber house. You have to read the Scriptures," Ellayne said. "Most days, my mother reads them with us."

"I've read a little bit of them," Fnaa said. "Ryons has to read them every day, and sometimes I read with him. But I don't remember reading anything about heaven."

"Well, it's in there," Jack said. "God calls people's souls His jewels. We read that part just a few days before you came to our house. When we get back home, we'll read it to you, and then you'll see."

Before the day was over, they knew about the ghosts of witches that guarded the Thunder King's gold and made terrible noises in the night and had even killed a man. Everyone knew better than to speak of these things in front of the baron's daughter, but they couldn't help muttering about them while they worked. Although they stopped whenever they saw the children draw near, the children still managed to overhear much of it.

"This place is not as safe as it looks," Jack said.

"Who says it looks safe?" Ellayne answered.

Prester Jod and Captain Joah arrived at the city the same day. Jod met with Constan at the seminary, but Joah and Gallgoid had a clandestine conversation in a boarded-up house that Gallgoid had secretly bought for his own use. As far as any of the neighbors knew, it was still deserted.

"I hurried to get here," Joah said. Grey-bearded, leathery-skinned, he wasted no time getting down to business. "The troops will be here in two days. No need for a forced march—Chutt made no effort to pursue us.

"Either he's a bigger fool than anybody thought he was, or he's out-guessed us all. He wasn't coming to Obann. No—as soon as he had five thousand men together, he took off into the east. His force is mounted, and they're making good time, I hear. But I'm chopped potatoes if I can fathom what he's up to."

"He's heading east, you say?"

"On a straight line that would take him to King Oziah's Wood." Joah frowned. "I don't understand it. He can feed his army by pillaging towns and farms—they're used to that!—but there's nothing in that country worth conquering. If he wants to overthrow the king, he needs to be south of the great river, not north of it."

Lord Reesh used to collect maps. Gallgoid used to draw maps, based on the reports of the Temple's intelligence service. In his mind's eye, Gallgoid plotted a course from Market City in North Obann to Oziah's Wood, just across the river from Ninneburky. It was farming and herding country, thinly populated. East of the capital, Obann's cities hugged the Imperial River.

"There's nothing up there," Gallgoid said softly, "and

nothing to draw him to Oziah's Wood. What can he be thinking?"

"Well, he hasn't force enough to take this city, even against an undermanned defense," Joah said. "I thought there might be traitors here who'd open the gates to him some night. That was General Hennen's biggest fear. But it looks like Lord Chutt has something else in mind."

———————

Wytt did not come into the big camp with Ellayne and Jack.

He remembered the Golden Pass from the last time they'd been there, with Chillith. Now it was a place that stank of death. Only humans would be dull enough not to notice. No bird would fly directly over the ruin, if it could be avoided. No wood mouse nested there. Nothing would live in that vast pile but worms and insects.

Wytt knew nothing of gold, so it was a mystery to him why all those human beings were there, toiling away like ants. But then they seldom behaved in a way that made any sense at all, and Wytt didn't try to understand them.

He was comfortable alone in the woods. And there he waited.

CHAPTER 26

When the Scriptures Came Alive

Foxblood's next prey was an encampment of Fazzan warriors, three hundred of them. They wouldn't last long against two thousand Abnaks.

Foxblood limped from his wound, but he wouldn't let that slow him down. "I have to strike while my warriors' blood is up," he explained to Orth. "They won't be in this mood forever. I'm surprised they've stayed together this long. My people are like a fire that burns hot, but won't burn for long."

As swiftly as they moved down the hills, the Fazzan still managed to learn that they were coming. But when Foxblood and his first rank of warriors emerged from the trees and looked down on the camp, they saw something they didn't expect.

"That's a dead man hanging from the top of the stockade," said a subchief with keen eyesight. "It's their mardar, by the look of him. His face is painted red and blue."

Two men in wolf's-head caps came out the gate and raised white shields over their heads. Foxblood sent for Orth to join him from the back ranks where he'd been placed for protection.

"They want to parley," the chief said, "and it seems they've slain their mardar. Let's go down and find out what's what."

He chose half a dozen warriors as a guard for Orth, in case of treachery, and led them down to the fort, holding his stone axe high in one hand and displaying the other palm-outward. It meant he came in peace, for the time being.

They stopped within shouting distance of the gate.

"If you wish to parley with us, speak!" Foxblood called. "What is the meaning of that dead man on your wall and those white shields in your hands?" He spoke in Tribe-talk, and they answered him in kind.

"Chief of Abnaks, we wish only to leave here with our weapons and our lives—to leave your country and never come back. We know how you overcame the Zeph, who had a much stronger camp than ours, and let them go. A few of them stopped here yesterday and told us all about it. Our mardar commanded us to kill them as traitors to the Thunder King, but it seemed best to us to kill him instead."

The other Fazzan spoke. "We've heard the God of Obann is with you, and His chief of holy men. This was the God who swallowed up King Thunder's host that marched to Obann to take the city. Not a man of them returned! We don't want the same thing to happen to us."

Orth asked Foxblood, "May I speak to them?" The chieftain nodded.

"Fazzan," Foxblood said, "we will let you go and do you no harm." The warriors of the guard shot their chief sharp glances: this was not the Abnak way. But he glared back at them, and none of them dared speak. "Come out of your camp, and we will come down from the hill and make peace with you. I, Foxblood, give my word."

As the Fazzan filed out of the fort and the Abnaks assembled in a sprawling mob, Orth plucked at Foxblood's elbow. "I'll need a speaker's platform," he said, "so they can see me and hear me." Foxblood ordered a few men to see to it.

"Chief," asked a warrior, "why do you let these people go without a fight? Their scalps are ours for the taking!" Among the Abnaks, any grown man could question any chief, and they obeyed a chief's commands only when they chose to. Foxblood led by consent.

"I let them go because we still have multitudes of enemy warriors in our country," he said, "and we'd be fools to think we could kill them all. But every man we spare will tempt others to do as these Fazzan have done. Besides, it pleases God. Or have you forgotten Him already?"

They were ashamed to answer that.

Someone found a good-sized stump for Orth to stand on, and they rolled it into position. Foxblood beckoned the Fazzan to come closer. Orth remembered seeing wolf's-head caps like theirs among King Ryons' men in Lintum Forest. With Foxblood translating, Orth spoke to them.

"I will not keep you long, men of Fazzan. But know this: the sins of the Thunder King have come up before the living God, and God has pronounced judgment on him. He will not escape the judgment, and his works will not survive his fall.

"God, the God of all nations, will give you back your homeland and your liberty. Remember that! It is God who has preserved your lives today. This is God who created the heavens and the earth, and all that live. You have not known

Him. But He knows you, and someday you will learn to know Him well. Go in peace, and be thankful for God's gifts."

The Fazzan were too amazed to venture any questions, but Foxblood asked, "How will they come to know God?"

"His word will come to all the nations of the East," said Orth. As he said it, he understood that that was why he himself had come into the East.

So the Fazzan shouldered their weapons and marched away, eager to return to their homeland in the valley of the Green Snake River. And the Abnaks tore down their fort.

———————

In a land emptied of inhabitants by the wars that swept across it, King Ryons' army raised another cairn. No natives were on hand to see it.

A few of Looth's scouts returned, after having come within sight of the first of the Great Lakes. Looth reported in person to the other chieftains.

"We'll have fighting when we get there—maybe sooner," he said. "There are some Zephites, with bulls' horns on their heads, and a lot of very big men who carry clubs and swords. They are all gathered around a big stone house beside the water. So much water! You can barely see the farther shore. Men are crossing it on long boats."

"Those big men will be Zamzu—King Thunder's favorites," Shaffur said. He made an ugly face. "Eaters of men! They won't be satisfied with killing us."

"It was a giant of the Zamzu who lost this sword after Helki felled him with his rod," said Uduqu, tapping the weapon with his palm. Not a few men in the army had seen that fight and remembered Shogg the giant. "Well, I don't think they're all as big as he was."

"My people are afraid of them," said Tiliqua, the Griff.

"Not mine!" spoke up Xhama. "We have fought them before, in Lintum Forest, when we became King Ryons' men. They are cruel and ruthless, like their master. But not one of them came back alive from that adventure."

It was Helki who led the destruction of the Zamzu invading Lintum Forest. At the moment, everyone felt his absence keenly, but no one said so.

"We are almost there, then," Gurun said, "for the castle of the Thunder King lies on the far shore of the farthest lake." And Ryons shuddered, because one of the Thunder King's chiefs once told him that King Thunder wished to capture him alive, put out his eyes, and keep him in a dungeon for the rest of his life. They were marching straight for that dungeon now.

He was ashamed to be afraid. How many times had he been told that God was with him? But it wasn't always easy to believe it.

Ryons slept a deep sleep that night, and so did all his men, except the sentries. They had come a long way and they were tired, and the night over that empty land was very still. Cavall slept next to him, with one of Ryons' hands nestled in his fur.

A voice speaking in a whisper woke the king.

"Ryons, King Ryons—awake."

When he opened his eyes he saw a man sitting beside him, an old man with a long white beard, wearing a farmer's work-stained clothes. Ryons' heart leaped because he'd seen the man before. Cavall picked up his head and whined softly, but the man patted him once, and he lowered his head and was quiet. He wagged his tail because he, too, had met the man before.

"I told you we would meet again, King Ryons. Indeed, I have been with you all the way from Lintum Forest."

"You're the servant of the Lord," Ryons answered, still lying on his back. "But who are you, sir? You've never told me your name."

"I'm only one of the Lord's messengers. You would have a very hard time trying to pronounce my name!" The old man smiled. "It is my charge to speak to you and give you courage: for the Lord knows you're afraid.

"Fear not! You are as a man traversing a fragile bridge, one step at a time. But wherever your foot touches the bridge, the Lord strengthens it to bear your weight. All the way to Kara Karram you'll go, because the Lord is with you. His eyes shall delight in you, and His right hand shall uphold you."

Ryons felt like springing to his feet and dancing a jig, but he could only lie still.

"Do you see those stars, O King? Behold!"

As hard as it was not to keep looking at the bearded face that had such love and comfort in it, Ryons shifted his gaze to the stars. They shone in such a multitude that the very number of them impressed his heart with fear—not a fear of something bad, but a fear of such grandeur and goodness that it defied his mind to take it in.

Then one of the stars fell. For the briefest of all moments it streaked across the sky, as a slash of flame against the dark.

"That was the star of the Thunder King," said the man of God, "and it has fallen. As the Lord has upheld you, so shall the Lord cast him down, never to be seen again."

"But what must I do?" Ryons wanted to cry out, but could only manage a whisper.

The old man smiled at him and answered, "Get some sleep!" And Ryons closed his eyes and slept till morning.

The first thing he saw was Gurun's face framed by a blue sky. She knelt over him.

"I saw him!" she whispered. "He turned and looked at me and smiled, and then he was gone. But what did he say to you?"

"That we're going to go to Kara Karram," Ryons answered, "all the way to the castle. And when we get there, it'll be the end of the Thunder King. His star fell last night."

"I saw it," Gurun said. "Ryons, it has been a long time since anyone has seen such things as we have seen! The Lord has sent His messenger to speak to you—and I have seen him. It's like the Scriptures are not just stories in a book any-more, but are coming to life all around us. And we are in the stories!"

That thought frightened Ryons, although he could not have said why. He didn't have to say as much to Gurun; she read it in his face.

"Yes," she said, "I'm frightened, too."

CHAPTER 27

A Predator Strikes

Lord Chutt drove his army hard, eating up the miles beneath their horse's hooves. No one who knew him would have thought him capable of it—unless they also knew that rumor of the Thunder King's gold had reached his ears.

As a member of the High Council of the Oligarchy, Chutt had been in charge of revenues. "He's a natural for it," the governor-general, Lord Ruffin, used to say. "He can squeeze taxes from a stone." That some of Obann's revenues stuck to Chutt's fingers was an open secret in the city. Had it become any more open, Ruffin would have called for his removal from the council. But the Thunder King's invasion put a stop to that line of thinking.

Chutt fled the city just before it was encircled by the Heathen and was the only one of the High Council not to die in its defense. As he had established himself in the north, he'd lost weight: his colleagues might not have recognized him, if they could see him now. He had thinned down to a short, sturdy figure of a man, with sharp, sly features and a brown beard shot with grey. His stamina and his horsemanship had improved to the point where he could ride all day, and he'd grown accustomed to rough fare. And the thing that drove him now was the thought of all that gold at the top of the Golden Pass, with only Roshay Bault and a few hundred militiamen to guard it.

He had some thousands of Wallekki and other riders and had promised their captains shares of the gold. "Stick with me," he said, "and you'll all be big men in a new Obann." And they believed him. To the thousand Obannese who followed him, he said, "It'll be like the old days, only better. Those of you who don't wind up as oligarchs or generals will at least be rich—richer than you ever dreamed!" They believed him, too.

Hennen remained in Market City, chained to a post in a cellar. Why Chutt hadn't had him killed, he couldn't imagine. But his officers had not forgotten him, and neither had Gallgoid.

"Now that Chutt has galloped off into the east, we might send a force to Market City to rescue Baron Hennen," the spy said to Captain Joah. "There'll be no one there to stop you."

"I've been thinking the same thing," Joah said. "Chutt's left no one minding the store in Market City, my scouts tell me. It doesn't look like he plans on coming back. What do you suppose he's up to?"

By now Gallgoid thought he knew: it could only be the gold. Chutt had worked hard to set up his little fiefdom in the north. He would only leave it for something that lured him irresistibly. People in Obann City were whispering about the gold of the Golden Pass. How they'd ever gotten wind of it, even Gallgoid couldn't say. But to Joah he only said, "I don't know what Chutt's plans are." If the troops caught gold fever, there might not be any left to defend the city.

Obann was quiet now. Jod gave public readings from the Scriptures, old and new, and no one seemed to be worried by the First Prester's absence. Constan carried on the work of translating, copying, and distributing the sacred books. Most of the farms around Obann were functioning again; most of the refugees had returned to their villages to rebuild; and most of the stragglers from King Thunder's host had either taken service with King Ryons, starved, or been hunted down by the militia. The river was alive with fish, prices had come down, and there were no shortages worth complaining about. Life in Obann these days was calm and peaceful.

"That's the time to keep the sharpest watch for trouble," Gallgoid thought.

━━━━━━━━━━

Ysbott couldn't get back into the baron's camp with the guard doubled. So that night he led his band in wailing and babbling—but not for long, in case armed men came out to investigate.

The noise unnerved the camp, but Jack laughed at it.

"Anyone can tell it's only someone trying to scare us," he said. Ellayne and Fnaa joined him in making fun of it.

"I used to make noises like that when I wanted people to think I was loopy," Fnaa said. "But I was better at it. Listen!" And he cut loose with an ululation that would have terrified the men, if they hadn't seen a boy producing it.

"I can do better!" Ellayne said, and let out a piercing shriek that would have caused an avalanche, were the mountains under their winter coat of snow.

Roshay Bault started toward them with fire in his eyes. But when he heard some of his frightened men begin to laugh, he changed his mind.

"There's your ghosts, you pack of softies!" he roared.

"A couple of kids playing a game! Now you can be properly ashamed of yourselves."

Jack plucked a blade of grass, stretched it between his thumbs, and blew. It made a sound like a bird being pulled apart by its wings. Ellayne, having never mastered that trick, ignored it. But the men who saw him do it had a good laugh. And a mile away, in the dark beneath the trees, Hrapp the cobbler looked wide-eyed at Ysbott and stammered, "What in the world was that! It's horrible!" All of Ysbott's men froze at the sound. "It's only a cuss't bird," was the only answer he could give them.

"Oh, that's loud!" someone said. "I'll bet they could hear it all the way back home!"

"I'd rather not hear it again," Roshay said. "My father gave me a good thumping once, for doing that while he was trying to balance his books." He raised his voice. "But I hope you all can see now that what you were so afraid of was nothing!"

"We've got a dead man to show for it, though, don't we?" someone muttered.

"A dead man who was murdered in the night by human hands," Roshay answered. "It won't happen again."

A mile off, Ysbott struggled with his men's failing courage and realized he would have to change his plans again.

In the morning Roshay announced his decision to send half his troops back down the mountain to bring up carts. But first he consulted privately with Martis.

"There is a killer waiting for a chance to kill again," Roshay said. "He won't get that chance, but I'd dearly love to see him caught. He may have interesting things to tell us before he's hanged. I was hoping you would hunt him down for me."

"I'm not much of a tracker in this kind of terrain," Martis said.

"Well, what about that Abnak—Trout?"

"He could do it easily, if his ankle were better."

"Maybe he can do it in spite of his ankle," said the baron. "Let's ask him."

Trout said his ankle wasn't so bad, now that he'd had some rest. "I can hobble around and look for signs," he said, "but I won't be able to catch anyone who runs away. I wouldn't be at my best if it came to fighting, either."

"Maybe you and Martis together, with whatever help you need from my men, could catch these fellows," Roshay said.

"It's worth trying," Trout said.

"I'm going to send the children back to Ninneburky," said the baron. "They'll have a safe trip with Sergeant Kadmel to watch over them."

"I've sworn an oath to protect them," Martis said.

"But I need you here, Martis—for a little while, at least. They're my children, after all, and they ought to be all right with two hundred armed men around them."

With some misgivings, Martis agreed. He didn't like to be separated from the children, but he trusted the baron's judgment.

———

Wytt hadn't yet ventured into the baron's camp, not even to cuddle with Ellayne as she slept. Hundreds of big, clumsy, noisy human beings: he'd rather have no part of them.

He spent hours watching Ysbott and his men. They were hungry and uncomfortable. But up in the trees, unperceived by their dull senses, an even hungrier animal was watching them—a hunter hoping for a chance to make a meal.

Wytt saw it. A human might have thought it was a giant-sized tree marten, almost as big as a grown man, but Wytt knew better. It was no marten, nor any other kind of beast he knew. It had great, sharp claws on its thumbs—whatever it seized with those claws would never get away. Wytt caught a glimpse of huge front teeth that would punch through the thickest skull, with bulging jaw muscles to back them up. The creature was black all over, black as night, except for a pair of sharp green eyes. Wytt guessed it must ordinarily be a night-time predator, drawn out into the daylight by hunger. Wytt heard its belly rumbling: it must not be satisfied, feeding on birds and rodents. It needed bigger game to fill its belly—and the only large game available was Ysbott and his men. The animal had been stalking them all day, and Wytt thought the beast might be hungry enough to act rashly.

The men slept during the day as best they could, too tired and worn-out to post sentries. One of them, a little space apart from the others, had fallen asleep sitting up against a tree, with a piece of dried beef in his hand.

Wytt crept up close, tugged at the meat. He could have easily whisked it out of the man's grasp and run away, but instead he kept on tugging at it, sharply, until he woke the man. Only then did Wytt snatch the meat from his hand. He stared into the man's astonished eyes and made a face, showing his teeth.

"Slowpoke! Son of a slug!" He chattered softly, so as not to wake the others. As a final provocation, he sank his teeth into the unappealing man-food and tore off a piece. "I am mighty!" he scolded. "I take your meat!"

With a curse, the man grabbed for him—and missed. Wytt danced backward, brandishing the stiff piece of meat, taunting him. The man lunged and missed again. He got on his knees and scrambled to his feet.

"You give that back, you thieving little skrayling!" The poor fellow was so upset by the loss of his ration that he forgot to be afraid of Wytt. The others were waking up, but now it didn't matter. Wytt made some rude noises and the man came after him, stumbling through the underbrush.

Wytt fled, just out of reach, straight for the tree where the great predator waited. Tempted past the bounds of caution, angered by the noise, the beast sprang from the tree onto the man's back. The prey screamed as the powerful claws sank into his flesh—a scream that was suddenly cut off as the beast's fangs drove into the back of his neck, a bite that killed him instantly.

All the others saw what happened. Too shocked and terrified even to try to rescue their comrade, they fled into the woods, roaring in their terror. Even Ysbott ran. He'd never in his life seen anything like this, and it shattered his nerve.

Wytt ran a little ways up a tree and, from the safety of a branch too frail to bear the predator's weight, looked down and watched.

The hunter was already feeding.

Two of the panicked fools ran blindly into Roshay's camp, just as the men who were to go back for the carts were saddling their horses. Guards tackled the fugitives and brought them to the baron.

"And who the devil are you?" he demanded. It took some hard shaking and several slaps to get any sense out of them.

"Mercy, lord baron—mercy!" one begged. "We're poor men from town; we came up for the gold. But there's a monster in the woods; it's hunting us!"

"It killed Vonnic," said the other—"jumped on him from out of a tree and killed him right in front of us. You should have seen the blood!"

"It was a giant cat or something," said the first. "Not a natural animal, not natural at all. I don't know what it was: no one ever heard of such a thing. It just jumped out of nowhere."

"These must be the ones who've been making spooky noises in the night," Kadmel said. "Maybe they killed poor young Willy, too. Give 'em a thrashing and string 'em up."

"No! No, my lord—it wasn't us! We never hurt a soul; we swear! It was Tobb; yes, it was Tobb who did that. And he made us do the noises. All we wanted was some of the gold."

"Martis, see if you can get truth out of them," Roshay said.

"But we are telling you the truth, my lord! As God's my witness! It was Tobb; he's the one. He made us do it!"

"He would've cut our throats if we hadn't," added the other.

There wasn't much story to come out. The two men

didn't know who their leader, Tobb, was—just a hunter who'd taken charge of them, led them up the mountain, and bullied them into obedience.

"I think they're telling the truth. They're too scared to lie," Martis said. He had expertise in such matters, and the baron knew it. "It seems there were only ten men in their band, and now it's down to seven."

"I wish we could get our hands on Tobb, whoever he is," said Roshay. Meanwhile, he ordered the two captives placed under guard. He didn't want to hang anyone in front of his daughter.

But they weren't going to get their hands on Ysbott. He was already two miles deeper into the woods. He ran down Hrapp the cobbler and smacked some sense into him, and the two of them pulled Gwawl out of a bog where he'd gotten mired up to his hips. He would have died there, if they hadn't found him. The rest of the band had bolted in several different directions and there was no hope of catching up to them.

"Let them blunder around until they starve," Ysbott said. "It'll serve them right for losing their heads."

"I'm sorry, Tobb—I couldn't help it!" Hrapp said. "We don't belong out here. What was that horrible thing that jumped on Vonnic? You said these woods were safe!"

"They are—for ten grown men who stay together."

"But now there are only three of us," Gwawl said. "What was that thing that got Vonnic? A lion?"

"That mud you've bathed in stinks," said Ysbott. "A lion! There are no lions in Obann. But we'd better find some place to settle down and get a fire going, if we can."

"We're lost," Gwawl said. Ysbott sneered at him.

"I'm not lost, you half-wit!" he said. "Do as I say, and I

won't let you get lost, either. But if you give me any trouble, I'll just go away and leave you here."

They followed him closely as he went off looking for a camping spot, almost treading on his heels.

CHAPTER 28

The Return of the Lions

Ellayne didn't want to be sent back to Ninneburky.

"Why can't we stay here with you?" she asked her father. Jack would have liked to stay, too, but he doubted the baron would respond well to wheedling.

"I would be easier in my mind if the children stayed with us, my lord," said Martis.

To Ellayne's surprise, her father reconsidered. "Maybe it's better for you to stay where I can keep an eye on you," he said. "But you're not to leave this camp! That goes for all three of you," he added, including Fnaa. "We have a lot of work to do up here that doesn't include baby-sitting. If you can't obey me in this, Ellayne, it's off to finishing school for you."

The business of the camp resumed. Two hundred men rode off to fetch carts, and Roshay Bault went back to supervising the work of those who remained. Martis continued to question the prisoners, who now seemed eager to cooperate.

"It was nice of your father to care about me, even though he doesn't know me," Fnaa said.

"My father is a great man," said Ellayne. "He feels responsible for you because you're our friend—and because you're just a kid."

"But we'd better do as he says, this time—all of us," Jack

said. Having been kidnapped once before and carried off to Silvertown and from there all the way to Obann City, he had no desire to repeat the experience.

———————

Helki made his way slowly back to the Golden Pass. The baron would be there by now, he thought: no need to hurry. He stopped to collect what news he could whenever he met a trapper or a hunter. But he was higher up than anyone had cared to plant a settlement, so those encounters were few and far between.

Even so, by now everyone in the hills seemed to know the First Prester was campaigning with the Abnaks. "And they're doing pretty well for themselves, or so I hear," a trapper said. "Not that anyone hears much—but it doesn't look like the Thunder King will be able to come back across the mountains anytime soon."

"That's good news," said Helki. If the Abnaks could drive the Thunder King out of their lands, then other nations might be emboldened to rise against him.

Helki didn't like to hurry through this country. It was new to him, and he had much to learn. Nevertheless, he thought, Ryons and Obst and all the rest of them were down there, somewhere in the East, "and I reckon I ought to be with them. No telling what might happen to them."

As he made his way toward the pass, he saw signs that the summer, up here in the high country, was wearing thin: black ink-berries that had been red or green not long ago and some of the leaves already turning yellow on the trees. The days were warm, and even hot; the air was full of insects; birds still fed their chicks; but some of the nights were get-

ting cool. He kept a careful eye on certain kinds of cater-
pillars whose behavior and color changes might presage an
early winter. So far, they showed no signs of it.

All of that aside, he thought, the Abnaks had better
hurry up and win their war. Depending on the situation, the
arrival of winter would either finish off the Thunder King's
dominion in their country, or else give his forces a breathing
space that they might use to good advantage.

As for King Ryons and his little army—"Well," said
Helki to himself, "that's in God's hands, and no one else's."

———————

As Helki prayed for them, Ryons and his men halted in
their march because they saw strange beasts on the grassy
plain before them—a dozen of them holding their ground
against two thousand men and horses.

"We'll soon have them out of the way—and some good
sport, too," said Chagadai, drawing an arrow from his quiver.
But Obst cried, "Hold! Stand still."

"What are they?" Ryons wondered, standing up in his
stirrups for a better view. The tawny beasts stood twitching
their tails, glaring back at him. "They're beautiful!" the boy
king thought. "Please don't shoot them," he said to Chagadai.

"As our father pleases." The Ghol put away his arrow.

"Send for Tiliqua," Obst said.

Tiliqua and his Griffs came to the front of the army, the
Hosa making way for them.

"Do you know what those are?" Obst said.

Tiliqua looked at them for some moments, then broke
into a grin. "This is a marvel!" he said. "If our old songs and
rhymes of lore speak truth—why, those are lions! There were

lions in this country, in ancient times, long, long ago. Their images are cut into certain rocks, hard to get at; but when I was a little boy, I used to climb up and look at them.

"See that big one, with the shaggy mane? That's the male, their king. We Griffs wear our hair after the manner of the lion's mane. The others are his wives and offspring. And it has always been said, among our people, that some-day the lions would return. And here they are! Where could they have come from?"

"We have lions in our country, far away," Xhama said. "Sometimes they kill our cattle."

"The Wallekki in the south hunt lions," Shaffur said, "and sometimes the lions hunt them. These must have come up from there. But it's a long way."

The maned male let out a low roar, turned, and began to walk away, slowly. The others, with an occasional backward glance at the men, followed. Held back by Obst, the army stood in place until the lions, with great dignity, passed out of sight. But Perkin had a hard time holding on to Baby. The giant bird fidgeted, clacked his beak angrily, and squawked. The lions paid him no heed.

"We ought to rejoice," said Gurun, "because the lions have given way to us of their own free will. It is a sign that God is with us."

"Well said!" Obst answered. "For it's written in the Book of Ika, 'For our God is a mighty God, a lion among the lesser beasts.'"

"Then I would say this is a good place to camp," Uduqu said, "seeing as how the lions have left it to us."

There would be no more big fights, Foxblood said, until the Abnaks came farther down toward the lowlands. There they would meet larger bodies of the Thunder King's troops and the greater part of his strength in their country.

"But first," he said to Orth, "there's something else I'd like you to see."

Being an intelligent man and having been a scholar all his life, Orth was quickly picking up the rudiments of both the Abnak language and Tribe-talk. "Someday," he said to Foxblood, "we will have the Holy Scriptures for the Abnaks in their own language—and in all the languages men speak this side of the mountains."

"All well and good," said Foxblood, "but come and see this."

The Abnak camp sprawled all around the ruins of the Fazzans' fort. As he followed the chief, Orth heard singing and the beat of leather drums. Soon he saw a fire, with a handful of warriors sitting around it in a circle, two of them pounding a rhythm on their drums.

In the midst of them danced a single man—an old man with a white scalp-lock and faded tattoos on his bare chest. As he danced, he sang.

"Can you make out what he's singing?" Foxblood asked.

Orth listened carefully. "He's giving thanks for something. He's rejoicing. But I can't quite understand his words."

"He's giving thanks to God—the Obann God," said Foxblood. "His voice is cracked with age, and he speaks a southern dialect that must be strange to you. But this is what he says.

"His name is Krahok, of the Mud Turtle clan, and he

thanks God because he has been sick, and he expected to die. His firstborn son was killed this spring, fighting against the Thunder King. So he is thanking God for raising him up from his sickness and giving him new strength and letting him live to see the day God came to the Abnaks to fight for them against their enemies.

"He thanks God for making him strong so that he fought well, as if he were young again, when we took the Zephites' fort. He promises God that he will fight courageously. He thanks God for allowing his son's wife and children to find refuge in Obann. And finally he thanks God for letting him know that He is God, a mighty God, who will not leave the people to be wiped out by their enemies. This is the song of Krahok, the Mud Turtle."

To see the old man dance so vigorously, and to hear him praise God with all his heart, brought a tear to Orth's eye—many tears, in fact.

"You have a tender heart, Et-taa-naa-qiqu," Foxblood said. "No Abnak would shed tears for this."

"I can't help it," Orth said. "But I weep for joy, not sorrow."

"It's because you are so different from us that my people are coming to love you," Foxblood said. "God must be strong indeed, to have a tender heart like yours. My people are used to gods that have no heart at all."

"When the mother forsakes her suckling child," Orth quoted from the Sacred Songs, "then I the Lord will take him in my arms, and he shall live."

He couldn't be quite sure of it, but he thought the chief's eyes had begun to water, too. But that was not something he thought fit to mention.

CHAPTER 29

How Gallgoid Learned to Pray

Angel the hawk liked to stretch her wings and fly for the joy of flying, covering ground in minutes that would take the army all day to traverse. Sometimes she flew so high that Ryons could see her as only an infinitely tiny speck. Sometimes she flew off in this or that direction until he couldn't see her at all, and stayed away for an hour, or even half a day. But she always came back. Her savage little heart treasured her roost on the boy's shoulder and loved the very sight of him.

How much can a hawk understand of the affairs of men? Angel knew the men who rode with Ryons were attached to him, as she was. She'd seen battles: Ryons' men fighting against other men, their enemies. That much she understood well enough.

Lately she'd been seeing some things that made her uneasy. Soon there would be more fighting. Her boy would be in danger. But there was no way she could tell him what she'd seen; he simply couldn't understand her when she tried. Even Chagadai the Ghol, who taught the king the finer points of hawking and knew more about hawks than any other man in the army, couldn't understand. "She seems a bit edgy. I don't know why," was all he could say.

The king's great dog, Cavall, understood. Even the big, stupid bird that couldn't fly, Baby, understood a little. But Cavall couldn't make the humans understand, no more than Angel could. Frustrated, she grew short-tempered enough to peck Chagadai's hand when he stretched out a finger to pet her.

"Did you see that, Father? She nipped me, the little devil!"

"Why?" asked Ryons. He was just as obtuse as Chagadai, but Angel would never peck him. It was the sort of thing no decent hawk would ever do.

"I don't know what's the matter with her," said Chagadai. "Something troubles her, but I don't think she's sick. If only she could talk, then we'd know."

Angel tried and tried to tell them, but they couldn't understand.

They were being followed.

———

Baroness Vannett expected to have a quiet time, albeit a lonely one, with her husband and children away to the Golden Pass. She thought she might get some things done around the house that couldn't be done so easily with everybody there. Jack's room ought to be repainted. Now that her eldest son, Josek, had his own house a few miles upriver, his old clothes ought to be sorted. Floors needed waxing, and so on. On top of all that, she had to see to the day-to-day running of the baron's logging business. A workman at one of the camps had gotten his foot crushed between two logs and some other duty would have to be found for him, so his family would be provided for. Breaking the news to the man's wife had not been easy.

So the baroness was hardly ready for it when a forester from King Oziah's Wood arrived in town, breathless, demanding to see the baron. They brought him to Vannett's front door.

"The baron's many miles away," she said. "Tell me your tidings."

"Tidings? I guess you could call it that!" he panted. "It's a huge mob of Heathen horsemen, thousands of 'em, heading straight for the Chariot River from the northwest. God knows where they came from! They're probably crossing the river right now. There's nothing in Oziah's Wood that they'd be interested in, but I don't think they'd pass up a tidy little town like Ninneburky. You've got walls and all, but I don't see enough men here to defend the place for long.

"We'll be all right in the wood, ma'am—but this town has got to be defended!" He ran out of breath and stared at her.

Once upon a time she would have panicked. Now she brought the man into the house and gave him something to eat and sent the groom to fetch the captain in charge of the militia remaining in the town. Her mind raced, but raced efficiently.

"I need your best riders on your fastest horses," she told the captain, and told him why. "Send to the baron up at the Golden Pass and tell him to come back down with all his men, quickly. Send to Lintum Forest. King Ryons left half his army there to deal with emergencies. We need them here at Ninneburky."

"I'll do it right away," the captain answered. "God help us, we've hardly enough troops to man the walls."

Now, Vannett thought, she had to mobilize the town without causing a panic. Roshay had greatly strengthened the defenses. If no one ran away, if the women and the elderly and some of the children pitched in so that every able-bodied man could defend the stockade, they might just keep the Heathen out until help arrived. As long as no one ran away.

———

Up in the pass, the work went on. There were no more nightly noises, no more murders—nothing to do now but pile up the gold and wait for the men to come back with carts.

Martis took Ellayne aside and asked, "Where's Wytt? I haven't seen him since we came here."

"He doesn't like to be around so many people, but he's somewhere close by—watching out for us, like he always does."

"If you and Jack and I went a little ways into the woods, do you think he'd come if you called him? I want to know what he knows, whatever that may be."

"He might," said Ellayne. Wytt always made up his own mind whether to come when you called him.

Roshay Bault gave his permission, on the condition that they wouldn't go far and that Trout would go with them. Trout said his ankle was much better. "I'm fit to fight," he said, brandishing his tomahawk. "But I think those people who were troubling the camp have gone away."

The four of them went a few hundred yards into the woods and sat down on a fallen log. From there they could hear the men working, although the sound seemed to come from far away.

"Wytt!" Ellayne called, a piercing cry that carried. "Wytt, come here, we want you!"

He jumped right out of the underbrush, startling them all. "You were here all the time, weren't you?" Ellayne said, as the Omah hopped into her lap. "Wytt, what's been going on out here? Martis and my father want to know."

Wytt chirped and chattered. Ellayne translated.

"There were a few men who got here first," she said. "Wytt can't count like we do, so it's no use asking exactly how many. One was killed by an animal. Two we've caught. The rest have scattered, and there are only three of them left together. They have a camp a ways from here—no good asking him how far."

But their leader, Wytt reported, was the same man who'd carried Jack to Silvertown to sell him to the enemy, thinking he was Ryons.

"Ysbott the Snake! He's a bad one," Jack said. "He was an outlaw in Lintum Forest, until Helki chased him out of there. Those were his men who attacked us, Martis." Martis nodded, remembering: they'd left him for dead. "What does he look like?" he asked.

When Jack described Ysbott, Ellayne cried out, "Why, he's the one who kidnapped me and Enith, right outside Ninneburky! I thought he was dead."

But he'd been staying right in Ninneburky for a while, Wytt said. The Omah had been waiting for a chance to kill him as he slept. The children knew that was no idle boast.

"You should've told us he was in town, Wytt!" Ellayne said. "The last time I saw him, he was practically blind. I didn't think he'd recover."

"I've heard of Ysbott," Martis said. "Helki was anxious to get him." Ysbott was a murderer many times over, Helki said, but Martis didn't mention that: the same could be said of me, he thought. "Ask Wytt if he'll take Trout and me to Ysbott's camp." And to Trout, "We should finish him off. It would save lives."

Wytt would be happy to do just that. He made jabbing motions with his pointed stick.

Ellayne and Jack understood such things. They'd already seen much more of the world than most see in all their lives—and not just the nice parts, either. They were older now. A good chunk of their lives had been spent in wild and perilous places. They knew what kind of man Ysbott was and understood what kinds of things he did. Martis was right: finishing off Ysbott would save lives.

"We'll take the children back to camp," he said to Trout, "and then we'll go find Ysbott."

———

Gallgoid woke in a sweat, every muscle tensed, from a dreadful dream that left but a single image in his mind—a blank, expressionless face in gleaming, beaten gold, eyes filled with a devouring blackness. He knew it for the golden mask of the Thunder King.

Gallgoid had never been let in to the golden hall, never seen King Thunder with his own eyes. But his master, Lord Reesh, had—with and without the mask.

"The man is mad," Reesh had said. "He truly believes himself to be a god. He expects me to believe it, too—me, the First Prester of Obann!"

Gallgoid had known his master well: Lord Reesh had believed in nothing. Not in gods, at any rate—not even in the true God, whose Temple he had ruled for most of his long life. He'd believed in the Temple and its mission, as he conceived it—to lead the nation of Obann, or even the entire human race, back up to the heights of power and wisdom and pride as the world was in the time of Obann's Empire, before the Day of Fire had consumed it all. For the sake of that future, Reesh had betrayed his city. For the sake of a greater Temple in the future, he'd allowed his Temple to be burned to the ground.

When he had spoken of his meetings with the Thunder King, Reesh had only been talking to convince himself, trying to find words that would give him courage. Gallgoid had seen through it. There was a part of Reesh's mind that had surrendered to the Thunder King and believed him to be a god, or that he just might be. Behind his bluster, the old First Prester had been afraid. So afraid, indeed, that his fear had moved Gallgoid to desert him, to flee alone from the Golden Pass into the howling, killing cold of a winter night.

The dream brought it all back. But it also taught Gallgoid what he ought to do.

He had to recover the golden mask of the Thunder King. He must present it to King Ryons. If the whole world could see that Obann now held it as a trophy, the Thunder King would be truly unmasked. A false god: a tyrant and a murderer whose great power rested on nothing but a great, towering lie—yes, thought Gallgoid, the whole world ought to see that.

They had a new Thunder King in Kara Karram, doubtless with a new golden mask as well. It was the same Thunder King, the mardars said: he was a god, he would never die. But if Obann had the mask and held it up for all the world to see, maybe the great lie would finally collapse. The Heathen would rise; the mardars would be slaughtered.

"And if God is good to us," thought Gallgoid, "that's all that would happen."

He understood that it was dangerous to get involved with something like the Thunder King's golden mask. You really never could calculate what would happen. It would be like removing stone blocks to create a door into a huge, complicated mass whose full extent you couldn't see. Maybe the blocks would slide out and you could go inside, as you intended. Or maybe the whole thing would come crashing down on top of you, because you had unknowingly removed the one block that held it all together.

Gallgoid never prayed. In his heart of hearts, he, who feared so little else, was afraid to pray. He'd done terrible things at the bidding of his master, Lord Reesh. He doubted God would want to hear from him. But now he remembered something Prester Jod had told him recently.

"All men are sinners, Gallgoid: there is no one truly righteous. Hear what God says to us through Prophet Ezah. 'I the Lord cover your sin with my own righteousness: else no man would live. Proclaim my word: if a sinner should repent, and leave off sinning, and do right, I the Lord will not hold his sins against him; that man, in his repentance, shall live. But if a righteous man should abandon his righteousness, and take up the way of sin, he shall die; his former righteousness shall not save him.'"

So Gallgoid knelt beside his bed and prayed, and then he made ready to leave Obann and go to the Golden Pass.

CHAPTER 30

The Laws of Obann

The Abnaks moved down toward the lower hills. By now there were three thousand of them. Two new warriors arrived to replace each one who drifted away. They'd heard of Foxblood's victories and were eager to follow him. Soon there would be hard fighting indeed, and they didn't want to be left out of it.

"But see us lose a battle," Foxblood confided to Orth, "and watch what happens to our numbers."

Orth spent as much time as he could in mixing with the men, marching with them, eating with them around their cooking-fires. As he sat and listened to their talk, his grasp of their language grew by the hour. Now he could even speak a bit of it himself.

One thing greatly puzzled him.

"Why," he asked Foxblood, "do so many Abnaks say things that can't possibly be true? This morning I heard a man say he'd been to a place where the trees spoke to one another and could move from one spot to the next, like men. And then someone else said his father once speared a big fish that turned into a woman, and when he nursed her back to health, he took her to wife and had a son by her. But the boy dived into a pool one day and turned into a fish and was never seen again.

"No one called these stories lies. They just nodded their heads and seemed to think the tales were true."

Foxblood laughed, hard. "Sunfish, my friend—never call an Abnak man a liar! No one believed those stories. They just enjoyed them! My people take great pleasure in fanciful tales—the wilder, the better."

It was not a practice that would be esteemed in Obann, Orth thought. "But how will the people believe me," he asked, "when I tell them about God—that I'm not just telling wild stories, too?"

"Don't worry about that," said Foxblood. "They will know you speak truth. Except when we're telling tall tales, we are a very truthful people. You'll come to know that, by and by."

———————————

With just two followers who weren't of much real use to him, Ysbott realized it wasn't his plan that he now had to save, but his neck.

"We have to get back down the mountain, and fast," he said. His outlaw's instinct was fairly screaming at him to move on. "We can't manage our gold with just the three of us. We'll have to lie low until Roshay Bault returns to Ninneburky. Then maybe we can come back with a cart."

"If we can ever find our gold again!" said Gwawl.

You can't find it, thought Ysbott, but I can. But aloud he answered, "It's perfectly safe where it is, and there it can wait for us for as long as need be. I know exactly where it is. I'm no pampered townsman!"

"Tobb knows what he's doing," Hrapp said. What a fool, thought Ysbott.

He'd heard the baron's two hundred horsemen go back down the road, and crept close enough to get a glimpse of them. "Right now it's safe for us to go back to Ninneburky," he said. But he didn't tell his men that he intended neither of them ever to see their homes again.

Short of rations, they made what speed they could. The way was all downhill, which helped. During the day they only stopped while Ysbott foraged for food. Their only meat was snakes he caught by overturning logs.

"I never dreamed I'd ever eat a snake," Hrapp said. "But they're really not bad, cooked."

Ysbott, of course, had eaten stranger things than that. Here and there, in his foraging, he'd found edible mushrooms. He had also found some fatally poisonous ones, which he'd hidden in his bag. These he would serve to Hrapp and Gwawl when he didn't need them anymore. But if they could somehow obtain a horse and cart before emerging from the foothills, he would let them live long enough to help him load the gold.

For the time being there was nothing he could do against the baron. This galled him, but he comforted himself with the thought that someday he would get a better opportunity.

———

Lord Chutt had lost several hundred men whose horses simply couldn't keep up with the pace he'd set.

"Never mind," he told his men. "If your horse tires, just follow the rest of us up to the Golden Pass as best you can. Be sure to pick up any carts you find along the way."

From various farms and herdsmen he'd commandeered several dozen carts: nowhere near enough, he supposed. But the important thing was to get to the gold and drive off anyone he might find there. The carts would just have to come up later.

They stormed across the Chariot River and onto the plain between the rivers, bypassing King Oziah's Wood. Going on to sack Ninneburky was very far from Chutt's mind. He would have been surprised to learn that the king's men in Lintum Forest had received the baroness' urgent plea for help and were already on their way. Indeed, the chiefs were glad to be called to action again, at last.

"I hadn't thought there were any Heathen armies left in Obann," said Zekelesh, chief of the Fazzan. "I hope we're strong enough to deal with this one."

They were some two thousand, all told—Fazzan, Abnaks, and Dahai. They left behind some five hundred Obannese, Lintum Forest men, whom Helki had trained, to defend Carbonek. Zekelesh would have liked to hear their prophetess, Jandra, tell them they were doing the right thing, going to Ninneburky, but no message was forthcoming. There being such a need for haste, they couldn't afford to wait for one. The Wallekki horsemen, under Shaffur, had all gone east with the king, so it would be a hard march to get there on time with everyone on foot.

"No fear," Chief Buzzard said. "Baron Bault will have to come down from the pass, and he'll have plenty of horsemen with him."

It took them two full days to get clear of the forest, but they expected to make much better time on the plain.

"We could use our long-legged Griffs, just now," said Tughrul Lomak. "We Dahai don't mind a long walk, but we're not built for speed. Still, it's better than sitting idle all this time at Carbonek."

━━━━━━━━━

The two hundred Obannese militiamen came out of the hills just in time to run into Chutt's hands. Outnumbered ten to one, and quickly surrounded by Chutt's Wallekki, they had no choice but to surrender. Chutt had their captains disarmed and brought before him.

"You've come down from the Golden Pass, haven't you?" he demanded. "But I don't see Roshay Bault among you. Where is he?"

"Who wants to know?" a captain snapped. A Wallekki started toward him with a blade, but Chutt wouldn't let him strike.

"I am Lord Chutt, of the High Council of the Oligarchy, the rightful governors of Obann," he said. "I was duly elected by the other oligarchs under the laws of Obann, and I am entitled to civil answers to my questions. No one has harmed you, sir, and no one will. But you have a duty to answer me."

"And what of the king—King Ryons?" said a second captain.

"He's no lawful king," said Chutt. "War has unsettled many things in Obann, but I never heard that we've repealed our laws. Roshay Bault is Chief Councilor of Ninneburky, under the ruling Oligarchy. Obann has not had a king since King Ozias was driven from his throne a thousand years ago. Or was it two thousand? We have no law in Obann recognizing any king."

Most of these militiamen had never laid eyes on King Ryons or had only a glimpse of him when he'd passed through Ninneburky. None of them was at Obann when the Heathen were about to take the city but were scattered like chaff by the great beast with Ryons on its back. They'd heard of it, but hadn't seen it. They'd lived their lives under the laws of the Oligarchy. Who were they to defy a lord of the High Council?

"I ask you again," said Chutt. "Have you come down from the Golden Pass? And is Roshay Bault there now?"

A captain licked his lips nervously, then answered. "Yes, my lord, he's there. He sent us down to fetch carts for the gold."

It may be a figure of speech to say a man's eyes gleamed, but if any man's eyes ever truly gleamed, it was Lord Chutt's at the mention of the gold.

"It's up there—all of it—the gold of the Thunder King?" he said. Suddenly his voice was raspy. "How much? How much gold?"

A captain shrugged and spread his arms, palms out. "How much, my lord? Why, more than I ever thought existed! A great shining hill of gold—no telling how much!"

"It must all be brought to Obann," Chutt said. "Gold—to rebuild the Temple and make it greater than it was before! Gold to build a new Obann!"

"That's what the baron says, my lord. Bring it down from the mountain and use it to rebuild."

"Then he won't object to another three thousand men to help him," Chutt said, "and a high councilor to take charge of it! That's what we've come to do. But we'll have to hurry, won't we? In case the Thunder King tries to get it back. He'd be a fool not to! Indeed, I've come along just in time, haven't I?"

Careful, now, he told himself: mustn't get overly excited. He forced himself to smile at his prisoners.

"I'm sure you're all loyal, law-abiding subjects of Obann," he said, "who only want to do the right thing for your country. Very well! You came down to find carts and bring them up to the pass: I release you to carry out your mission. Come back up with as many carts as you can find. Understand?"

When it dawned on the captains that they and their men were to be released unharmed, free to carry out their baron's orders, they were delighted and amazed. Who would blame them for obeying one of the High Council of the Oligarchy? If it seemed strange to any of them that this high councilor had gathered to himself a host of Heathen warriors—well, had not King Ryons done the same? All they had to do was round up carts and bring them up to the Golden Pass. Why trouble themselves with questions of high politics?

The first captain saluted. "My lord," he said, "we understand and will obey! We'll bring up all the carts we can."

After they were released, the boldest of Chutt's Wallekki chieftains asked, "Why did you let them go? They'll only make trouble for us later."

"I can hardly hope to win back Obann if I start by slaughtering Obannese militia," Chutt said. "They were too few to do us any harm—much better if they just bring us carts instead. Once we have the gold in our possession, you'll see. What we cannot conquer, we can buy."

─────────────

One captain, a man named Kerdig, took a trooper aside and ordered him to ride back up the mountain as fast as his horse could carry him.

"Tell the baron everything," Kerdig said. "He must be given time to decide what to do, so hurry!"

"But if it's a high councilor—"

"The baron will decide how to deal with him. Now go!"

CHAPTER 31

How News Came to the Baron

Uduqu marched beside Obst, toiling along on tired legs, hard put to keep up with the old man's long strides.

Obst no longer knew how old he was, having lost count of the years he'd lived in Lintum Forest as a hermit. Uduqu had formed a habit of studying Obst's face when Obst wasn't looking. He was sure some of the deep lines around Obst's eyes and mouth were filling in with flesh and a few more hairs in his beard were turning black. But that was something Obst didn't like to talk about.

"This is going to have to be my last campaign," Uduqu said. "My legs just can't stand it anymore. I feel like I've hiked to the end of the world and back.

"I always thought I'd die in a battle, somewhere—a good end for an Abnak. But I find I'm not content with that anymore. Now I want to live long enough to read and write. I want to read the Scriptures, like Ryons does. I was coming along pretty well in Obann, with Ryons' teacher teaching me. But then we had to leave, and I've had no more lessons. And we haven't brought along any books with us, so I don't know when I'll be able to get back to it—if ever. I wanted to be the first Abnak who ever read a book."

Obst winced. "Oh, my friend—I've let you down!" he cried. "I should have been teaching you myself."

"You were busy with a few other things. I'm not complaining."

"But I'm sure we can manage something," Obst said. "A piece of charcoal can always serve you as a pen. Or you could practice on bare ground with the point of your knife. We can resume your lessons this evening, after mealtime."

Uduqu usually fell asleep right after eating, sometimes even before the sun went down. "But I'll stay awake for that," he said. "All these years, old man, I've written the story of my life with axe and scalping knife. But that's no way to write the Scriptures."

"No," said Obst, "it isn't."

———

Gallgoid set out alone, on a mule selected more for endurance than for speed, having first appointed one of his agents to act in his place and introducing her to Constan, Jod, and Joah.

"This is Jilly," he told them. "She works as a maid in the house of Evrach Hoyl, the wool merchant. She also shops for him and gets around the city. I've told all my people to report to her instead of me. She has the sharpest eyes and shrewdest ears in all Obann, and you can rely on her."

Prester Jod was gracious; Constan responded only with a nod, but Joah the captain had his doubts.

"She looks too young for this sort of work," he said, young, fair-haired, and pretty, he didn't need to add.

"You don't want a spy who looks like a spy," said Gallgoid. "I've trained her myself. She now knows everything I know." And much that the three of you don't know, he thought.

"I'm sure we can place our trust in her," said Prester Jod. "Besides, the city is quiet now."

"We want to make sure it stays that way," Gallgoid said. There were still many Obannese who wanted to rebuild the Temple, despite First Prester Orth's insistence that a Temple built by human hands would no longer serve the people's need—a position with which Prester Jod fully concurred. The burned ruins of the Palace continued to remind people of an old order that had passed away but not yet been replaced.

"There's a great deal of uneasiness in this city," Gallgoid said. "If Lord Chutt puts himself forward as a man to restore the Oligarchy, and all the old ways, there are many who will be disposed to follow him."

"But Chutt has gone east, not south," said Joah.

"He will come back someday," Gallgoid said. "Be ready for him."

Prester Jod sighed. "The Lord has shaken the earth," he said, "and many great things have fallen down. We can only put our trust in Him and do our best."

———

Helki the Rod made camp a single day's journey from the top of the Golden Pass.

A flight of birds told him there was trouble coming. They weren't migrating: it was too early for that; they were getting out of the way, heading for some place more likely to be peaceful.

He knew from the faint smell of smoke that Roshay

Bault was camped by the ruins of the golden hall, with many men who needed many cooking-fires. But the birds had come from the west, from Obann's side of the mountain. The trouble, whatever it was, wasn't at the baron's camp.

Helki kept a watch for crows and eagles. If there was a battle in the offing, they would seek it out. But so far those birds had not appeared.

"Tomorrow I'll come a little closer," Helki said to himself, "and then I'll hunker down and see what's what."

━━━━━━━━━━

Thanks to the Thunder King's road, Vannett's messenger and Kerdig's trooper arrived one right after the other, just hours apart.

"Lord Chutt has a host of Wallekki, Baron, and some Obannese, too—a good three thousand, all told," Kerdig's man reported. "He has come for the gold. He's one of the High Council and says he's going to take charge up here. He says it's not lawful for King Ryons to be king."

Roshay grimaced. "Of all the High Council, trust Chutt to be the only one still living!"

"He says the law is on his side, my lord. Is it?"

"Where was his reverence for the law when he ran away and left the rest of the High Council to die, trying to defend the city?" Roshay's face reddened. "It was that boy, who is now our king, and the power of God, that saved the city—no one else, and least of all Lord Stinking Vulture Chutt! He wants the gold to set himself up as a tyrant. Well, it might not be as easy as he thinks!"

"They're coming right behind me," said the trooper.

Which meant, thought Roshay, that they weren't going

to Ninneburky, and his wife and his town were safe.

"What am I to do?" he said softly. "Surrender to him, just like that? No, by God!" He made the trooper jump. "If Chutt wants this gold, he'll have to fight for it." The baron turned and bellowed to his men. "Stop work—now! I want a trench dug across this road and a barricade behind it."

The trooper stared at him, wide-eyed. "My lord, there are too many of them! We'll all be killed."

Roshay seized him by the neck of his mail shirt and shook him. "I don't allow that kind of talk!" he roared. "Chutt is a coward and a traitor, and we have work to do." The men were already gathering around him. "Half of you start digging—I'll show you where—and the rest, cut a lot of stakes and make them sharp. We have all the timber that we'll ever need, right here. Captains, get these men working!"

Jack, Ellayne, and Fnaa heard everything. Suddenly everyone was hacking at the earth with swords and spears and axes, or dragging heavy timbers from the ruin. The routine of the camp was shattered. Roshay Bault was everywhere, barking orders, shoving men who weren't moving fast enough. No one paid any attention to the children. Martis, Trout, and Wytt were off hunting Ysbott.

"I've never seen a battle," Fnaa said. "Maybe this is a good place for one."

"It's not as much fun as you think," said Jack, who had seen a battle once—the one that had started with Helki killing the giant. Jack and Ellayne had seen the battle from the top of a cart. Sometimes he still saw it in his dreams.

"What about Martis?" Ellayne cried. "Someone ought to go and bring him back!"

But there was no one available to do that.

Guided by Wytt, Martis and Trout found Ysbott's camp abandoned. "Only three camped here," Trout said, as he studied the ground and the remains of a campfire. "They left here yesterday morning, I'd say."

Wytt, of course, could track them easily, by scent. It would be hard for Ysbott to go where they couldn't follow. But now Wytt didn't want to follow Ysbott, and neither did Trout.

"There's something brewing that this little fellow doesn't like," Trout said. "I don't understand his chattering like the kids do, but look—the hair's standing up along the back of his neck. And it's standing up on my neck, too! I think we ought to head back to the baron's camp."

Martis nodded. He used to get such feelings in the city. If an enemy were following him secretly on a busy street, Martis would know it, even if he couldn't see the enemy. So he listened to Trout.

Besides, Wytt was scolding both of them, noisily, trying to tell them he smelled men and horses, as many as the leaves on the trees, coming from the wrong direction. It maddened him that the humans couldn't understand him no matter how simply he tried to put it, but he was satisfied when they turned from the camp and headed back up to the pass.

CHAPTER 32

The Door of the Sun

It wasn't necessary to dig a trench all around the ruins of the hall. That wouldn't even have been possible. The Thunder King had built around it a high stockade, sealing off the pass except for two great gates, one facing west and one, east. The avalanche had smashed this stockade, creating a jumble of fallen, broken timbers impassable to horses and dangerous for men on foot. Roshay's men had only to dig in front of where the west gate used to be.

Behind the trench the militiamen raised an abatis. It wasn't very high or very deep, but it would do: Chutt's cavalry wouldn't be able to charge them. Even so, it would be hard for two hundred men to hold off an attack by thousands.

"We should've brought more archers," Sergeant Kadmel said.

"We'll do our best with what we have," said Roshay Bault. "Chutt's no man of war. He's only good at counting money. And his Wallekki won't relish a stiff fight against a fortified position."

"Once they get a peek at all this gold, they won't go home without it," Kadmel said.

"We'll make them lose their taste for it, if we can. If worst comes to worst," the baron said, "we have enough gold to buy our way out of trouble. And by the way, Kadmel, you are now a captain."

"Thank you, sir!" Kadmel grinned. "I hope I live to spend my raise in pay."

Toward the end of the day Martis and Trout returned, winded and soaked with sweat, but otherwise unharmed. Wytt leaped into Ellayne's arms and told her enemies were coming.

"Yes—we know," Ellayne said. "They'll be here tomorrow morning, my father says. They won't find it easy to budge him off this spot!"

Roshay took Martis aside.

"Once we see how things are," he said, "I'd appreciate it if you and Trout would take the children into the woods and make them scarce. I don't want them caught up in a battle."

"We'll get them back to Ninneburky, Baron. I promise," Martis said.

———

While waiting for King Ryons' men to come up from Lintum Forest, the baroness had not been idle. She'd sent messengers up and down the river and had collected another hundred fresh militiamen. Meanwhile, scouts from King Oziah's Wood reported that the invaders had turned east and wouldn't be coming to Ninneburky, after all.

That could only mean they were making for the Golden Pass, where her husband was with only a few hundred men. What could he do? Where could he go? But she didn't give in to panic. She had no time for it, nor would she tolerate it in her cook.

"Pull yourself together, Lanora!" she said. "The king's

men are coming, our own people are coming, and they all have to be made ready to go and save the baron."

"But, my lady, they'll be too late! Can't you send some of them now?"

"It'd be folly to send out a little force that would just be swallowed up—the baron wouldn't thank me for it!" Vannett said. "We're better off doing all that we can do and praying to the Lord to do the rest."

Lanora went about her kitchen duties sniffling and teary-eyed. Nywed the housemaid, Enith's grandmother, did all she could to calm her. Nywed's husband, Master Harfydd, put out calls to his boats to come down the river as fast as they could. "They'll be another three hundred men," he told the baroness, "if only we can find arms and armor for them. If not, most of them have axes and other tools that they can fight with."

Vannett found a little time to sit with Enith and read Scripture.

"My grammum says it's a wonder you're so brave, Baroness," the girl said.

Vannett laughed uneasily. "Me—brave? I certainly don't feel brave, Enith! But there's so much to do, so many messages to send out, to say nothing of finding places to stay for all the men who are going to be here soon and seeing that they'll have enough to eat. There's just no time to mope."

Besides: ever since she and Roshay woke one early morning to hear Ozias' bell tolling from the summit of Bell Mountain—they'd had no idea what it was until much later; there was no such bell in Ninneburky—Vannett had come unexpectedly into possession of a conviction, or a feeling, that it was all going to be all right. It meant, she believed, that

God had taken charge: that her daughter and her daughter's friend had obeyed God, no matter how difficult and dangerous it was, and that the Lord would remember it. Because the children had obeyed God, there was a blessing on their house. The man who'd been sent out to kill them, Martis, would protect them with his life. More than that, God would protect them. And had He not delivered all of Ninneburky out of the hands of a Zephite army?

But she couldn't explain it to Enith, not without revealing the secret of Bell Mountain and Ellayne's part in certain great events. It wasn't safe to speak of it. So Martis said, and she believed him.

"Well, let's do something that'll do us good," she said to Enith. "I'll read a Sacred Song to you, and you can read one to me. And then we'll go back about our business."

The crows were gathering, Helki noted from his hiding place. Their general flight was up the mountain, west to east, when they weren't otherwise just going around in circles. Pretty soon, he thought, he'd be seeing eagles, too.

There was going to be a battle, and at no place more likely than the top of the Golden Pass. "Reckon I'd better move a little closer," he said to himself. But if there was going to be a full-scale battle, he supposed he'd be able to do more good if no one knew he was anywhere nearby. He put out his fire and began to move toward the pass, exercising all his stealth. Not even the blue jays noticed him.

By and by he came close enough to smell smoke, sweat, and the dung of horses, and to hear raised voices and the thump of metal blades on wood, when the wind was right.

It sounded like Roshay Bault was working his people hard. "Which means they know an enemy is coming, and they're getting ready for a fight." They weren't going to be taken by surprise, Helki thought.

What enemy could be coming from the west? Helki never thought it might be a friendly force, coming to join the baron in his labors. The crows were never wrong.

And then, high up in the sky, much higher than the crows, he saw an eagle circling: slowly, patiently, just keeping an eagle eye on things until the battle had been fought and it was time for eagles to feast on the dead. The eagle wouldn't be there unless it thought there would be many dead.

Helki decided to shift his position to the west, so that when the enemy, whoever it was, came up before the baron's defenses, he, Helki the Rod, would be behind them.

———

Without anyone ordering it so, Ryons' army slowed the pace of its advance as it drew nearer to the first of the Great Lakes. The lake had many names. The Griffs knew it as the Door of the Sun—"Because the rising sun must pass through it every morning," Tiliqua explained. "We don't believe that anymore, but the name has stuck"—so that was what the army called it.

Uduqu, meanwhile, had an idea. "I'm not much for ideas," he confided to Obst, "but when I get one, I stay with it."

In Obann, studying along with Ryons, he learned the alphabet and how to write his name. One evening, with two more days to go before they were to come within sight of the Door of the Sun, after thinking about it all day on the march,

Uduqu took a piece of charcoal and scrawled something on the blade of Shogg's sword.

"Now find me someone who can read," he said to Obst, "but who doesn't speak a word of Abnak."

That someone was a grey-haired Griff named KoOmah, who in his youth went west and served some years in Obann's army. Uduqu showed him the writing on the sword.

"Can you read that?"

"I can," said KoOmah, "although it makes no sense. It says, 'Wattaki Uduqu sa,' whatever that may mean."

"Aha! It works!" Grinning, Uduqu sheathed the sword and swatted KoOmah's shoulder. "It's Abnak, man! That's why you don't understand it. 'Wattaki Uduqu sa' means 'I am Uduqu.' I can use the letters of Obann to write things in my language!"

"I could have told you that," said Obst, smiling. "But I didn't want to spoil your fun."

"But it means that I can write things that other Abnaks can learn to read," Uduqu said. "Why, I can write my whole life's story now, without having to learn Obannese, which is a devilish hard language. Not only that—I could write down everything that you've been teaching us. That might be more useful than the story of my life. Any man could tell a tale of fights and scalpings and women."

"I couldn't!" Obst said. He ran his fingers through his beard. "I don't know why I hadn't thought of this," he said. "Between us, old friend, we could render the Holy Scriptures into Abnak—or any other language spoken by men. What a blessing that would be! If only we live long enough to do it."

"I'll make it my business to stay alive," said Uduqu. "And you do the same."

That, he thought, would get trickier and trickier the farther east they went. Already the broad plains of Griffland were giving way to lands that rose and dipped. The day's march up and down these low hills had not been an easy one. Uduqu longed for the forested hills of Abnak country; he'd even be glad to see Carbonek again. He wondered how his people were doing in their war. As long as the Abnaks could keep fighting, he thought, that would mean fewer and fewer warriors available to the Thunder King to bar Ryons' way to Kara Karram. "But by the time we get there," he supposed, "they'll have prepared a hot reception for us."

CHAPTER 33

Treachery Ahead and Behind

When the door at the top of the cellar stairs opened and two men came down instead of just the one who'd brought him bread and water, Hennen was sure they'd come to kill him. He was in chains with no way to defend himself. "A pretty miserable end for a soldier," he thought. And he prayed a brief prayer: "Lord, receive my soul! I've done my best."

"On your feet, General!" said the man who carried the lamp. "We've come to turn you loose."

Hennen didn't believe it, but he struggled to his feet: he preferred to die standing up. But the second man produced a key and unlocked his fetters.

"Where is Chutt?" Hennen asked. It had been quite a few days since Chutt had sent any word to him. How many, he'd lost track.

"Who knows? And who cares? He's gone off with his Wallekki bully-boys and left us to deal with an army coming up from Obann. We don't feel like dealing with it! So if they've come for you, they can have you."

Why had Chutt left Market City? Where was he going?

Hennen asked, but the guards didn't know.

"Rumor has it that he's heard about some gold stashed somewhere and galloped off to get it," said the man with the keys.

"You'll put in a word for us, won't you, sir?" said the other. "Market City belongs to Obann, and they're welcome to it. We won't fight for it."

They had to help him up the stairs and then wait for his eyes to get accustomed to the light of day. Hennen insisted on a good meal before he left the building, and the guards gave him one. It was wonderful to eat at a table for a change, seated on a proper chair. The beef stew went down like the food of angels. When he'd finished it, Hennen was able to rise without assistance.

"There's a horse waiting for you, General, and your sword and your armor, too. Try not to be too mad at us! It wasn't our idea to lock you in the cellar. Who could go against Lord Chutt, once he had all those Heathen at his beck and call? Good riddance to him and them!"

"I think I'm able to ride," said Hennen. "And then we'll see about securing this town so Chutt can't get it back."

———

Ysbott pushed his two men off the road and into the shelter of the trees. At first they didn't understand why he was doing this and would have resisted, if they'd dared. But soon enough they heard the racket of several thousand armed men on horses, and soon they got glimpses of Chutt and his horde.

"I never heard them coming!" Gwawl marveled. "How did you know they were coming, Tobb?"

"I felt it through the soles of my feet, of course," Ysbott said. Any woodsman would have felt the vibration of thousands of horses' hooves battering the earth well before he heard it. He might not have known what it was, but he would have known to get out of the way.

"Who were they?" said Hrapp. He was trembling, Ysbott noticed. Why was it, he wondered, that you just couldn't find good men anymore?

"A lot of Wallekki, by the look of the feathers in their hair," he said, "but with some Obannese mixed in. King Ryons has Wallekki cavalry, but he took them with him when he went east. I don't know who these could be. That bothers me!"

That was an understatement. The passage of the cavalry reminded him that he was Ysbott the Snake, outlaw: every man's hand was against him. Whoever was leading that body of horsemen up the mountain, he had the power to hang Ysbott from the nearest tree, if he so desired.

Even so, Ysbott's mind began to work.

"Come—let's turn around and follow them. From a safe distance!" he said. "Something's happening, and I want to know what it is."

"Well," said Gwawl, "but if they catch us—"

"Will you try to show a little courage, just this once!" Ysbott snapped at him. "Whoever those men were, they've come for the gold. They'll either help Roshay Bault or try to take the gold away from him. I want to see what happens!"

"Whatever you say, Tobb," Hrapp said. He wished with all his heart that he'd never left his cobbler's shop, but didn't say so.

"Father, what are you going to do?" Ellayne asked. Night was coming on, but still the men labored at the camp's defenses.

"I'm going to try to save our lives—and save the gold for Obann, if I can." Shirtless, covered with grime, the baron had put in a full day, but Ellayne knew he'd work all night, if necessary. "I want you and Jack and the other boy to be ready to skedaddle out of here with Martis and Trout at the first sign of trouble. Maybe there won't be any—but we must be ready, if there is."

He'd done this before, Ellayne knew, when an army of Zephites attacked Ninneburky and he defended it against fearful odds. There were men here, like Kadmel, who'd been with him in that fight. They had confidence in him.

"Lord Chutt really is a traitor, then?"

"I remember how he bought the votes to be elected to the High Council," Roshay said. "Lord Gwyll couldn't stand him, but Lord Ruffin thought they could make use of him. They all said he was a wizard when it came to bringing in the taxes. But no one ever would have thought he had it in him to raise an army. Yes, he's a traitor. I wish King Ryons and his men were here with us." And then he went off to get the ditch dug deeper, now by torchlight.

Wytt was edgy. "He smells a battle coming," Jack said. "I wish I knew how he knows these things! He thinks we ought to leave right now and not wait till the morning."

"It'll be a hard battle, if there is one," said Fnaa. "I wouldn't want to try climbing over those timbers with people throwing stones and poking spears at me."

"My father wins his battles!" Ellayne said. But if what that trooper said was true, and there were thousands of

Wallekki coming, what chance had Roshay Bault with only two or three hundred men? She didn't want to be there in the middle of a battle, but she didn't want to leave her father, either. He might be killed here—a thought too terrible to hold for long.

"We'll find paths to take us down the mountain," Martis said, looking ahead. "They'll catch us if we try to use the road."

"They'll be sorry if they do," said Trout. He'd bound his ankle tightly and said he didn't think it would hold them up. He'd also spent a little time honing the edge of his scalping knife—not that Abnaks ever let their knives get dull.

Jack feared for his foster-father, but thought it would only make Ellayne feel worse if he said so. But he couldn't remain entirely silent.

"There's always traitors, aren't there?" he said. "One goes down, and another one pops up somewhere else. Will King Ryons ever be able to be safe on his throne? Or will he have to keep fighting for it until he's old and grey?"

———————

"Tomorrow you will see the great water," Looth told the other chieftains. But Chagadai had bigger news than that. Some of his Ghols had been out since the middle of the night before and had only just come back with tidings.

"We are being followed," Chagadai reported. "Something was troubling the king's hawk, something she saw from high up in the sky. So I sent four riders to see what it was.

"We are being followed by an army of Zephites, with at least as many men as we have. They're all on foot, but they're coming on quickly all the same."

"Ungrateful sons of dogs!" said Shaffur, showing his teeth. "This is how they pay us back for letting them go when we had them at our mercy!"

"And the big men, the Zamzu, are waiting for us at the lake, with a lot of Dahai, too," Looth said. "We'll be caught between two armies."

"And if we wheel around to attack the Zephites, the Zamzu will take us in the rear!" Shaffur said. "Is there any good ground for us to hold? Anyplace where we might make a stand and live to tell of it?"

Pitched battles involving large numbers of men had never been the Attakotts' way. They fought—mostly against the Abnaks—as small raiding parties, mostly from ambush. They wouldn't think in terms of finding a good defensive position and holding it. But Looth had learned a thing or two about the art of war.

"There are hills overlooking the water," he said. "The big men and the Dahai are camped right on the shore with the water at their backs. But I have seen one hill big enough for all of us. If we can get there first, it will be hard to drive us off it."

"We'll still be surrounded," Shaffur said. "Curse those Zephites for their treachery! But I suppose we'd better make all speed to that hill—and it means we'll lose any advantage that our strength in horse might give us."

Ryons understood enough to understand that his people were in grave danger. But what else could they do? It was the hill or nothing. He didn't dare interrupt the deliberations of his chiefs.

"Praise God that the king's wise little hawk has warned us," Xhama said. "At least we won't be taken by surprise. Nor do I believe that God has led us all the way out here just for the Thunder King to kill us."

"We ask too much of God!" Shaffur muttered. Gurun heard it.

"My lords," she spoke up, "I know nothing of wars and battles. But I do know that God has brought me to this place farther than any of you. I came from across the sea, and I don't know how to get back! All I know is that we must go on—by faith, because we cannot see the way. Ask Obst if it is not so."

Obst stood up and sighed. "It's so," he said. "When the Children of Geb walked on little islands that rose up in the sea and sank again when they'd passed over them, they had only faith to guide them. And God brought them to a wide and pleasant land, which is now Obann and all these countries in the East.

"What else can we do, but go on? First to Looth's hill, and there await deliverance. We came here in obedience to the Lord. He won't desert us now. Let us rest while we can and then make all speed to the hill as soon as it's light enough for us to travel."

All the chiefs murmured their approval. But then Tiliqua shook his head and said, "We never should have trusted the Zeph! I wish you hadn't healed that chief of theirs, Gurun. I wouldn't be surprised if he's leading them in person."

"If he comes within reach of my sword again," said Uduqu, "he'll get a wound that will be very difficult to heal."

Gurun said nothing in reply. She couldn't find it in herself to regret the healing of Jiharr. That had been, after all, a sign that God was with them.

She exchanged a look with Ryons and knew he felt the same.

CHAPTER 34

Blood Money

When Roshay Bault finally sat down to rest and eat and drink, the children sat with him. The night was well under way, but the captains were still busy shoring up the defenses. "Unless Chutt's Wallekki got around them somehow," the baron thought, "we're as secure as we can be. We'll see what they're up to. If they do try to outflank us, it'll take them some time." But he worried because that was exactly what he would do if he were Lord Chutt.

Not wishing to alarm the children, he talked about what a coward Chutt was and how the Wallekki had never been known to have the stomach for a really stiff fight—forgetting that his daughter and Jack had actually seen Wallekki fight and knew how brave they could be.

But then Fnaa said something that none of the others had thought of yet.

"I wonder how the Thunder King ever got to have so much gold," he said. "Vallach Vair was a rich man—my mother and I were slaves in his house—but he never saw so much gold as this. He was crazy for gold, and he'd do just about anything to get more of it. But all the gold he ever had wouldn't be a drop in the bucket, compared to what's up here."

"The Thunder King must have a lot more gold, though, where this came from," Ellayne said.

"How did he get to be so rich, Baron?" asked Jack.

Roshay had never thought about that, and at first he answered casually, "Well, he must have taken it from all those people he conquered in the East. He must have plundered whole nations and sacked a lot of cities."

Had Lord Orth been there, or Obst, he would have said that that made it blood money, and that God had commanded the Children of Geb, long ago, "You shall not take a price for men's blood." But Orth wasn't there, and just for the moment, Roshay had forgotten the law against taking blood money. That would not have surprised Lord Orth. It had been a long time since God's laws were preached in Obann's chamber houses.

"I don't like to think of it," Jack said. "When we were with King Ryons' army, they all talked about the terrible things the Thunder King did to their countries. He killed off their cattle, poisoned their wells—and a lot of other things. That's why all those different peoples are so afraid of him."

To sheathe his great hall in sheets of gold, Roshay thought, must have cost only a fraction of King Thunder's wealth. Even so, the gold they had up here—how many murders, how many robberies, how many blood crimes had to be committed to amass it? The baron shook his head.

"Everyone wants to be rich, Jack," he said. "I'm considered a rich man, myself. But several generations of my family worked for it! Felling trees, sending God knows how many rafts of lumber down the river to Obann; building docks and saw-mills; and paying a good price to get the best labor, but robbing no one. And yet just a few of these gold sheets would be more wealth than we could have earned in all that time. But at least our hands are clean."

"But won't this gold make them dirty, sir?" Fnaa said. "I'm just a fool of a boy, and I don't know much. But I wonder if it'd be bad luck to take the Thunder King's gold." And that was when the baron remembered the law.

"Not bad luck," he said. "I don't believe in luck. But I don't suppose God would be pleased with us for taking it. He wouldn't bless blood money. But what else can we do? We can't let the Thunder King just have it back! He would use it to shed more blood—here in Obann."

There they let the matter rest. The baron needed sleep.

———

With all the men busy with the defenses or else asleep already after their hard toil under the blazing sun, the ruin stood deserted in the night. But not entirely deserted.

As silent as a shadow, Wytt crept through the camp eager to explore the vast pile over which so many men had labored like ants. He'd never seen humans behave like that before, and it had aroused his curiosity. Besides, the heap was sure to be full of tasty insects.

Compared to a man, Wytt weighed hardly anything at all. It was safe for him to go where no man dared. He could pick his way along the timbers without upsetting them, through the maze of interstices between them, deeper and deeper into the ruin.

He couldn't imagine why the men were so interested in this place. They weren't eating any of the creatures that lived in it. Could it be they wanted the dead men lying under it? For most of his life Wytt had lived in a flat-topped hill that used to be a city, along with hundreds of his kind. That hill was full of dead men's bones. The Omah never gave them a second thought, except to pull them out of the way when necessary, as if they were just sticks or stones. They held no meaning for the Omah.

There were dead men here, too, down at the bottom of the heap. Wytt smelled them long before he saw them. A lot of them were not yet skeletons, but getting there.

Their presence didn't trouble him, but something did, and he didn't know what it was. It made him proceed cautiously. It wasn't anything he smelled or saw or heard. It was just a certain sense he had that this was a bad place and that, if he stayed too long, something bad would happen to him. He didn't like that feeling and he knew better than to ignore it. Why was it that the human beings acted as if there were no danger here? Were their senses so dull? But then they often behaved as if their heads were made of solid wood. Certainly their noses were of no use to them.

Wytt could see in the dark, but down here it was so dark that even an Omah couldn't see. Guided by his nose and ears, and by other senses unknown to human beings, Wytt went on, just a little deeper.

He stopped when he came into contact with a human hand.

His hair stood up on end. The hand was dead; it couldn't hurt him. Nevertheless, it was time to retreat back up to the clean, open air. Maybe he could make Ellayne and Jack understand that the men should not be digging here. They probably wouldn't understand, but he could try.

Wytt backed away from the hand, growling under his breath. He couldn't shake the feeling that the fingers would try to close on him. That he knew they couldn't didn't seem to help. He gripped his sharp stick tightly, ready to thrust at anything that threatened him. He wanted no more part of any of the crawling things that must have been feeding on the dead. Slowly he retraced his path back up to the rest of the world. With each yard he gained, the scent of fresh air encouraged him. Had he been a human being, he would have danced for joy when he finally emerged into the night. But he did finger the lock of Ellayne's hair that he wore around his neck.

When he found them again, Ellayne and Jack were already asleep. He crawled under Ellayne's blanket and cuddled with her for a while before returning to his safe nest in the woods.

―――――――

Foxblood, of course, had scouts prowling all over Abnak country, and tonight they were bringing him good news.

"The Thunder King's men have had just about enough of us," he told Orth. "We were wise to spare some of them. That was good advice you gave us, Et-taa-naa-qiqu. Now that they believe they can get out of here alive, a lot of them don't want to stay in our country any longer. Just a few days' march from here, two hundred Dahai burned down their own fort and deserted. Some Zamzu caught up to them and tried to force them back, and there was a fight. The Dahai got away, and many warriors on both sides won't be fighting anymore. I think we're going to win the war! At least for the time being. Come next spring, I suppose King Thunder will send more armies here. But we'll deal with that when the time comes."

All around, men talked and laughed and sang around

campfires, plucked on harps made from tortoise shells, and blew on flutes and whistles that sounded shrill and barbaric until you got used to it. Orth was used to it by now. The solemn music of the great water organ in the old Temple at Obann would have been out of place here, he thought. "They will need hymns and sacred songs in their own language, to their own kind of music," Orth thought. But then Foxblood spoke again.

"Abnaks will remember, forever, that the king of Obann gave them a safe refuge for their wives and children in his own country," he said. "They will remember that God fought for them; nor will they ever forget you, Sunfish. My chiefs want you to ask for a reward. Whatever you ask them for, they will give you."

That surprised Orth. "For me? But they don't have to give me anything! And yet," he added, as the thought came to him, "there is something I will ask for, but not for myself.

"I would ask leave to build a chamber house in Abnak country—a place where all the people can go to hear God's word preached and to be instructed in His ways. The house will send out teachers to all the tribes and clans, and one day Abnaks themselves will be the teachers."

Foxblood considered it. "Hm!" he grunted. "Abnaks aren't much for building great houses like you have in Obann. But we could try to build one."

"I wasn't thinking of a great house—not at all," said Orth. "It would be up to the people to build whatever suits them best. Indeed, I'd rather it were not a proud, imposing building. It should be just a place where a prester and reciter can assemble the people and teach them.

"We in Obann made a great error when we allowed the

Temple and its chamber houses to become more to us than
God's word itself. I share in the blame for that. We mustn't
let it happen here. Our Temple collected worldly riches and
became, as it were, a false god in itself. It'll take us many
years to correct that error. But here in your country, we can
make a fresh start. The important thing is that the people
learn to know God and love Him and keep His commandments—to serve the Lord, and not a Temple. For that I think
some ordinary tents and shelters will suffice."

Foxblood nodded, thinking along with him.

"Will you send us a prester?" he asked.

"Oh, yes!" Orth said. He smiled. "In fact, I know just the
man for the job—not a man of Obann, but an Abnak." He
was thinking of Hlah and pleasurably imagining the look on
Hlah's face when he proposed the appointment to him.

CHAPTER 35

The Race to the Hill

The other half of King Ryons' army arrived at Ninneburky to find it busy, but not under siege. The baroness met with the chieftains in her parlor to explain the situation.

"My husband, the baron, is at the top of the Golden Pass with just a few hundred men. Some three thousand warriors, most of them Wallekki, are on their way after them. I have since learned that Lord Chutt is leading them—a traitor to the king. I don't know how long the baron can hold them off, or even if he can hold them off at all. I have five hundred Obannese militia, all mounted, to go with you—should you choose to go up to rescue the baron. We've had no word from him. It may already be too late." Vannett didn't know how she was able to say that without breaking down, but somehow she did.

"The Golden Pass—that's the way King Ryons took to cross the mountains," said the Abnak chieftain, Buzzard. "That's where the Thunder King's gold is."

"The baron went up to get it," said Vannett. "Lord Chutt wants that gold. If he gets it, he may be able to overthrow the king."

"We won't let him do that," said a kilted Dahai chief. "Lady, we'll march as soon as we can replenish our supplies."

"I've collected provisions for you and loaded them in wagons."

The Fazzan chieftain doffed his wolf's-head cap. "Then we can set off right away!" he said. "All of the best of the Wallekki are with King Ryons. Those up on the mountain won't be good for much. We'll bring the baron home to you. He's a good man who deserves to be rescued."

Vannett's eyes finally filled with tears, but they were tears of gratitude.

———————

Knowing that whatever might happen at the Golden Pass would happen long before he could get there, Gallgoid traveled slowly along the road that paralleled the north bank of the Imperial River. It was his plan to offer his services to Lord Chutt and then see what he could do to bring about Chutt's downfall. Chutt might remember him as a servant to Lord Reesh; he could easily pose as someone who wished to restore the old order. Chutt used to dine with Lord Reesh occasionally, and the two of them had always been on good terms.

Chutt and his following had passed through the country well to the north of the road. No one along the river had heard anything about him. As far as these folk knew, Obann was at peace. Gallgoid let them go on thinking so.

Chutt would get the gold—Gallgoid had no doubt of that. If Chutt's ambition ran so high, he would use the gold to raise armies and purchase the support of great men. Indeed, he had set a course that would force him to do that. If he failed, he would die a traitor's death. He was probably so caught up in his lust for the gold that he hadn't thought that far ahead, but he was not so big a fool that he would never think of it.

"He's a dangerous man," Gallgoid thought, "and possession of the gold will make him a deadly menace to the king.
Jod and the others underestimate him." Gallgoid knew him
as a shrewd man with an uncanny gift for raising revenue. If
he proved as wise in spending money as he was in getting it,
he might make himself master of Obann.

But as Lord Reesh was wont to say, "Every man has a
flaw in his character that turns him into a fool when he most
needs to be wise"—an observation that the old First Prester had failed to apply to himself. Reesh's flaw was a sheer
inability to distinguish his own interests from the Temple's.
Chutt's, as Gallgoid well knew, was unbridled greed.

Before the sun rose, King Ryons' army dashed with
all speed into the east, to the lake and to the hill that they
hoped would be their stronghold. Looth's men skirmished
many miles ahead, but the chiefs warned them not to loose
their poisoned arrows except in dire need. "We'll need as
many arrows as we have," said Shaffur, "once we're on that
hill." It took only a single Attakott arrow to kill a man, even
if it only grazed his flesh. The poison's composition was a
secret even from most of the Attakotts themselves.

Some of the Ghols stayed far to the rear to keep an eye
on the army of the Zephites. "Whatever you do," Chagadai
commanded them, "don't let yourselves be seen. We don't
want them to know that we're aware of them."

Uduqu refused the offer of a horse, let alone a seat in
a supply wagon. "You'll be wanting to carry me to battle in
a wheelbarrow, next!" he snapped. He toiled along beside
Obst, keeping up the pace with his teeth clenched, his face

already shining with sweat. "These old legs will get all the rest they need, once we're on the hill."

Cavall trotted along with Ryons, barking now and then until Chagadai bade him to keep silence. Being a wise dog, he obeyed. Behind the king came Perkin, practically dragged off his feet as he tried to restrain Baby. The giant bird sensed excitement; the feathers on his neck stood out, and he clashed his beak. The Ghol bodyguards on their wiry little horses gave him a wide berth.

"Sorry!" Perkin gasped. "By my head, if there's any man looking for a fight, Baby will give him one!"

Looth's scouts ran back and forth with reports to the chiefs. The Zamzu still slept in their fort by the lake; the hill was still unoccupied. Looth himself was up there now, they said. Dahai stood guard over the multitude of boats overturned on the lake shore, but showed no sign of being ready to do anything else. With any luck at all, the army would be atop the hill before anyone could prevent it.

"We'll only have to charge back down," Shaffur said, "as soon as we run out of water."

"True," Chagadai agreed. "But if the Zamzu try to charge up first, we'll make them pay."

Gurun and Ryons rode side by side. Gurun had all she could do not to fall off her horse as it was trotting. She was thankful that she had to concentrate on that instead of on the coming battle.

To Ryons it seemed strange for the army to be advancing without chanting "His mercy endureth forever." The chiefs had ordered it so: they didn't want to alert the enemy. But Ryons missed the anthem and wished he could hear it now; it would uplift his spirits. Being surrounded on a hilltop didn't appeal to him. It didn't seem like the kind of thing his ancestor, King Ozias, would have done. But it never entered his head to overrule the chieftains' strategy.

And then, surprising him, the sun peeked over the horizon, gleaming off the bottoms of the clouds and painting them a golden hue, turning the grey grass to a lustrous green. There should have been a trumpet to announce it, Ryons thought. He remembered a verse he'd learned from the Book of Beginnings: "And God kindled the sun, to give light to His creation; and all living things rejoiced in it."

Up and down, up and down, over one low rolling hill after another: horses' hooves and men's feet ate up the ground. Thick grass muffled the thunder of their passage. Now the Hosa would have loved to clash their spears against their cowhide shields, beating time, but Hawk and Xhama restrained them. They formed a dark, solid square at the center of the army, easily keeping up with the horsemen on the wings.

There was something grim and terrible about this silent advance, Ryons thought. And suddenly Angel took wing from off his shoulder and flew overhead with a shrill, exultant cry: her way of welcoming the morning. It heartened those who heard it, and the Hosa saluted her with their spears. She was a great favorite of theirs.

An Attakott scout came running.

"There it is, just up ahead—the hill!" he cried, in Tribe-talk. He pointed with his bow to a great hill that rose ahead of them, standing alone above the other hills. "Hurry! The big men are coming out of their fort."

"It's a race, then," shouted Shaffur, "and we'll win it! Forward at the gallop!"

No more silence now. The Wallekki spurred their horses, the riders whooping their tribal battle cries. The Hosa broke into a run, wondrously maintaining their formation and pounding on their shields for all they were worth—a dreadful, daunting sound. Behind them the Griffs, as was their custom before a battle, chanted their death-songs.

Uduqu only puffed and panted.

"Now, Father! Now, honeysuckle! Now!" cried Chagadai; and the Ghols, with Ryons and Gurun in the mist of them, swept around the mass of infantry to chase the Wallekki up the hill.

The sun rose higher. Now Ryons could see Looth and some of his men on the hilltop, waving to them. Cavall howled, running flat-out.

Before the sun came fully over the horizon, the Wallekki had joined the Attakotts on the hilltop. King Ryons and his Ghols arrived a minute or two behind them. Up came the Hosa, five hundred strong, and then the Griffs. The army's supply wagons rumbled up the slope.

Obst had to take Uduqu by the arm and help him the rest of the way.

"We've done it!" Ryons said. "We've won the race." But other words froze in his mouth when he laid his eyes on the water down below—an endless flat sheet of it, dyed gold by the rising sun. It stretched as far as you could see. He had not known there was that much water in the world.

There, almost at the water's edge, stood the fort—like a little shed, from this distance. The Zamzu and the Dahai, scurrying like ants, deployed in front of it. They'd made no effort to win the hill. To Ryons it looked like a very great host of men down there. But Shaffur, who had experience in such things, said they could be no more than four thousand. He sat on his horse and studied them.

"Twice our number, I would guess," he said, "but no cavalry. We would beat them in a stand-up fight—if only we could have one!"

The Hosa assembled on the top of the hill, looking down on their enemies, and began to drum on their shields again: a slower beat this time. For now they raised their voices in the anthem, and all the rest of the army joined in, in all their different languages—"His mercy endureth forever!" And it seemed to Ryons that the sun shone brighter, hearing it.

Shortly, the Ghol scouts came trotting up the hill to report to the chieftains. By now the black tent had been set up in the middle of the hilltop, with the wagons parked around it.

"How many of the Zeph?" asked Chagadai.

"At the very least, a thousand—maybe more. I would say a thousand and a half."

Shaffur grimaced. "I'd like to charge right down there as soon as they come in sight—wipe out every last one of them, the dogs!"

"But then we'd lose this hilltop," said Chagadai, "and without the hill, we'd never take the fort. And then we'd never get across the lake."

"Let us pray," said Obst.

CHAPTER 36

How Ellayne Parted from Her Father

The sun rose also over the Golden Pass, and Roshay Bault rose with it.

"Get that ditch filled with broken branches," he ordered his captains. "That'll slow them up if they try to cross it. We might set it on fire, too. Chutt will be here soon; let's use every minute that he gives us." Tired as they were, the men fell to work before they had their breakfast, knowing that their lives would depend on preparations such as these.

Ellayne had an early breakfast because her father insisted on it, but she had no appetite. Still, she and Jack ate because they'd learned, in their adventures, that sometimes it might be long before you ate again.

"Do you really think there'll be a battle, Baron?" Jack said. "You've made the defenses mighty strong."

"I'm hoping they'll be strong enough to persuade Chutt's Wallekki not to fight at all, Jack. But you youngsters are going to go on your way as soon as you've had a good feed. Better safe than sorry! Give me a kiss, Ellayne."

She threw her arms around her father's neck. "Let me stay! I don't want to leave you."

"Not a chance," said Roshay Bault. "Be brave. I know you know how." He kissed her again, then peeled her loose. He understood that, for his sake, his daughter refused to cry. "Maybe, before this is over, I'll cry for her," he thought.

He took Jack into his arms, too, and kissed the top of his head. "We'll play chess when we're safe at home again, my boy," he said. "Meanwhile, obey Martis and take good care of my girl." He grinned at Jack and added, "After all, you're going to be married to her someday." Jack and Ellayne both blushed a deep red, and Fnaa laughed. Roshay released Jack and put an arm around Fnaa's shoulder.

"I don't know you very well, young man," he said, "but if you served as the king's double, I guess there's more to you than meets the eye. Be good, and don't get up to any tricks. I'll know you better someday."

Fnaa had never known his own father. His eyes began to fill with tears; he couldn't help it. "I'll be careful, sir," was all he could say.

Roshay clasped Martis' hand. "I'll see you back in Ninneburky, Martis. Thank you," he said. Martis only nodded; he didn't trust himself to speak. "Make sure these kids eat before you take them out of here." With that, the baron strode off to position his men for battle.

"Where's Wytt?" Fnaa asked.

"Once we're started, he'll find us," said Ellayne. "He always does."

Orth marched with the Abnaks. The nearest enemy outpost, Foxblood said, was a day's march down the slope. There they would find Zamzu with several hundred Wallekki.

Aside from offering up a prayer for victory, the First Prester wasn't thinking about the battle. In his mind, he was composing a letter to Prester Jod in Obann.

"I'll need as many copies of the Scriptures as you can send me," he addressed Jod mentally, "and if you can find any reciter who knows the Abnak language and is willing to come here, please send him, too.

"These people, who have for so long been our nation's enemies, are now ripe for the grace of God and hungry for His word. Do not send any money. Abnaks have no use for it, and why should we teach them to desire it? Let them be as God made them, with no foolish efforts on our part to teach them how to live like Obannese. They wouldn't want to! But I do believe God's word will take firm root in this country, if only we can plant it."

He would write the letter as soon as he could come by any writing materials, which were rare among the Abnaks.

Foxblood jostled him to get his attention.

"Pardon me," Orth said. "My thoughts were racing on ahead of me."

"I just wanted to warn you that the Zamzu won't give up without a fight," the chieftain said. "We'll have to wipe them out, and I know that will upset you. But the Zamzu are the Thunder King's favorites, and he's their god."

"Let their blood be on their own heads," said Orth. "Is it true they eat people?"

"Nothing truer. They've done it here, in Abnak country. They have eaten women and children, and they flaunt it. They think it makes us fear them, but it only makes us angry. Our warriors will need no encouragement to fight them. Every man will want to tuck a Zamzu scalp into his belt."

Orth shuddered, but this, he knew, was the way of the world. When had the Tribes of the Law ever lived by God's laws? The Heathen didn't even know the law. Men of the world lived by the promptings of their own lawless hearts, doing more evil than good. The Scriptures told of several nations of the ancient world whose destruction God commanded—because they were committed, heart and soul, to evil, and would not turn back from it.

"Don't be afraid," said Foxblood. "We'll win this battle, for we know God fights for us."

"Do you believe that, Chieftain?"

"I do! Haven't I seen it for myself? Before you came to us, what could we do? Not much! My people are fighters, but we couldn't drive King Thunder's servants out of our country. They kept coming and coming, and while all we were able to do was take the odd scalp, here and there, they ate up half our homeland. We gave them pinpricks while they hammered us with axes. But now it's different. If God is for us, no enemy can stand against us."

Orth smiled so broadly that Foxblood had to notice.

"Have I said something funny?"

"Not at all!" Orth answered. "But King Ozias wrote practically your very words in a Sacred Song, two thousand years ago."

Foxblood laughed. "Do tell!" he said. "I'll remember that."

━━━━━━━

Ysbott, Hrapp, and Gwawl followed Chutt's riders up the mountain at a safe distance.

"What if we get caught, Tobb?" Hrapp panted.

"We won't!" Ysbott growled. "Do you think they'll bother with three men on the road? It wouldn't be worth their while to chase us through the woods."

"But what are we going to do, once we get back up to the top?" Gwawl said.

"Nothing! Not until we see what happens there. Now stop complaining!"

The Wallekki were going to take the gold from Roshay Bault; Ysbott was sure of that. Would they kill him, too? He wouldn't be surprised if they massacred the baron's men. And after that, what? Probably go down the east side of the pass with all the gold they could carry, Ysbott thought. The Thunder King would get it back. But at least he could then retrieve the seven sheets that he had cached, enough to make him a rich man all his life.

And if they went west with the gold instead of east, back into Obann—well, he'd think of something.

———

They couldn't use the road because the enemy was on it, so Martis led the children into the woods with Trout bringing up the rear. Once out of sight of the camp, Wytt joined them. Ellayne yelped when he sprang out of hiding and scrambled up her leg. Once in her arms, he chattered excitedly.

"What's he telling you?" Martis asked.

"He says he crawled into the ruins all last night," Jack said, "all the way down to where the dead men are. He says it's a bad place, very dangerous."

"But he can't say why," Ellayne added. "Wytt, what did you see? Is it dangerous to my father?"

Wytt could have bitten her. Big people always wanted to know things that couldn't be known and didn't matter—even Ellayne and Jack, who had much more sense than other humans.

"He thinks the baron shouldn't stay there any longer," Jack said. "It's something about the place that he doesn't know how to explain."

"But that's easy!" Fnaa said. "It's just a bad place, isn't it? And the gold is bad, too, because it belongs to the Thunder King and he did wicked things to get it." Wytt couldn't understand Fnaa's words, but if he could, he would have agreed.

"Well, Father can't get down—not now!" Ellayne said.

"Shh! Listen!" Martis said.

For a long moment they all stood silent. But then they heard the noise of horses' hooves.

"That's Chutt with his army. They're coming," Martis said. "We'd better get a ways farther from the road, deeper into the woods. It seems we left just in time."

The noise grew into a racket, but they were already too far from the road to see anything. After what seemed a very long time, the clatter died away. A few jays protested from the treetops.

"They'll be up to the top in another hour at the most," said Trout.

"God save the baron!" Martis said.

———

Invisible to anyone who might chance to look in his direction, Helki, too, saw Chutt's riders pass. An eagle flew along with them, high up in the sky.

Helki was on the south side of the road, Martis and the

children on the north. As far as he knew, they were still in Ninneburky.

Nevertheless, the thought began to nag him that perhaps he ought to cross the road, once Chutt's army passed. Being Helki, he needed no better reason for action than his instincts. But he was here to help the baron, if he could, by positioning himself behind the Wallekki and waiting to see what he could do. At the very least, he could invade their camp by night and make them think the forest was full of enemies. No Wallekki ever born could track him through the woods. He could pick men off as he pleased.

After a sufficient interval, he turned and followed the Wallekki.

CHAPTER 37

How the Gold Changed Hands

In Obann, Joah sought out Prester Jod with a message from Hennen.

"It's good news," he said. "Hennen is alive and well. The men Chutt left behind have set him free. He's taken command of the force I sent to rescue him and has set about securing Market City against Chutt's return. But he doesn't think Chutt's coming back."

"Our prayers for the general are answered," Jod said.

"He'll be coming back to us soon," Joah said. "He thinks the north will be safe for a while. Chutt, it seems, recruited all the Wallekki who were on the loose up there and has taken them east with him. I don't think any Wallekki would care to spend a winter in North Obann if they could help it."

"Then the question is," said Jod, "where will they plant themselves? Or will they just decide to go back to their homeland, once they've got the gold at the Golden Pass?"

"Maybe Gallgoid can find out in his travels."

But they'd had no word from Gallgoid since he'd left Obann.

Chutt found the ride up the mountain hard to endure, even if there was a road. He was ten times the horseman he'd ever been before. "I should be!" he thought. "I've ridden ten times as much as I ever did in all the rest of my life." Still, he couldn't be compared with any man of his Wallekki. To keep their respect, he had to grit his teeth and pretend his bottom wasn't being battered into a paste by being rammed against the saddle. This mountain road was rough! He wondered if his legs would ever again function properly.

But the gold was worth any amount of hardship. "It'll be your downfall, someday, your lust for riches," Lord Ruffin, the governor-general, used to warn him. Back then, Chutt wouldn't listen: the pickings were too good to resist. As the high councilor in charge of collecting Obann's revenue, he'd become a wealthy man. But when the Heathen broke into the city, he'd lost most of his wealth. They'd burned down his house, and looters had made off with everything of value. Chutt had had to start over again. All they knew about him in the north was his great name as a wealthy man. The name was all he had, but he'd used it to recruit an army.

Now he would be able to pay that army and to do much more besides. But if the Wallekki had ever found out his famous coffers were empty—! Ah, well, that danger was past.

Ilfil, the chief of his Wallekki, clattered along beside him. "It can't be much further, lord," Ilfil said. "There's the top of the pass, straight ahead. Shall we do battle there?"

"Only if we have to," Chutt said. "I doubt they have sufficient numbers to make a fight of it."

An hour more of hard riding, and they were there.

At first the sight that met his eyes nearly broke his

heart. The way to the ruined hall was blocked: a ditch and a barricade in front with mail-clad men behind it, and on either side a chaos of heavy, broken timbers.

But beyond all that, the sun, now high in the sky, shot its rays off sheets of gold—more gold than Lord Chutt had seen in all his life: enough gold to make him the sole ruler of all Obann, if only he could take it.

His riders, three thousand of them, halted in a cloud of dust. Chutt paused to catch his breath, then moved out a few paces in front of his army. Now, if ever, he had need to speak with a commanding tone. He cleared his throat.

"I am Lord Chutt, High Councilor under the law of Obann. Who is in command here?" he called. "Let me see your face!"

A sturdily built, middle-aged man who needed a bath rose up to answer him.

———

Roshay Bault had thought long and hard about what he would say when this moment came. He knew that if he faltered, his men would falter, too. When Chutt called out his challenge, Roshay stepped onto a log so Chutt could see him clearly.

"I'm in command—Roshay Bault, Baron of the Eastern Marches by appointment of His Majesty King Ryons, King of Obann by the grace of God." There was no one in Ninneburky who had a voice to match his. "I'm here by commandment of my king, to retrieve this gold for the good of all Obann."

"I've heard of you," said Chutt. "You're the chief councilor of the town of Ninneburky, and well known as a man of valor and good sense. Come down from there, Chief Councilor. I wish to speak with you."

"My title is 'Baron,' Lord Chutt. And the High Council of Obann no longer exists."

"Must we shout at each other, Chief Councilor? Surely there's no reason why we shouldn't have a parley. As for my rank, it's true that my colleagues on the High Council are all dead. But someday the oligarchs will elect new ones to replace them. I am here lawfully. And so are you—even if there is no law of Obann recognizing any such rank as Baron of the Eastern Marches. Let us reason together!"

"The other high councilors died defending our capital city," Roshay said. "You're still alive because you ran away when you had the chance. That won't help your reelection."

Roshay's men chuckled. "Good," thought the baron. They'd been more than a little edgy since they'd first heard the rumble of Chutt's host coming up the road.

"You do me wrong, Roshay!" Chutt answered. "Someone had to go and secure the north. The council appointed me to do it."

"Too bad I can't ask any of them if that's true." Roshay was sure Chutt was lying, but didn't want to provoke him with the name of "liar." If Chutt lost his temper, men would die.

"I see you don't trust me enough to come down and parley," Chutt said. "I suppose that's understandable. Very well—will you permit me, and two or three of my officers, to enter your camp so you and I can have a civil discussion? I'm willing to trust you!"

That was unexpected. Roshay thought swiftly. Chutt's men would hardly launch an attack while their commander was on the wrong side of the barricade and sure to be killed. As chief councilor of Ninneburky for many years, and as a man of business, the baron was used to negotiations of all kinds. That was how things got done. Try as he might, he could think of no reason not to negotiate now.

"Let me confer with my captains first," he answered.

"By all means," said Chutt.

————————

Ilfil spurred his horse up next to Chutt's.

"Are you mad?" he said. He spoke fluent Obannese and had understood every word that passed between Chutt and Roshay Bault. "He has only a handful of men to hold that barricade! We can slaughter them all in a matter of minutes. By the face of the moon, we haven't come here to talk!"

Chutt kept his temper. "Talk is cheap, Ilfil," he said, "but combat is expensive.

"We'll get the gold, one way or another. Have no doubt of that! But this man, Roshay Bault, is a hero. The people in this part of Obann love him. What would they think if I killed him and massacred his men?

"Oh, we will do that, if there's no other way. But if we manage our business skillfully, all Obann will be ours for the taking. Why settle for a little, if we might have it all? I've not yet done anything against the law. That will help us greatly, when we seek to buy the support of all the great men in the country. Can't you see that?"

Ilfil scowled. "It seems like wisdom," he conceded, "but I hope it doesn't turn around and sting us when we least expect it."

"If we're going to have a battle here," said Chutt, "we

can have it any time we please. Don't be in a hurry! You must learn to understand these things, my friend. After all, when all is said and done, you're going to be a lord of Obann and a very, very wealthy man."

———

Roshay had never met Lord Chutt before, although he'd seen him and heard much about him. He remembered Chutt as a rather pudgy man, but he wasn't pudgy anymore. As they shook hands, the baron sized him up: a hard man who would be very shrewd and canny when it came to getting what he wanted.

He came with two of his captains, an Obannese soldier from Market City and a Wallekki chieftain in a headdress of black and white plumes: a renegade and a brigand. Chutt introduced them. "This is Captain Born, commander of the regular army garrison at Market City, and this is my ally, Chief Ilfil. Gentlemen, this is Roshay Bault, who defeated a great army of the Zephites when they attacked his town." And so Chutt adroitly sidestepped the sticky issue of Roshay's proper title.

Too late, the baron realized he'd made a mistake in letting Chutt into his camp. "I've lost a rook for nothing!" thought the chess player in him. He'd allowed Chutt to have a good look at the gold: now Chutt would take it no matter what he had to do.

"My dear sir," said Chutt, "what we have here is a practically infinite supply of money! Such a windfall as this has never come to Obann, not in all her history. It's enough to rebuild the Temple, rebuild the Palace, fortify every town along the river, and raise and equip armies able to defeat the Thunder King—with enough left over to repair all the damage from his last invasion."

"I'm aware of that," Roshay said. "That's why I came here to collect it."

"With these few hundred men? It would take you a whole year just to load it onto wagons! It will be a major project even for my thousands of men.

"I think you must agree that this gold belongs in the treasury of Obann, in the capital. As a lawfully elected member of the High Council, all I seek to do is put it there! Why should you oppose me?"

"Because you're a liar," Roshay thought, but he only said, "First Prester Orth does not wish to rebuild the Temple."

"Surely that is a matter for the whole College of Presters to decide," Chutt said. "We needn't concern ourselves with it. I will bring up many carts—they're a day or two behind me. I have the manpower to remove the gold—and it's only a matter of time before the Thunder King tries to get it back. He may well send a force that will be too strong to resist, even for me."

"First he'll have to get past King Ryons and his army."

Chutt sighed. "Although I don't recognize the boy as king, there being no lawful basis for a monarchy, I do admire him for the valiant part he's played. And I grieve for him. His march into the East was an act of folly that can only have one outcome. He may be already dead."

"That's in God's hands," said Roshay, "and I believe in God."

"Of course, of course—and so do I! But in the meantime, the gold must be brought all the way back to Obann. I can do that, and you can't. There's no reason under the sun why we should quarrel over it! I'm only carrying out my lawful duty as high councilor in charge of revenue."

"I can think of a reason," Roshay said. "I believe you mean to kill us, one way or another. We'd be fools to come out from our defenses."

"But I don't want to kill you!" Chutt cried. "I haven't come here to kill anyone. We encountered a body of your men down below, rounding up wagons as you ordered. Not one of them has been harmed. Once we ascertained what they were doing, we released them all to carry out their mission. You'll see them soon enough."

"Then why don't I just stay here and wait for them?"

"Because, while we're waiting, the Thunder King may come!" Chutt leaned forward on the stump that served him as a chair. His two captains watched him intently. "Dear sir, if I meant to attack you, what could possibly stop me from doing it? You can't put your men back to work; they have to man your defenses. If you think we mean you harm, you can't let my men in to join in the work. And so no work gets done.

"As disagreeable as it is to me to say so, I must tell you that unless you let my men work here, so we can remove the gold before the Thunder King can send an army for it, I shall have no alternative but to attack you. This gold will guarantee the safety of our country, and that's more important than your life or mine. Of course you can stay and help us in the work, or you can lead your men back home to Ninneburky. But one way or another, I must take charge of this gold."

Roshay was tempted to give the order to have Chutt and his two captains slain on the spot. Leaderless, what would his followers do? He could at least take the leaders hostage.

But then he thought, "Blood money! That's what it does. Much blood has been shed for it, and now it works to shed more." The gold was seductive. Even now it was seducing him, King Ryons' man, to commit murder. This was a parley. What he had just imagined himself doing was nothing less than treason. He ground his teeth, disgusted with himself.

What was it Obst so often said? "Walk by faith"—not faith in gold, but faith in God.

And so the baron said something he never thought he'd say.

"I'll surrender this gold to you, Lord Chutt—all of it—if you can convince me that you will not attack us when we come out of our defenses. I don't know how you can guarantee that, but maybe you can think of something."

Roshay's captains flinched. Only Kadmel showed no sign of surprise. But Lord Chutt fairly beamed.

"That's talking sense!" he said. "Naturally, we'll give you hostages—"

"The three of you will do very nicely," Roshay said.

Ilfil the Wallekki reached for his knife, but Chutt caught his wrist.

"You can't have us, dear sir," Chutt said. "That would leave no one to command my army, and then I couldn't guarantee their good behavior. Indeed, I'd say you might be better off without hostages. If you're going to trust me this far, you may as well trust me all the way. You have my solemn oath that you and your men will be allowed to go in peace, and unmolested."

Roshay doubted Chutt's Wallekki were so attached to their commander that fears for his safety would restrain them, should they choose to attack. "They can kill us all, no matter what we do," he thought. "What would they care for hostages?"

"I think my men will be too busy admiring the gold, once they get in here," Chutt added, "even to think of chasing you down the mountain. They'd have nothing to gain by it."

Roshay nodded. "Let the blood money do its work on Chutt, not me," he thought. "I'm well rid of it."

"Take your oath in front of your men and mine," he said, "and we'll be on our way." He turned to Ilfil. "Will your people abide by such an oath?"

"I will take the oath myself," said the chief, "and cut the throat of any man who breaks it." Martis could have told the baron that Wallekki chiefs set great store by their oaths. No oath-breaker could remain a chief for long.

"And you?" Roshay asked Born.

He shrugged. "I'm a soldier. I obey my commander's orders."

They made arrangements. Chutt and Ilfil stood in the space between the army and the camp and swore to let the men of Ninneburky go peacefully. Chutt's army withdrew a little ways and dismounted. The baron ordered his men to gather up their gear, saddle their horses, and prepare to leave. A crew pulled the deadwood out of the ditch, while another tore a gap in the barricade.

Leading his men on horseback, with the disappointed townsmen bringing up the rear on foot, Roshay Bault rode forth from his defense, sword in hand. Enemies lined either side of the road. As the baron's men passed through their midst, there was nothing to be heard but the snorting of the horses, the clip-clop of their hooves, and the jangle of equipment. Roshay prayed silently that he would live to see his wife and children. But none of Chutt's men moved or even spoke. They hardly looked at the retreating militia. They all seemed to have their heads turned upward, where they knew the gold lay waiting for them.

It seemed to take all afternoon, but it didn't, for them to pass out of sight and hearing of Chutt's men. Kadmel spurred up next to the baron.

"They're not following us," he said.

"Good."

"They're crazy for the gold, sir. Their mouths are watering. It does seem a shame to give it up to them after all our hard work."

"It's the Thunder King's gold, Kadmel. It wasn't ours to give away." Roshay let out a long sigh. He suddenly felt very tired. "It's dirty money. The rightful owners have been robbed or murdered. I don't believe that gold will be good to anyone who tries to keep it. It certainly wasn't good to the Thunder King whose bones lie at the bottom of it."

Down at the end of the line, Donn Decker grumbled about the baron's cowardice. Two men marching with him beat him into silence.

CHAPTER 38

Hold or Die

Helki watched from cover as Chutt's army halted before Roshay Bault's defenses, and listened as the baron exchanged words with the enemy. Helki didn't know who Chutt was, but surely he was a man of Obann. Other than King Ryons himself, who in Obann had such a host of Wallekki to follow him? And why were those Wallekki mixed with Obannese soldiers?

The commander, whoever he was, along with two others, went into the baron's camp for a parley. The crows settled into the treetops, waiting for a battle. "They sound as confused as I am," Helki thought. Had they sensed more surely that fighting would break out, they would have made more noise.

That man leading the Wallekki had called himself a high councilor of Obann. "I thought they were all dead," Helki mused. "Could there be a new council?"

He was still watching when the baron led his men out of the camp. At any moment he expected the Wallekki to pounce on them and was surprised when they didn't. Would they wait until the militiamen had passed and then give chase? But they didn't do that, either.

The Wallekki's commander reappeared, standing on the barricade.

"The gold is ours!" he cried. "Come and clear away these obstacles!" When their chiefs repeated it in the Wallekki tongue, the mass of men whooped like drunken witches and surged forward to obey.

So Roshay Bault had given up the gold! Helki would have expected him to fight for it. But it wasn't worth dying for, was it? The baron had used it to purchase his men's lives. That was only good sense.

The Heathen tore down the barricade, hurled the deadwood out of the ditch, singing and cheering, shrill songs of triumph. But the crows stayed right where they were, quiet now, waiting. They didn't think things were quite what they seemed, and Helki respected their judgment. As long as they stayed, he would stay.

———

Chutt and Ilfil ran to the nearest stack of golden sheets.

"It is all as you said, O Chutt!" cried the Wallekki. "We are all rich men!"

Chutt couldn't speak. The gold dazzled his eyes and stunned his soul. And there was still plenty more of it, incalculably more, shining amid the tumbled mass of logs that had been the Thunder King's golden hall.

"With just a fraction of this wealth, I could make myself king of all the Wallekki," Ilfil said. That jarred Chutt's mind back to work.

"The Thunder King would only come and take it from you," he said. "But on this side of the mountains you'll be safe. You'll have to settle for being a great lord of Obann, my friend—with a palace, slaves and servants, a stable full of fine horses, and gems and jewels for your toys."

"I bow to your wisdom," said Ilfil.

Born had gone back to organize the removal of the barricade. Some of the men had already hurt themselves. Before another hour passed, they had undone enough of the defenses to let the whole army come through. They had to lead their horses carefully across the ditch, but with the deadwood removed, it posed no problem.

As soon as they crossed, the Wallekki charged to see the gold. They shoved each other out of the way. As members of various tribes, some of them hereditary enemies, they weren't gentle with one another. The Obannese troops came in for more than their share of the jostling, and they resented it. Someone drew a sword and struck. A man fell dead. And suddenly there were many swords flashing and spears thrusting, and cheering turned to cursing, cries of woe.

"Stop it, stop!" Chutt cried. The men couldn't hear him. "Ilfil, make them stop!"

But it took a long time to restore order, and the crows had their feast, after all.

Helki waited to see what would happen next.

———————————

All morning the Hosa taunted the Zamzu. But the Zamzu wouldn't come up the hill, and King Ryons' army wouldn't come down.

"We ought to charge them," Shaffur said, dissenting from the other chiefs. "We would scatter them like dead leaves."

"Maybe," said Chagadai. "But if we don't—for the Zamzu are not men who scatter easily—and we're locked in a battle with them when the Zephites come, well, we would be caught between two forces and likely to be burned."

"Chieftains, stand still," said Obst, "and wait for deliverance by the hand of the Lord! We are here by His command. He has not forgotten us." And Shaffur was overruled by the votes of all the other chieftains and had to make the best of it.

Ryons didn't like just standing on the hill, but he didn't want to rush headlong into a battle, either. He'd heard stories of the Zamzu and their ferocity. The smallest of them, he could see with his own eyes, was bigger than the biggest men in his army. The Zamzu had formed up with their Dahai allies on their flanks, and the Dahai were no mean fighters. Ryons wished he had his own Dahai with him, Tughrul Lomak and his men. They might have something to say to their countrymen to move them to desert the Zamzu. But there was no profit in wishing for that.

Early in the afternoon, a lookout on the other side of the hill called out the dreaded news: "The Zeph are coming!" Ryons and Gurun walked over to see, along with Chagadai and Tiliqua.

The Zeph came in a mass, with bulls' horns on their heads. The Zamzu couldn't see them because the big hill was in the way. Looth's archers ran to take good positions: the first Zephites up the hill would die from poisoned arrows.

"I can't believe they've turned on us," Ryons said. "Not after the healing of their chief."

"That's the Zephites for you," said Tiliqua. "Not that they were ever on our side, my king." But Gurun said, "God healed that man, and God is always right."

The Zeph made no attempt to assault the hilltop.

Instead, they turned aside and went up another hill perhaps a quarter of a mile away. Up they went like ants, all of them. It was a long, low hill, and when they were all gathered on top of it, they raised a battle cry.

That was when the Zamzu finally noticed them, and when they did, they cheered loud and long, waving swords and spears and clubs to salute their unexpected help. Ryons looked for Jiharr, but couldn't pick him out of the crowd.

"Now we face enemies in two directions," Chagadai said. "That man Jiharr knows that we have archers. That must be why he hasn't charged us."

"The Zeph have a saying, 'Arrows don't kill,'" said Tiliqua. "Still, no one wants to get shot, eh? But they'll get more than wounds from Attakott arrows."

"I think Jiharr knows that," said Chagadai. "Oh, well—the question of strategy that faces us is an easy one to answer. All there is to do is to hold this hill. Hold it or die."

———————

They would have been surprised by the news Foxblood received from his scouts that same day. Contrary to all experience, the Zamzu had abandoned their fort and retreated, making for the lowlands at the edge of Abnak country.

His warriors danced when they heard the news, but Foxblood was thoughtful.

"They haven't retreated because they're afraid to fight. I'm sure of that," he said to Orth. "They just didn't have enough men to resist us. I suppose they expect some of our people to drift away, if there's no fight in the offing."

"Do you think they will?" asked Orth.

The chieftain shrugged. "This is something new—an

Abnak army," he said. "Never before have so many warriors from so many clans come together. It may never happen again. The Thunder King had nothing like this to deal with when he first invaded our land.

"So we must make all the speed we can, chasing the Zamzu down to the low country before too many of our warriors leave us. But there are still more men joining us than are leaving. Pray that it continues, Et-taa-naa-qiqu! We'll need them all."

"Amen!" said Orth. Inwardly, he was glad the great battle was delayed. "I am a man of peace," he thought. "I'll never get used to war." But there could be no peace as long as the Thunder King's Zamzu remained in the country. And down in the lowlands, Foxblood said, the Zamzu would have Wallekki cavalry to help them. Even a man of peace could see that the Zamzu's retreat had made things harder for the Abnaks.

What neither Orth nor Foxblood knew was that they had a secret ally that preyed on King Thunder's forces in the south—rumor.

Down from the north, filtered through the lips of wanderers and traders, and distorted by each man in his turn, came rumor of a great invasion launched by the king of Obann—the same king who'd destroyed the mightiest army ever raised in the East. Some said he came riding on a great beast that was like a walking mountain; others, that he commanded a host that was like the blades of grass in number. Rumor reported that he came with certain death for all who opposed him. Rumor had it that the great God of Obann went before him like a tempest, a black cloud, full of lightning, that blotted out the sky. Rumor credited him with battles never fought, victories never won, and wrath insatiable. And many of King Thunder's men believed the rumors and feared the conquering king of Obann.

Ryons' chieftains would have laughed aloud, could they have heard even the mildest of rumor's imaginary terrors.

But they were on a hilltop with enemies on two sides, and didn't laugh at all.

CHAPTER 39

The Next King of Obann

They hadn't gone far before Wytt darted into the underbrush and disappeared.

"Where's he off to now?" said Trout.

"He's looking for trouble," Jack said. "It's always better for him to find it before we do."

A trick of the wind had brought Ysbott's scent to him, and Wytt ran after it. Ysbott should have been far away by now, but he wasn't. He was coming closer.

A man would have told the others where he was going before he left them, but Wytt just acted. There were many men and horses coming up the road. Even the dull humans knew that. But Ysbott was coming, too, not far behind the horses. Had Martis and Trout not found a path deeper in the woods and farther from the road, the two parties would have met. Now they would pass each other, just a little ways apart. Wytt thought that was funny and bared his teeth in a grin. You might have thought he was scowling, but it was only Omah laughter.

Meanwhile, Martis kept the children moving.

"What if Wytt can't find us again?" Fnaa asked.

"Don't worry," said Ellayne. "He always finds us."

275

When the camp changed hands, and Roshay Bault led his militia down the road, Ysbott was amazed.

"He's surrendered the gold!" he whispered to his two companions. "I never thought he'd prove a coward! Why didn't he fight for it?"

"How could he?" Gwawl answered. "Those people would have wiped him out. I wonder who they are."

"I thought they might be the Thunder King's men," Ysbott said, "only they never would have let Bault go. It may take a while to find out who they are."

When Chutt's army broke down the barricades and pushed into the camp, Ysbott crept a little closer—close enough to hear the tumult when Chutt's men started fighting over the gold.

"Who are they fighting?" Hrapp said. "Who's there for them to fight?"

They heard loud cries and the clash of weapons. "They must be fighting among themselves," said Ysbott. "Good! Maybe they'll kill themselves off." But it didn't go on long enough for that. It sounded like there were plenty of them left alive, and Ysbott dared not advance any closer.

"Somehow we will profit by this," he thought. Then he shot a glance at Hrapp and Gwawl and corrected "we" to "I."

It was Ilfil who quelled the mutiny, with help from Captain Born. The Wallekki chieftain waded into the melee and hacked off a man's head—one of his own tribesmen. Roaring, he held it up by the hair. The fighters lowered their weapons.

"You sons of dogs! You fools! Must I behead you all? Put down your weapons!"

Born clubbed a soldier who was slow to obey. He put a shoulder to another man and knocked him down. The fighting ceased.

"Do you see this man—Lord Chutt!" Ilfil cried. Chutt stood alone beside the stack of gold. He'd never been in a fight in his life and didn't want to start now. "Without him, we are nothing—like a snake without a head. Do you see the gold? This gold shall make him king of all Obann, and us his favored men!

"Come to your senses! We can't go home again, to be killed off by the Thunder King. We're here in Obann now and here we'll stay—either as masters of Obann, or leaderless outlaws to be picked off one by one or two by two. The whole country is ours for the taking. But not if we behave as jackals fighting over the carcass of a camel!

"On your knees, you dogs! Do homage to Lord Chutt— King of Obann!"

This stunned them, and at first nobody moved. But then, three or four at a time, and then together, the men dropped to their knees and raised their hands.

"Chutt! Chutt! King of Obann!" They chanted, making a noise like stormy surf. Chutt drew his sword and held it high. When he could finally be heard, he addressed his troops.

"My lord Chief Ilfil speaks the truth. With all this gold, and with the swords that it will buy for us, and the friendship of great men, Obann is ours—but only if we all stick together and conduct ourselves wisely. If you break up into smaller bands, you'll only be hunted down by armies and killed for the gold.

"Why fight among ourselves? There's more than enough gold here for each and every one of you—much more than enough. But first we have to bring it down from the mountain, and then we'll have to work very hard to keep it. You can leave all the complicated business to me. I'll never fail you there. But you men are my sword, my bodyguard—you must not fail me! United, we shall stand. Divided, we must fall. Are you with me? Are we all united in this enterprise?"

"We are! We are! Lord Chutt, King of Obann!"

The chiefs put the men to work removing the dead bodies from the camp and slaying a few men too badly wounded to be saved. Ilfil said they were dogs and rebels who didn't deserve a proper burial, so the crows got them. The Wallekki believed the ghosts of men left unburied would be blown away on the wind and find no rest forever. Those who threw the bodies into the woods went about it with grim looks on their faces. All told, a hundred men or so had died in the brief riot. It could have been worse, Chutt thought.

As order was established in the camp, Chutt took Ilfil aside.

"I'll never forget what you've done for me today, my lord," Chutt said. "I'll make you the commander of all my armies, Lord General of Obann."

"I am yours," said Ilfil. "But also you are mine, my lord! Remember that."

"We shall grow old as the rulers of Obann," said Chutt. It wasn't quite what he had planned for, but he would learn to live with it.

———————

If Helki had known that Ysbott the Snake was in a

hiding place just across the road, that would have been the end of Ysbott. But Helki didn't know, even though a blue jay and a cowbell-bird were loudly protesting Ysbott's presence. On a quieter day Helki would have heeded them and tried to find out what was disturbing them. Today he thought they were just responding to the tumult in the camp.

So now this high councilor of Obann, whoever he was, had the gold. He'd let Roshay Bault depart unharmed. To Helki, that was the most puzzling part of it: "No brigand chief would have done that," he thought. Maybe the high councilor and the baron had reached an understanding.

Roshay would be loyal to King Ryons—no doubt of that. Which meant, Helki thought, that he wouldn't do any-thing to hurt the king. As strange as it seemed, it must mean that the baron had judged that handing over the gold to this great lord would not betray King Ryons.

"Fah! It's making my head hurt, trying to make sense of these goings-on!" Helki said to himself. He clung to what he knew for sure: that God had chosen Ryons to rule Obann. He was sure Roshay Bault believed that. "This calls for a wiser head than mine. Too bad Martis isn't here!"

Silently he moved closer to the camp. He saw men car-rying out dead bodies, setting up campfires, following orders. Whatever the trouble had been, now it was over—at least for the time being. The high councilor was in command.

Helki didn't speak Wallekki, or he would have under-stood that these men had hailed the high councilor as king. He couldn't decide whether to follow Roshay down the mountain, and see what he could learn from him, or to go down the other way and try to catch up to King Ryons.

"I'd better stay here," he thought. "At least stay until I

understand what all this is about."

———————————

Wytt found Ysbott and his men hiding not far from the camp. He wouldn't attack them because they were wide-awake and cautious.

"What are we going to do?" Hrapp said. "If they ever see us, we're done for!"

"They aren't going to see us," Ysbott said. "Whatever we decide to do, we'll have to lie low until they're finished here and cart the gold away."

"I'm hungry," Gwawl said.

"Shut up. I've got some mushrooms in my bag. We won't starve."

Wytt didn't understand their talk, but he did understand that Ysbott meant harm to these men who followed him. They were blind and deaf to their danger, although to the Omah, malice radiated out from Ysbott like heat from the sun.

With thousands of men crowded into the camp, Wytt kept his distance. He wouldn't have chosen to come much closer, anyway: he knew something that none of them knew.

Within that sprawling heap of wood and metal, down deep among the dead men's bones, was something that would hurt you if you got too close to it and stayed too long. Wytt would have agreed with Shaffur, who said the treasure had a curse on it. Wytt knew nothing of curses. But in the flat-topped hills of Obann's plains, hills that had once been living cities, there were places where the Omah wouldn't go. They couldn't have told you why: they simply shunned those spots. Obst would have said they were particular locations that kept a residue of evil, and he would have cited verses from the Scriptures. "Lo, my judgment has made a desolation there; it shall never be inhabited, and its waters shall be bitter forever." Obst would have trusted the Omah's keen perceptions.

But none of the men now at the top of the Golden Pass, in their greed, in their rejoicing, felt even the slightest sense of danger.

Wytt turned back to help his own people travel safely down the mountain. Someday he would have another chance to kill Ysbott. For the time being, he dismissed it from his mind.

CHAPTER 40

The Battle of Looth's Hill

When they saw the Zeph lined up on the ridge flanking the hilltop occupied by Ryons' army, the Zamzu let out a deep, exultant roar. They blew on horns that had harsh voices and formed into a solid square, with Dahai in a looser formation to protect their flanks and sweep around the enemy once he was engaged with the Zamzu in the center. They saluted the Zephites with their weapons, and even Ryons and Gurun could see what the Zamzu saw: the Zeph would attack from that direction, once the battle was joined.

Shaffur ground his teeth. "We don't have enough men to hold on two fronts," he said. "We should have attacked first, when we had the chance!"

Obst knelt in prayer. Down below, the horns blared again. With a great shout the Zamzu began their advance up the grassy slope. The Hosa, ready to meet them at the top, took up the anthem: "His mercy endureth forever." The rest of the army joined in, drowning out the noise the Zamzu made. But Looth and his men skirmished a little ways downhill to shoot their poisoned arrows. Those few Zamzu who were hit laughed aloud and plucked the arrows from their flesh without missing a step. They didn't take many steps before they began to fall, one by one. But there were many more of them than the Attakotts had arrows.

"Here they come, the dastards!" cried Tiliqua, pointing to the other hill. Ryons turned to look. The Zeph were coming down at a run, like a herd of wild bulls stampeding.

Gurun could have wept. So it was true, then, after all. Jiharr and his people had betrayed them.

"All-Father," she prayed, "I do not grudge to die in your service." Ryons stole a look at her and thought it was wrong that she should die, unbearably wrong, but he was afraid to cry out against the Lord his God. He clamped his lips so tightly shut that they went pale. Chagadai, seeing that, reached out to pat his shoulder. "Be brave, Father," he said. Ryons only nodded.

"Look!" cried Tiliqua. "Look!"

The Zephites turned. They weren't charging Ryons' flank. They went around the base of the hill and came up in the Zamzus' rear. Before another two minutes passed, they were striking down the Dahai on the Zamzus' right flank.

Shaffur, the tallest of the chiefs, stood in his saddle, sword held high.

"Now! Now!" he shouted. "All of you—charge!"

The Hosa couldn't hear him, but they didn't need to. As one man they rushed down the hill. Uduqu followed, brandishing the giant's sword, and after him came the Griffs. Around them on both flanks raced Wallekki horsemen.

"This is it!" Chagadai said. "Conquer or die! Father, you stay here with Obst and Gurun." And the fifty Ghols spurred their horses to the rim of the hill and galloped down.

Cavall howled and took off after them. Baby tore free from Perkin's grasp and lunged after the hound. Ryons tried to rein in his horse, but couldn't. It wanted to run with the others; it carried him off with the Ghols, and all he could do was struggle to remain in the saddle.

The Zamzu halted in confusion, suddenly forced to go on the defensive. Behind them the Zeph hewed and clubbed their way into the rear of their formation. The Hosa took them head-on, smashing into the center of their line. And the Walle-kki were already driving the Dahai from their other flank.

Ryons saw Baby get there ahead of the Ghols. Not even the Zamzu would stand against the giant bird. His massive beak, more deadly than a lion's jaws, terrorized them.

What might have been a day-long siege on the hill-top turned into a boiling chaos on the slope. From then on Ryons saw little of the battle beyond his horse's head tossing in front of him and his own hands below, white-knuckled, clinging to the saddle horn. He couldn't let go to draw his sword. He couldn't control his horse, but at least it kept close to the others.

The Dahai surrendered as promptly as they could, throwing away their swords and small, round shields, fall-ing to their knees with empty palms held high. The Zamzu fought to the last man. They could advance no farther up the hill and couldn't go back down.

――――――――

Suddenly it was quiet. No more screaming of men and horses, no more clashing of metal. Suddenly Ryons' horse stood still among the Ghols, panting. For just that one instant, the world seemed as quiet as a tomb.

Ryons raised his head. The Zamzu lay everywhere, not a man of them left standing. He turned: Obst and Gurun were already coming down, slowly. Ryons felt as if he'd just awakened from a fearful dream.

Baby stood over a fallen Zamzu warrior, delicately picking at the carcass. He made no resistance when Perkin came and picked up his leather leash and led him away. Cavall trotted up to Ryons and sat down, red tongue lolling.

Ryons almost jumped out of his saddle when Chagadai spoke to him.

"It's over, Father. We've won. I don't think our losses are too bad. But why didn't you stay on the hilltop like I told you to? Far be it from me to chide a valiant heart, but my own old heart nearly stopped when I saw you charge down with us."

Ryons wanted to tell him that he couldn't help it, he couldn't hold back his horse from running with the others, but he couldn't summon up the breath to say any more than "Sorry!"

Gurun and Obst joined them.

"God has delivered us again," said Obst.

Already the Zeph, helped by the Wallekki, were rounding up the Dahai. But one of the Zephites, with his bull's-head helmet in his hand and his face brightly beaming, came striding up the slope.

"Well met, King Ryons!" he called. It was Jiharr. "And well met, my lady queen! In a good hour we meet again, as the God of Obann willed it."

Gurun dismounted. Now the tears, which she'd held back in the face of death and danger, filled her eyes. She hardly knew this man; but to see him again, here and now, was as if one of her own brothers had come to her from Fogo Island, far away.

"Well met, Jiharr!" she said. "By God's grace, you and your people have saved our lives."

"Who would have thought it?" said Chagadai. "We very

badly misjudged you, friend! We thought you'd come to help the Zamzu have us for their dinner."

"The Zamzu thought so, too!" Jiharr said, grinning. "But all the people who are left in Zeph-land have had enough of the Thunder King. His hand brought us only poverty and terror, and never-ending war from which we had no profit; but your hand brought healing, when I should have died."

"Not my hand," said Gurun, "but God's."

"I know! I understand. You told me so, and I believe you." Jiharr placed his hand on his heart and bowed his head—a Zephite act of homage. "When the Thunder King came, he took away our gods. They couldn't do anything to save us. Better for us now to follow Obann's God and fight for Him. He will take away the Thunder King! He will heal the nations.

"But where is your great warrior who gave me my death-blow when we fought? Does he still live? I haven't seen him."

Ryons' heart went cold. Uduqu! When he was still a slave, assigned to watch over Obst when Obst was a prisoner among the Heathen, and this army still belonged to the Thunder King, Uduqu had taken Ryons into his wigwam and laughed at the boy's sassy remarks: treating him not as a slave, but as a child to be jollied and protected by the men. Uduqu had always protected him.

"We'd better find him," Ryons said. He couldn't bear the loss of that old man. "But you're the king now," Uduqu would have said, "and so you ought to act like one." So Ryons didn't cry, although he wanted to.

They found Uduqu in the middle of the battlefield, lying on his back between the bodies of two huge Zamzu dead of terrible wounds from the sword of Shogg. Uduqu's hand still gripped the weapon.

"This is a great loss!" Gurun cried.

"They paid a high price for him," said Jiharr.

But Obst, who, like Ryons, had been protected by Uduqu and traveled far with him, couldn't keep his composure.

"Shaffur is right—we ask too much of God!" he said. "And maybe God asks too much of us!" Tears flowed down his cheeks. "It's too much! It goes too far! Lord, will you leave no man alive out of all your people?"

Uduqu's eyes slid open.

"Can't a man get a little sleep?" he said.

Ryons almost leaped onto his chest. "Uduqu! Are you hurt?"

With a yawn and a groan, the Abnak sat up and rubbed his eyes. "No, I'm not hurt—just so cuss't tired, I couldn't stay awake another minute. Had to lie down. The fight was over, and we won, and I thought my two arms were going to fall off—"

He had to pause because Gurun started laughing: laughed until she couldn't see through the tears, laughed until her belly hurt and she doubled over. Ryons had never seen her so, and it made him laugh, too. It made his head spin, and he had to sit down and laugh some more.

CHAPTER 41

Homeward Bound

Roshay Bault lost no time getting down the mountain. The townsmen he ordered to double up with riders on the strongest horses. It was an ordeal for most of them.

"Do you want to slow down and wait for the Wallekki?" he said. "They might change their minds about having let us go."

He would have liked to march right through the night, but he saw that too many of the men were too tired for it. The captains agreed that the road wasn't wide enough to allow any kind of attack but a direct assault upon a narrow front. With the last of their strength, the Ninneburky men cut down saplings and dragged and piled them into a tangled barrier across the road. It wouldn't stop such a mass of horsemen as Chutt had, but it would slow a charge. "Nothing much more we can do," said Kadmel. "But maybe they won't be coming after us."

"Chutt has nothing to gain by shedding Obannese blood," Roshay said.

Early in the morning they set out again, leaving the barrier in place. By riding all day without a halt, they were in the foothills by late afternoon, and tomorrow would see them on the plain, homeward bound.

It troubled the baron that he was making so much

better time than Martis and the children could make on foot through the thick of the forest. He trusted Martis, with Wytt and the Abnak, to find the safest path. But how safe could it be and how long would it take them to come down? If he were alone, he would turn back and look for them—"and probably get myself lost in the woods like a cuss't fool," he thought. No, that die was cast; there was nothing he could do except to pray the children came home safe and sound. In any event, he consoled himself, sending them off with Trout and Martis had to be better than it would've been to have let Chutt see them.

They camped another night, set out again at dawn, and when at last they came out onto the plain, they found an army waiting for them.

It was King Ryons' army, the half of it he'd left in Lintum Forest, who had come all the way from there to rescue the men at the Golden Pass. They'd been delayed because they'd captured Chutt's host of wagons and the men who drove them.

The chiefs were more surprised to see the baron than he was to see them.

"We didn't expect to find you still alive," said Buzzard, the Abnak chief. "Your lady sent us up to save you, but we only expected to avenge you. How did you escape?"

"They let us go in return for the gold," said Roshay.

"Wulloo! You let them take it?"

"We had to—it was our only chance. Besides, it's all blood money. It won't do them any good in the end."

"We can go up and take it back," Tughrul Lomak said. "And now we have all these carts to fetch it down."

Roshay shook his head. "We have a truce," he said, "and

the enemy has honored it. We must not be the ones to break it. By my advice, we ought to release these carts and let them go on up."

The Fazzan chieftain laughed. "Now there's pure foolishness, if ever I heard it! But it's just what our teacher would tell us to do, if he were here. I'm all for it."

"And then what?" said the Dahai chief. "March back to Lintum Forest without a battle?"

"I think that would be best," Roshay said. "Lord Chutt, who commands the Wallekki up there, is a traitor to Obann. The Thunder King's gold will be his undoing. Let him swallow it, I say. It's poison."

"Well, Baron," Buzzard said, "we came all this way to bring you back to Ninneburky, and that's what we'll do. Chief Zekelesh is right—this is what Obst would have us do. And I think we'll have a battle soon enough, after those people come back down the mountain."

Chutt's men with the carts were amazed when the chiefs released them. But the Obannese militiamen, who'd rounded up carts for the baron, would not be going with them.

"We'll return these carts to their rightful owners later, after we get home," Roshay said. "I'm relieved to see you all again. Chutt wasn't lying when he swore he hadn't harmed you."

Kerdig, the captain who'd sent the trooper back up the mountain to warn the baron, grinned. "Not half as relieved as we are to see you again, sir!" he said. "But is it true that this high councilor has the law on his side? Is that why you let him have the gold?"

"His law is a dead law, Captain," Roshay said. "There is

no more High Council of Obann. There's only King Ryons, and we are his men. But you acted prudently, and I commend you for it.

"Now let's go home."

———————

They were too far from the road to see or hear Roshay and his men pass down the mountain. Ellayne would not have believed her father had surrendered the gold. She and her companions plodded through the woods, always downhill, with Wytt going on ahead to find the best paths and sniff out trouble.

They'd had to stop once, for half a day, because there was a big animal in their way devouring a berry patch, and Wytt said they ought to keep their distance. He didn't know what kind of animal it was: a big, hairy beast with a horn on its head and a short temper was how Wytt described it. Something told him great caution was required.

"I've never heard of any animal like that," Trout said. But when the wind shifted, he caught a little scent of it and made a face. "It has a nasty smell," he said. "I didn't know there was any creature like it in these woods." Whatever it was, when it finally left, it made a racket in the underbrush. They waited until Wytt said it was safe to go on, and they found the whole berry patch pressed flat.

"I wish we could have seen it," Fnaa said.

"Your mother will have my scalp if I don't get you home in one piece," Trout said. "That means no adventures with funny animals."

"They're not all dangerous," Jack said—remembering the first time he and Ellayne saw the great knuckle-bears at dawn, shambling back to the fringe of Lintum Forest after a night of grazing on the plain. It was not a sight he would easily forget. Obst said they, and all the other strange beasts that people were seeing nowadays, were a sign that God had changed the world.

"It's still best to keep out of their way," said Martis. "Come on—we have a long way to go."

———————

Ysbott's two followers thought their plan was simply to wait until all those Wallekki departed, and then find some way to retrieve their own cache of seven sheets of gold and enjoy fabulous wealth for the rest of their lives. Hrapp and Gwawl weren't much for enduring hardships, but they'd endure more for the sake of the gold. "I'll move to the big city and buy a fine house there. No more cobbling for me!" Hrapp said. "I'll get me a beautiful young wife," said Gwawl, "and deck her out in jewels."

"You already have a wife," Hrapp pointed out.

"Well, I want a better one!"

Ysbott found it hard to bear, listening to their prattle, but they were well out of earshot of the camp and he let them go on as they pleased, knowing it was the only way they had to keep up their spirits.

His own plans seemed to be dissolving into a mist. Seven sheets of gold now seemed to him a paltry thing, when there was a hundred times as much, and maybe more, in the possession of the barbarous Wallekki. What a cringing cur Roshay Bault turned out to be, to give it up without a fight!

All Ysbott knew for sure was that he himself would never leave this gold, not if he had to stay up here all year.

He would never lose sight of it. If the Wallekki removed it, he would follow them to the ends of the earth. They had no right to it! What he could possibly do to get it all for himself, he couldn't imagine. His mind was stopped, like a traveler confronted by a towering sheer cliff he couldn't climb. But he would not turn back. He would not give up. He felt now that it was his gold and that the Wallekki had robbed him. He swore not to let them keep it.

He still had the deadly mushrooms in his bag, which he would feed to Hrapp and Gwawl when he deemed the time was right. That time had not yet come.

That first night in camp, Lord Chutt slept beside a stack of gold in a plain canvas tent he'd brought from Market City. Someday he would sleep again in a soft bed with silken sheets in a marble palace. Tomorrow he would put the men to work digging out the rest of the gold from the heap. Soon the carts would arrive, and they could start loading the gold.

And after that? What if there was a hostile army waiting for him at the bottom of the mountain?

"I'll have to send messengers to some of the great men, enlisting their support," he thought. Obann was full of oligarchs and rich men and military men, and quite a few of the presters, too, who would welcome a restoration of the old order. Chutt knew most of them by name. They would support him if he had the gold. They would interfere with any efforts to take it from him—always provided that he acted within the boundaries of the law. He must be able to justify anything he did.

Outside Chutt's tent, Chief Ilfil and Captain Born

posted guards. Neither of them wished to see the leader assassinated, and neither of them quite trusted the other.

"Your men shall watch mine, and mine shall watch yours," Ilfil said to Born.

"And you and I shall watch either other," Born thought, but didn't say.

Outside the camp, Helki slept in a nest made of piled leaves, under the shelter of an old uprooted tree. During the afternoon a few of the Wallekki, carrying dead bodies out of the camp, passed within arm's length of him. He let them pass unharmed, and they never suspected he was there.

Helki's ears and nostrils slept but lightly. If a predator approached, or anything else out of the ordinary, he would wake instantly, with his rod in his hand. Those who lived alone in the forest without this gift of instant wakefulness didn't live for long.

At any time he pleased, he could steal into the camp, strike a blow, and vanish back into the forest before the Wallekki knew he'd been among them. He hadn't yet decided to do that, nor had he ruled it out. It might be, he thought, a way to get them fighting among themselves again.

The Boats

The night following the battle—the Battle of Looth's Hill, they called it, much to the delight of the Attakotts—Ryons and most of his army slept inside the walls of the fort beside the lake. They slept soundly, lulled by the soft splash of wavelets on the sand and the calls of birds that hunted fish by night. Jiharr and his people, with some of Shaffur's riders, stood guard over five hundred Dahai prisoners outside the fort. The surviving chiefs of the Dahai said they wished to become Ryons' men and follow him from now on. "No one ever dreamed the king of Obann would come here," said their spokesman. "Until today, no one ever saw the Zamzu defeated in a battle."

"We defeated them before," said Hawk, "when they invaded Lintum Forest."

The chieftains would decide tomorrow whether the Dahai could be trusted and taken into service. Meanwhile, Jiharr promised to follow Ryons all the way to Kara Karram beyond the lakes, with as many of the Zeph as would go willingly. "But I think they all will," he added. "The time has come to make an end of the Thunder King."

When the next day dawned, most of Ryons' men lined up on the shore and stared out over the lake, the Door of the Sun. A body of water whose farther shore could not be seen—to many of them, that was something new in their lives.

"It's a good thing we didn't bring a lot of Obannese men with us," Obst said. "To them, this great lake would be like the sea. They'd be afraid of it."

"It's not so bad," said Chagadai. "A few of us Ghols crossed the lakes on ships when King Thunder sent us west, back when we had Szugetai to lead us. They were big ships, big enough to carry many men and horses. We could cross a big lake in a single day, when it would have taken many days to ride around it. But I see no great ships for us here—just these boats. I don't know what good they'll be."

The boats lay overturned along the shore, more of them than anyone cared to count. Gurun went down with her Blays and turned a boat right-side up. It took her and half a dozen of her men to do it, because the boat was heavy.

She climbed into it, bending over to study its planks, measuring it. After a few moments, she stood up and turned to beam at the chieftains.

"Why, these are very good boats!" she cried. "Look—this one comes equipped with a mast and a sail. And it's very solidly built! Bring me some of those Dahai prisoners, and they can tell us how long it takes to cross the lake."

This was of great interest to the chiefs. They gathered around to examine the boat.

"It looks dangerous," said Shaffur.

"Indeed not!" Gurun said. "On Fogo Island where I was born, we practically live on boats such as these all summer long, catching enough fish to feed us all through the winter. We catch whales in our boats, too. And that is on the sea itself, not a little lake like this.

"I can hardly wait to be out on the water! There is nothing to fear: a man will fall off a horse before he falls out of a boat. Or would you rather toil all around the lake shore and be months doing it?"

The Dahai came, half a dozen of their chiefs, under guard.

"My people built these boats," said their spokesman. "This lake we cross in half a day. It's much longer than it is wide. The Zamzu don't like the water, and quite a few of them were sick with fear. We enjoyed seeing that! The opposite shore of this lake is Dahai land. It would be no hard feat for us to ferry this whole host across the lake aboard these boats."

"What about our horses?" Shaffur demanded.

"Horses, too," said the Dahai, "as long as they don't make a fuss. But I think we will have to make two trips to bring all the horses."

"Your sails aren't quite as big and heavy as the ones we use in my country," Gurun said.

"We make them as our fathers taught us."

Gurun turned to the chiefs. "Well, then!" she said. "We have the boats we need to get across the lake, and men who know how to sail them. As for me, it will give me pleasure to sail and steer a boat again. I won't need anyone to show me how."

"What about Baby?" Ryons asked. The thought of the killer bird cooped up in a boat made him uneasy.

"Baby and Perkin shall travel in my boat, my king—and you and Cavall, too. Baby is a good bird. I'll sing him a Fogo Island lullaby, and that will keep him calm and peaceful."

Obst stroked his beard. "There are more lakes and

greater lakes than this one, Gurun."

"We'll cross them all, O man of God! By the time we cross the last of them, I'll have made sailors of you all."

———————————

With their number now swollen to three thousand, Foxblood and his Abnak warriors marched on the enemy stronghold in the lowlands. As the Battle of Looth's Hill was being won in the north, they were still a few marches distant from their own great battle with the Zamzu.

Feeding three thousand fighting men, along with an uncounted number of childless women who were following their men, was no easy thing to do in Abnak country, where there are no tilled fields, no storehouses. The women gathered in baskets everything edible that they could pick or dig up. Hunters fanned out for miles around the main body of the host, felling deer, spearing fish. They also had provisions they'd captured from the enemy. Somehow everyone had enough to eat.

"I'd almost call that a miracle," Foxblood said to Orth, "only these past two or three years, the land has been more fruitful than anyone can remember."

Orth nodded. "It's the same in Obann," he said. "Even with the war, we've had better crops, better hauls of fish, more lambs and calves and colts being born, more chicks hatched—all since King Ozias' bell rang on Bell Mountain. And the cloud that always used to hide the summit blew away that morning and has not returned.

"There is a Scripture that sheds light on this. The Lord spoke to Prophet Ika, 'Behold, I and I alone make all things new. As I renew the seasons every year, and call forth the new grass, and bring forth each new generation of both men and beasts, so will I make for my people a new heaven and a new earth, when the old have passed away.' All life is the work of His hands."

It was nighttime, and they sat around a fire with some of Foxblood's chiefs. A few of these, as they rested, smoked tree-beans and blew rings into the air. But Orth politely declined their invitation to join them in that pastime.

"Your Scriptures speak to me," said Foxblood, "although never in my life have I ever thought of such a thing as a whole new earth. Someday I would like to know those Scriptures."

"Someday you will," said Orth.

"One more battle to fight, First Prester; one more battle to win. And then I'm thinking we should send you home—get you back across the mountains well before the start of winter. You've been a great help to us, but I know you have duties to carry out in Obann. I wouldn't want them saying we kidnapped you."

This touched on something that Orth had been deeply pondering the past few days.

"I'm not so sure my place is in Obann anymore," he said. "I know a man"—he meant Prester Jod—"who would be a better First Prester than I can ever be. I've been wondering whether God has called me to remain here in the East, to plant His word and water it and see it grow. Not only here, among the Abnaks, but in other countries, too.

"I believe now that the destruction of the Temple in Obann was God's way of breaking the chains that kept His word bound there, as in a prison. I connived in that destruction; I was a traitor. The burden of that sin was so heavy that for a time it overthrew my mind. I was like a beast when

Hlah found me starving in the marshes. But my sin, which I meant for evil, God meant for good—and great good has come of it. And there will be more to come. I must have faith and let the Lord lead me step by step, one step at a time: I don't know where. But He does."

To this Foxblood made no reply. But, of course, he didn't need to.

CHAPTER 43

A Weapon Against the Past

When Roshay Bault came home again, he sent out his best men as scouts to see when Chutt would come down from the Golden Pass and where he would go from there. A few of them were to venture up the Thunder King's road and look for Martis and the children.

"Martis will keep them safe," Vannett said, "and that man, Trout, seems very capable. Besides, they have that little creature with them. Ellayne says he's better than any two men. I must take her word for it."

"We have to make sure we can defend the town, if Chutt decides to come our way," the baron said. "I won't let him and his Wallekki through the gates. I don't expect him to start a civil war—not yet!—but it's best to be prepared."

"You were wise to walk away from the gold, Roshay."

The baron kissed his wife. "Not everyone will think so," he said.

Guided by Wytt, Ellayne and her companions made their way down the mountain without incident. They didn't hurry. Trout needed time to collect food that Martis and the children could eat. Game abounded in these woods. Trout's snares kept them fed on roasted squirrel, wood-hens that didn't fly, and one or two animals that none of them had ever seen before. It took them a whole week to get all the way down to the plain, and then the baron's scouts found them and brought them home to Ninneburky just as King Ryons' men were about to return to Lintum Forest.

The scouts had seen no sign of Chutt and his Wallekki. They must still be at the top of the pass, loading their wagons with gold.

"If only we could have some word from Ryons!" Ellayne said, more than once. "It's as if he's vanished out of the world."

Fnaa and Trout departed with the king's army. By and by, Ellayne and Jack had time to sit with Enith behind the baron's stables and tell her all about their adventure in the mountains.

"I wish I could have gone with you," Enith said. "I would have liked to have seen all that gold!"

"You won't like seeing all the trouble that it causes, when it comes back down," Jack said. "The baron thinks they're going to use it to start a war and take King Ryons' throne away from him. He says we'll have to be ready for just about anything."

"The king is out there, somewhere. Maybe anywhere, maybe nowhere—with just half his little army," said Ellayne. "There's no news of him, no messages from him. He must be too far away by now to send a message. Maybe the birds in the air have seen him. I wonder if we ever will, again."

"Oh, well!" Enith said, trying to keep Ellayne from getting too gloomy. "While you were away, the baroness read me the rest of that story about the glass bridge." Ellayne already knew the story, but Enith told Jack what he'd missed. "It's a strange story, isn't it?" she added. "Imagine having to walk across a bridge of glass! Doesn't make much sense, does it? I wonder why anyone would ever make up a story like that."

"But wait—it does make sense!" Jack said. It had suddenly dawned on him. "It does, if you know how to look at it. Crossing the glass bridge that might fall to pieces on you any moment—isn't that what Ryons and Obst and Gurun are doing?"

"That's a terrible thing to say!" Ellayne cried. "You shouldn't even think it."

"But what if the bridge doesn't fall to pieces?" Jack answered. "What if they do cross over, just like in the story? All the way to Kara Karram!"

Ellayne thought it over. "I wonder," she said, "if we've all been walking on a glass bridge, all this time. Ever since you and I—well, you know." She remembered just in time that she mustn't tell Enith about the journey to Bell Mountain: that was still a secret. She shook her head and sighed. "That was a daft thing we did, Jack."

"Maybe—but we did it," Jack said.

"What are you two talking about?" Enith demanded. But they wouldn't tell her.

As for Wytt, he spent the day under the back porch with some bacon scraps from the kitchen to share with the old rat. The rat was glad to see him. While they were gone, a big brown snake had crept under the porch and forced the rat to hide outside, among the shrubbery, for several days. Happily, the snake chose to move on.

Wytt told the rat that there was something worse than

a snake under a huge pile of wood atop a mountain—which the rat couldn't grasp, not having any notion of what a mountain might be, but nevertheless shivered at the thought of it. They then abandoned the subject and enjoyed the rest of the bacon.

———

The half of Ryons' army returned to Carbonek without having drawn a sword or thrown a spear. Carbonek had had peace while they were gone: Helki's scouts, trained by him in person, forced the remaining outlaw bands to keep their distance. Still, the people of Carbonek missed their king and were distressed to have no word of him.

Fnaa's mother, Dakl, when she'd finished fussing over her only child, threw her arms around Trout's neck and kissed him.

"Be careful," Trout said. "Among my people, when a woman kisses a man as you've kissed me, it means she wishes to become his wife."

"And is that such a bad idea?" said Dakl. So Trout returned the kiss, and told her that, according to the custom of the Abnaks, they were married.

"Does that make you my father?" Fnaa said.

"No," said Trout. "But I've gotten into the habit of looking after you, and I guess I'll keep on doing it. Maybe I can teach you some sense."

The warriors had a feast that night to celebrate their homecoming and to hail Trout and Dakl as man and wife. There was still plenty of food on the tables when Abgayle rushed in to interrupt them.

"All you chiefs," she said, "and everyone else who's

here—come before King Ryons' throne, now."

It wasn't a real throne, but only a throne-shaped stone that had long ago broken loose from the ruined castle. What purpose it had once served, no one knew. It still bore some trace of ancient writing, which not even Obst could read. Ryons always sat on this stone when his chieftains assembled for a council.

Tonight, under the late summer stars, Jandra sat upon the throne—not as a little girl playing a game, but as a queen: straight and still, with a dignity that commanded silence. The chiefs lined up before her, the warriors and the settlers in a quiet mass behind them.

"Hear the word of the Lord," she spoke, and her voice was no child's, but that of a grown woman. "Behold, I shake the earth; I raise up kings and cast them down. I give honor and majesty to great men, and I take it away. I kill, and I make alive: I am the Lord.

"To my servant Ozias and to his seed, forever, I give the kingship of Obann: his throne shall be established here; it shall not be moved. If his seed keep my commandments and observe my laws, my servant Ozias shall never lack a man to sit before me on his throne. But if they turn from me, and go after other gods, I shall uproot what I have planted, and pull down what I have built. But I shall preserve his line, as I have preserved it in the hidden places of the earth; and of his blood I shall bring forth a man to be my son: the glory of Obann, and a savior to the nations of the earth; I will give him the Heathen for his inheritance. You shall hear of him again.

"As Ozias is my servant, so shall you be his servants, and mine. I shall delight in you, and never fail you or forsake you. Stand with him, and I will stand with you. I am the Lord."

Jandra's eyes closed, and she slumped on the king's throne, a little girl asleep.

―――――

Martis didn't sleep that night. He lay awake, his thoughts stretching out all the way to Kara Karram, the castle of the Thunder King.

He believed in his heart that Ryons would get there— Ryons, Obst, and Gurun, with as many of their people who weren't killed along the way. The Thunder King might call up ten thousand men to crush them, or tens of thousands: of course he would, thought Martis. He had but to stamp his foot and the king of Obann would be destroyed like an insect. But as obvious as that seemed, Martis didn't believe it. With his own eyes Ryons would see the New Temple and the fortress where the Thunder King kept the Heathen's idols as his trophies, so that he could be their god.

It wasn't the Thunder King's armies that chilled Martis' soul. It wasn't the armies that would devour Obann's king.

The last danger would come roaring out of the past, the ancient past.

In the Temple at Obann—it seemed so long ago, and yet it wasn't—Lord Reesh had a whole roomful of bits and pieces from the past. They inflamed his imagination, but they were only scraps and relics. They had no power in them.

But the Thunder King had burrowed more deeply into the ancient times and found things that did have power. He must have many such pieces because he'd given some to his agents. Jack and Ellayne had taken one. It had made music and showed a picture of a woman with unnaturally large eyes. When Ellayne tried to make it do more, it had destroyed itself.

The Thunder King's false First Prester, the traitor, Goryk Gillow, brought an ancient item with him to Obann. When its power was let loose, it ate up the whole palace in a colossal gout of flame. It, too, destroyed itself.

But they wouldn't all destroy themselves, Martis thought. Surely the Thunder King had kept the best of them for himself at Kara Karram. There was no imagining what he might have in his possession, nor what those things could do.

Many years ago, when the first Thunder King rose up in a country far to the east of Kara Karram, the Heathen said he had a sword that belonged to the War God, and with this he conquered nations. It had not been seen since the Thunder King occupied Kara Karram, but doubtless he still had it. Had its ancient power been exhausted? Or was he only waiting for a certain time to use it again—when Ryons stood before his castle?

"I should have gone east with Ryons," Martis thought. But how could he have done that when he'd sworn an oath to God to devote the rest of his life to protecting God's servants, Jack and Ellayne, who'd climbed Bell Mountain and rung the bell of King Ozias?

Such thoughts tormented him all night. In the morning, the baron sent for him.

Gallgoid was at the baron's house. He'd come along, riding on a mule. When Martis arrived, Roshay ushered them into his private study and shut the door.

"I've already told Gallgoid of all that happened at the

Golden Pass and that Lord Chutt now has King Thunder's gold," Roshay said. "But Gallgoid has something to tell us that we didn't know."

The chief spy nodded. "There is something else in those ruins," he said, "that may be worth more than all the gold. There is the gold mask of the Thunder King. He was wearing it when the avalanche buried his hall. He always wore it when he sat before his mardars. It must be there still, buried with him.

"If we can get it, we can use it against him. It will be proof that the Thunder King's a mortal man, and neither god nor devil. It may be enough to make his whole empire crumble."

"Have you seen this mask?" said Martis.

"I was never admitted into the hall. But Lord Reesh saw it many times and described it to me."

"And Chutt is unaware of its existence," Roshay said.

"I mean to get it, my lord. I know it's there."

"It won't be easy," Martis said.

"For Lord Reesh's two favorite spies and assassins, it shouldn't be impossible," said Gallgoid. "We dare this in the service of King Ryons."

"And of God," the baron said.

Follow the Entire Adventure
with the First Six Books
in this Exciting Series!

You won't want to miss a single moment of this thrilling adventure, so be sure to get *the first six volumes* to complete your collection. These engaging stories are a great way to discover powerful insights about the Kingdom of God through page-turning fantasy fiction.

Ordering is Easy!
Just visit
www.ChalcedonStore.com